SHONA

BOOK 1

VICKY JONES
CLAIRE HACKNEY

Hackney and Jones
HACKNEY & JONES

GRAB YOUR FREE BOOK NOW

Chloe - A prequel to Meet Me at 10

What if a life-shattering family tragedy forces you to completely rethink your future? Destined for a different path in life, twenty-year-old Chloe Bruce's world is shattered after a tragic accident on her father's plantation in Alabama.

Ok, so how do I get my FREE book?

EASY! See the next page

GRAB YOUR FREE BOOK NOW

Instructions:

1. Open the camera or the QR reader application on your smartphone.

2. Point your camera at the QR code to scan the QR code.

3. A notification will pop-up on screen.

4. Click on the notification to open the website link

JOIN IN!

If you would like to receive regular behind-the-scenes updates, get beta reading opportunities, enter giveaways and much, much more, simply visit the site below:

http://hackneyandjones.com

CONTENTS

ABOUT VICKY JONES

Vicky Jones was born in Essex, England. She is an author and singer-songwriter, with numerous examples of her work on iTunes and YouTube. At 20 years old she entered the Royal Navy. After leaving the Navy realising she was drifting through life with no sense of direction, she wrote a bucket list of 300 things to achieve which took her traveling, facing her fears and going for her dreams. At the time of printing, she is two-thirds of the way through her bucket list.

One item on her list was to write a song for a cause. Her anti-bullying track called "House of Cards" is now on iTunes to download.

Writing a novel was on her bucket list, and through a chance writing competition at her local writing group, the idea for *Meet Me At 10* was born. Vicky hopes she can change hearts and minds due to some of the gritty themes of the book.

Vicky is a keen traveler, stemming from her days traveling the world in the Royal Navy, and has visited around 50 countries so far. She has also graduated from The Open University after studying part time for her degree in psychology and criminology—another bucket list tick! She is currently writing a book series about her bucket list adventures, the first of which is entitled *'Project Me, Project You'*, alongside planning and writing more fiction books and book marketing guides for self-published authors.

Also in the pipeline is a writing course, put together to help aspiring authors plan and write their first novel.

She now lives in Cheshire, splitting her time between there and visiting her family and friends back in Essex.

For more information on upcoming book releases, to tell us what you think of the books, or just to say hi, visit the sites below:

facebook.com/VickyJonesWriter
twitter.com/vickyjones7
instagram.com/vickytjones

ABOUT CLAIRE HACKNEY

Claire Hackney is a former English Literature, Drama and Media Studies teacher who, after attending a local writing group with Vicky and writing several of her own short stories over the years, has now decided to focus her career on full-time novel writing.

She is an avid historian and has thoroughly enjoyed researching different aspects of the 1950s for the 'Shona Jackson' trilogy of novels.

Claire is very much looking forward getting started on the many future writing projects she and Vicky have in the pipeline, including the 'DI Rachel Morrison' thriller series and several standalone novels.

For more information on upcoming book releases, to tell us what you think of the books, or just to say hi, visit the sites below:

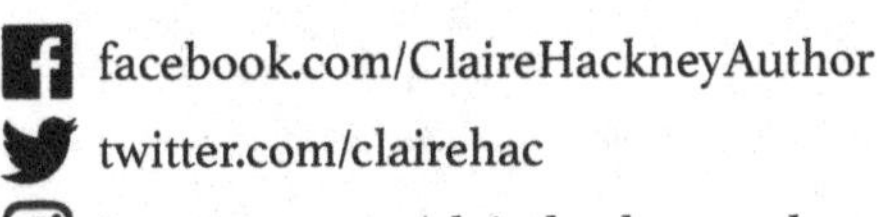

facebook.com/ClaireHackneyAuthor

twitter.com/clairehac

instagram.com/clairehackneyauthor

New town. New life. Old enemies. With the past and present colliding and threatening their future together, can Shona protect her new life and the lives of those closest to her?

GRAB THE SHONA JACKSON SERIES HERE

Instructions:

1. Open the camera or the QR reader application on your smartphone.

2. Point your camera at the QR code to scan the QR code.

3. A notification will pop-up on screen.

4. Click on the notification to open the website link

SHONA

Chapter 1

"Get the *goddamn* hell outta here, you filthy varmint! Before I put my boot through your ass."

It was sunset and the humid Mississippi heat was waning as Shona Jackson shrank down to her haunches behind a parked car, startled by the man's shout. Peeking through the gap between the fender and the wheel arch, hardly daring to breathe, she watched as the screen door to the house flew open and a stocky, greasy-haired, forty-something man wearing oil-stained work pants and a grubby undershirt appeared at the top of the porch steps, his bloated face red with fury. He took a swig from his bottle of Budweiser and scratched at his unshaven chin, his eyes scanning the area below him for any signs of movement. Large magnolia trees lined the wide street as far as the eye could see, and each garden in the neighborhood was heavily fringed by shrubs just beginning to flower again in the late-March climate. Shona slowly crept out from the car and hid behind the rotting wooden slats of the fence at the side of the man's property, taking advantage of the cover provided by the overgrown bushes.

As the opening theme tune of *This is Your Life* drifted from the house, tempting him back to his TV, the man's eyes narrowed when he noticed that at the end of his garden path, his trash can lid was lying upside down. A shadow beside it became the sole focus of his interest. He picked up a piece of grit and threw it at the can, yelling again.

"What you pitchin' a fit for, Bob?" a shrill voice rang out from inside the house.

"That damn stray again," Bob replied, casting his gravelly voice backward over his shoulder towards his wife.

"Well, don't let it get your feathers ruffled. Get back in here. Ralph's about to bring out Reverend Tucker," she hollered.

"Comin'," Bob grunted, taking one last look around.

Shona ducked out of sight again. She pulled her burgundy pageboy cap down over her eyes and peeked through the slats and weeds, waiting for Bob to disappear back into his house. After making sure the coast was clear, she slung her satchel over her shoulder, crept over to next door's trash can and lifted its lid.

"Whoa... You gotta be kidding me," she whispered to herself.

In her twenty-two years of life, she'd rarely smelled anything more repugnant. She rested the lid on the ground as quietly as possible and began sifting through a heap of sweet potato peelings and fish heads. Next to them, she spotted a hunk of bread and some fresh-looking dinner scraps. After picking them out, she flicked off the bits of debris clinging to them. She slipped the food into her pocket, swept back her long blonde bangs and tucked them underneath the peak of her cap. Rolling up the sleeves of her dark brown jacket, Shona rifled deeper.

She spotted a glint of silver on the ground. She reached down to pick it up but, in her urgency to find out the coin's value, her boot struck the lid and sent it crashing to the side-walk. Startled, her blue eyes widened, seeing the neighbor's porch light illuminate. Stooping low, she swiped up the coin and scuttled back behind the fence. After a few heart-pounding moments, the light clicked off and Shona relaxed her shoulders. Remembering the coin now pressed inside her clammy palm, she unclenched her fist. With her eyes shining as brightly as the Franklin half dollar did in the dim amber glow of the streetlight, she flipped it over, then ran her fingertips along the 1955 date stamp, the Liberty Bell raised proudly on its reverse side. Shona grinned. It was brand new, minted only a year ago.

"In God we trust indeed," she whispered to herself, tucking the coin into the top pocket of her blue denim overshirt. Scanning the quiet street, Shona stood up and stretched out, brushing the powdery dirt off her taupe khaki pants. She was already filthy from her long journey, but habit was habit.

Following the signs towards town, hoping to find a grocery store still open, Shona began to notice in more detail the deprivation of the neighborhood she'd somehow wandered into. For the most part cars were parked neatly in driveways, but some, in various states of disrepair, had been left languishing in front yards, rusting and redundant. Clotheslines were hanging by bent metal poles and some front gates were hanging by only one hinge. It wasn't the sort of place Shona wanted to hang around for long in and so she quickened her pace, her body beginning to shiver as the darkness of the evening started to surround her. She walked as quickly as her leaden legs could carry her, nibbling on the corners of the stale hunk of bread, with only the cold gravy pools it had previously sat in softening the crust. After a mile or so, Shona saw a large painted sign: *WELCOME TO RIVERSIDE*

A little further on was a crossroads where the town's truck repair garage sprawled its vast area across one corner. The paint on the dark green weatherboarding was pristine, the concrete forecourt scrubbed spotless before the solid wooden doors had been closed for the night. Given its appearance, Shona couldn't help but smile as she mouthed its strange, incongruous name. *Wreckers?* She raised an eyebrow at the irony before continuing her walk along the main road into Riverside.

The noise emanating from Chasers, a darkly lit saloon across the road about fifty yards away, caught her attention and, as she looked over, she located the grocery store adjacent to it.

Seeing the light go off inside, she forced her aching legs into a run, watching helplessly as the owner stepped outside to lock up for the night. Oblivious to the figure approaching quickly behind him, he placed his keys back in his pocket and began whistling as he strode away.

"Damn it," Shona panted. Pressing one hand against the wall and the other on her growling stomach, she grimaced and clamped her eyes shut. Composing herself, she opened her eyes to assess her new surroundings. Between the grocery store and Chasers was an alleyway and, with no better idea of where to shelter for the night, Shona trudged down it.

There wasn't much around to make a bed, but it certainly wasn't the worst place she'd ever slept in. Spotting a pile of flattened cardboard boxes lying on the dirty ground about halfway down next to a green dumpster, Shona traipsed towards them. Kicking the bits of broken glass and rotting vegetables off the largest piece of cardboard, she slid her back down the wall and pulled one of the flatter pieces over her legs. She wanted to stay alert but began to lose her battle, her eyelids too heavy to hold open any longer. Every few seconds, with every slight sound, she jolted back awake. Sitting bolt upright, fighting to stay vigilant, Shona wrapped the cardboard around her for warmth as effectively as she could and sat quietly, resting her head against her satchel and watching the entrance to the alleyway like a hawk, wishing she could just melt into the bricks behind her.

It had been a long time since Shona had had a restful night.

Chapter 2

Squinting into the bright Thursday morning sunshine, Shona groaned, feeling her gritty eyes sting as she forced them open. With her backside completely numb from sitting on the cold, hard ground all night, she shuffled her legs to get the blood flowing properly again. Her thin cardboard mattress had provided little comfort to her during her almost sleepless night.

As she coughed and rubbed her face, the events of last night came flooding back to her. Finding the last of her foraged bread in her jacket pocket, she took a hungry bite, wiping crumbs off her grubby chin. Leaning back against the bricks, she heard a purring sound and looked down to see a pair of green eyes fixed on her every chew. After being kept awake for most of the night with the unnerving feeling of being watched, Shona was relieved to see only a mangy old cat there with her in the alleyway. Suppressing a smile, she swallowed down her mouthful, her expression hardening as it edged closer.

"Don't eyeball me like that," she scolded, flicking her hand at the stray, but it crept closer and then nuzzled her. She stroked the cat for a moment and fed it her last few crumbs. Standing upright, she stretched out her aching back and felt for the rounded edges of the half dollar coin against the fabric of her overshirt, praying it hadn't fallen out.

"Well, it's been nice knowing you, kitty, but I got a hankering for some proper food," she said, tipping her cap and slinging her satchel over her shoulder.

Walking to the end of the alleyway, Shona, to her relief, saw the grocery store was now open. Hoping her dirty, disheveled appearance wouldn't attract too much attention, she took a quick look through the window to see how many people were in there. The inside of the grocery store was separated by two main aisles, with a bakery counter situated at the far end. To the left of the entrance was the cash register and to the right, by the soap powder stand, three women wearing gingham check print house dresses, white gloves and cardigan sweaters were standing chatting with each other, holding boxes of Omo. A businessman in a gray sack suit and fedora was reading the headlines of the newspaper he'd picked up off the rack by the door. Talking to the owner behind the cash register was an old lady wearing a green full skirt, white blouse and pale green cardigan sweater. After heaving in a large breath to steady her nerves, Shona pushed open the door.

The little bell above tinkled as Shona entered, causing the housewives to look over at her. They wrinkled their noses, sniffing as the scent of body odor and unwashed skin wafted over on the breeze. Trying to be as nonchalant as possible, Shona took off her cap, ruffled the back of her short, matted blonde hair and swept her hand through her long, greasy bangs. Replacing her cap, she wandered over to the far end of the store and began browsing the cakes that were sitting proudly behind the glass partition. The women tutted to each other, then carried on with their conversation. The owner kept one eye on Shona and the other on the old lady standing at his register. Half-listening to her story about the bits of gutter on her house that were falling down, he finished bagging up her items and totaled up her bill.

Shona licked her lips as she stared at the delicious-looking mud pie behind the glass, adding up in her head what the half dollar could buy her. With her common sense overriding her desire for the pie, she headed over to the bread section and, feeling many sets of eyes on her, began to pick up a few of the cheaper items she saw, including a loaf of Wonder Bread, a lump of cheddar, a couple of green apples and a Holloway's Hi-Noon bar. As she walked over to the counter, she overheard the old lady still in full flow of her story and, after lowering her eyes, stood in line behind her.

The old lady finished her conversation and pushed her bags to the end of the counter while she put her wallet back in her purse. Shona approached and laid her goods down, sending an apple rolling across the counter until she shot out her arm to catch it. The owner stared for a moment as Shona flashed him an embarrassed smile, then he pulled out a brown paper bag from under the counter to start bagging up her items.

"Right, that'll be forty-eight cents then," the owner announced.

From her top pocket, Shona pulled out the coin she'd been treasuring all night and handed it over. Nodding her thanks, she picked up her bag and turned to leave, unnerved by the stares that were fixed on her every move. Reaching for the handle of the door, her attention was caught by a Highway Patrol car cruising past the store. Feeling an innate surge of panic grip her, Shona twisted her body, her back now flat against the wall next to the door, her bag hugged closely into her chest.

"Hey," the shop owner called out. Shona looked over, terror etched on her face. Her eyes flicked a second time to the black and white Dodge Coronet outside that had now rolled to a halt.

"You forgot your change," he continued. He held out two copper coins as Shona looked back at him.

"Keep it," she replied.

As her fingers reached down for the cold steel of the handle, another customer came through the door quickly, knocking Shona's grocery bag flying out of her arms and scattering her items on the stone floor, the paper bag shredding in her shaking hands. Shona sank to her knees to retrieve her precious food. As she did so, her cap fell off. Bending down next to her, the man who'd caused the melee reached to grab what he could to help.

"Hey, man, I'm so sorry. I didn't even see you there." The young man stopped mid-sentence and stared at Shona's messy blonde hair, her high cheekbones and ocean blue eyes. "Oh, my... I'm so sorry, ma'am. But your clothes... I thought you were a guy." He laughed nervously as Shona pocketed an apple and the candy bar, and, in her haste, left the other, bulkier items on the floor.

"Don't sweat it," Shona replied, replacing her cap and tucking her hair underneath the peak. Jumping to her feet, she slipped out of the grocery store and back down the alleyway. Hearing the roar of the Dodge's engine, she ducked down behind the dumpster and peeked around, watching as the Coronet drove straight past.

"Relax. They won't find you," she whispered to herself over and over again until her raging heartbeat finally calmed down.

~

Dorothy leaned on the counter, looking at the young man who'd caused Shona's swift exit. His keen green eyes were staring through the glass door as he ran a hand through his light brown hair.

"You see where she went, Jonny?"

Jonny turned around, a downcast look on his boyishly handsome face. He sank his hands into the pockets of his dark blue mechanic's overalls and sauntered over to her. "Oh, hey, Mrs. Clark. No, she disappeared." He placed on the counter the rest of Shona's groceries and the newspaper he'd come in to buy.

"Well now, I reckon a young girl who dresses, and smells, like that can't be too hard to track down now, can she?" The old woman smiled as Jonny blushed. "Bag that girl's stuff up, will ya, Jake, there's a good fella," she ordered, nodding her head to the items on the counter, minus the newspaper which Jonny held out a coin for to Jake.

"Sure thing, Mrs. Clark," Jake replied, placing the coin in the register. He wiped his hands down on his white apron and took out another brown paper bag.

Jonny looked down at his watch. "Well, you know I surely would help you with your bags, but Harry wants me to help him open up, so I'd better skedaddle. He'll tan my hide if I'm late again..."

"It's fine, go," Dorothy replied. "Just slow down. You ain't gonna get a lick of work done for Harry if you keep running around like a headless chicken."

Jonny waved, forgetting to open the door before attempting to walk through it.

"How that boy's made it to twenty-five years old I'll never know," Jake muttered through his bushy moustache as he handed over the bag to Dorothy.

~

Dorothy walked over to the alleyway entrance. About halfway down, a pair of scuffed brown leather boots sticking out from behind a green dumpster caught her squinting eyes.

"Hey. I got the rest of your food here," Dorothy called out.

Receiving no reply, she rested her walking cane against the wall, then shook the brown bag. The peak of Shona's cap emerged, then whipped back almost immediately. The old lady sighed.

"Well... I reckon I'll just have to leave this here. I ain't running no delivery service."

She leaned forward to put the bag down, her eyes still levelled at the dumpster. The peak appeared again.

"I don't need no charity," Shona snapped back, rubbing her shaking palm over the back of her neck.

"I ain't offering you none," Mrs. Clark replied flatly, standing back up straight. "You paid for these, remember? You can do what the hell you like with them. But I wouldn't leave them too long down here, your furry little friend over here looks mighty interested. Hey fella, you want some cheese?"

She bent over to entice the green-eyed cat. It crept closer and sniffed around her ankles. The wrinkly corners of her mouth twitched at the flurry of movement behind the boxes as Shona jumped up and flew towards her.

"No, wait..."

Shona snatched the bag up off the ground before the cat could tear his claws into it, almost dropping it again in her haste.

"Why, you're as nervous as a long-tailed cat in a room full of rocking chairs," Mrs. Clark exclaimed. "You running from the law or something?" Her smile vanished when she saw the look that flashed briefly across Shona's pale face. Setting her thin lips in a straight line, the old lady returned to her matter-of-fact tone. "Well, one good turn deserves another—help me load my bags onto the truck, will ya?"

Grabbing her wooden cane, she walked back out of the alleyway to the street where her rusting blue Ford pick-up truck was parked. Shona obeyed, but as soon as she reached the sidewalk she paused, back on high alert. Mrs. Clark turned to glare at her, prompting Shona to quicken her step, fearing the wrath of the cantankerous old lady coming her way for the second time.

~

Across the street, two young men wearing navy blue turn-up jeans and plaid shirts laughed and jostled each other as they swaggered along the sidewalk.

"Frank, quit bein' a son'bitch and gimme that back," the taller, stockier of the two men complained as his gray newsboy cap was swiped off his sweaty, balding head. Tossing it up in the air, Frank's stubbly face broke into a huge grin as he transferred it from hand to hand behind his own back. Eventually the cap was wrestled from him.

"Jeez, Chuck, what's with the hissy fit? Can't a guy have a little fun around here?" Frank protested, straightening his collar and running a comb through his jet-black hair.

"Yeah, but your idea of fun's to be an asshole," Chuck's deep voice whined as he put his cap back on. Looking up, he caught sight of Frank's glare. Dropping his shoulders, Chuck mumbled an apology, his thick lips quivering. He'd known Frank since they were five years old and was just as wary now of his unpredictable moods as he ever was, even though Chuck had grown to be over a foot taller.

As Frank opened his mouth to remind Chuck who was boss, two blonde-haired women in their early twenties carrying shopping bags and chatting quietly to each other walked up behind them. Stepping aside to let them pass, Frank's leering gaze lingered on the front of one woman's fitted pink blouse, then traveled downwards over her pencil skirt and shapely legs. The two women continued on their way, ignoring Frank's lame attempt at conversation.

"If only you knew where your husbands were last night," he

11

muttered to himself, spitting on the ground to the side of him. Chuck slapped him on the arm with the back of his hand and pointed over to the light blue Ford truck parked on other side of the street.

"Boss, look what we got here. Check out over yonder, the broad standin' with the dotty old bag from across town. Now, that's a fine-lookin' specimen, don'tcha think? I mean, she's dressed a little funny but, well, damn." Chuck grinned.

Frank let out a low whistle of agreement. His eyes drifted up over Shona's slender body, which was now jacketless. He watched as she bent forward to pick up a bag, exposing the curve of her bosom beneath her undershirt.

"I ain't seen her around here before. Reckon that's her grandma?" Chuck asked.

"Maybe. You know what? I like to see new faces in town. You know why?" Frank raised an eyebrow at Chuck, who shrugged. "Because they don't know my reputation around here."

"Yet," Chuck replied, curling his lip.

"Normally I'd get Jake in there to help me load up, but you look strong enough. Sling that wood there on the back of the truck, will ya."

"Jeez, lady, don't you ever say 'please'?" Shona huffed as she threw her jacket and satchel down over the back of the truck.

"Well now. I do apologize. Please will you help me load my truck?" Mrs. Clark asked, stifling a smile.

Shona clenched her lips, trying to mask her own grin. "Alright, well... that's a little better." Reaching down to grab the bag of coal, she heaved it over the tailgate of the truck, then placed the string bag of kindling next to it.

"You staying with family while you're in town?" Mrs. Clark asked.

Shona froze. "Um..." she mumbled, running a fingernail over the handle of the bag.

The old lady watched Shona's reaction closely. "Well," Dorothy continued with a twinkle in her eye, "while you're trying to think up a name for which long-lost relative it is that you've come here to visit, you can load up the rest of the stuff. Then come and help me into the truck. I'm a little unsteady these days."

Mrs. Clark climbed into the driving seat with the help of her cane and Shona's arm. Struggling to swing her stocking-covered legs over the threshold, she maneuvered her feet into the footwell. When her legs were clear, Shona slammed the door, causing the windowpane to clatter. Within seconds of the ignition being fired up, the battered old diesel engine began kicking out plumes of white smoke behind it, the morning breeze blowing it back into Shona's face. Coughing, she wiped her face with the back of her hand.

"When did you last get this heap of junk serviced?" Shona asked, slipping her jacket back on and her satchel over her shoulder.

"It runs, don't it," the old lady snapped back. "Well, what are you standing there bellyaching for? Get in!"

Shona opened her mouth to argue but thought better of it. Drawing attention to herself was the last thing she needed right now. "No, I gotta get moving. I got places to be," she replied, pulling her cap down over her eyebrows.

"What? You don't expect me to be able to unload all'a this when I get home, do ya?" Mrs. Clark asked. "What's your name anyways?"

"Shona," she mumbled, climbing into the truck.

"Shona? Strange name. Shona *what*?"

"Just Shona," she replied, a little firmer than before as she scanned the horizon.

"Alright. Well, I'm Mrs. Clark. I live just on the edge of town. What do you do for a living, Shona?"

"Um... well..." Shona began, trying to think of the quickest way out of that question too. The truck hit a pothole, bouncing Shona up in her seat and smacking her head against the roof. The black tape precariously holding the passenger side wing mirror on ripped off, sending it bouncing along the tarmac of the highway.

"Jeez," Shona exclaimed, rubbing the bump on her head. She leaned out of the window and watched as the wing mirror smashed into pieces. "Lady, your truck's falling to bits. You really need to get this thing seen to."

Mrs. Clark looked in her rear-view mirror at the debris in the road and nodded. "Yeah I know, but it's expensive taking her into the garage." She paused as her face clouded over. "It ain't easy, me being on my own."

Shona looked over at the old lady, who was turning the wheel more widely than she needed to, her arthritic fingers gripping the leather as tightly as she could manage. Her eyes were squinting as they concentrated on the road ahead. Shona remained quiet and leaned against the truck door as the world trundled past her. They weren't moving very fast; the truck simply wouldn't have managed it but, even at thirty-three miles per hour, the panels still felt close to disintegrating with every mile of highway the balding tires ate up.

After about a mile, the truck wheel-spinned into the front drive of a rickety old cottage and crunched on the gravel below as the tires rolled to a halt. The little cottage had whitewashed weatherboarding on the outside and green timber framed windows. Mrs. Clark pulled the gear lever up, cursing under her breath as she cranked it into place.

Shona stepped out of the truck and took a closer look at the cottage. It had a porch swing on the veranda and a chicken pen on the far right hand side. On the top right of the roof there was a chimney. The front yard was a grassy lawn, with a gray cobblestone path parting it right up to the three steps that led up to the front door. She smiled as she took in the view of this cute little house that was in desperate need of some TLC.

"Nice place you got here," Shona remarked, a glimmer of light shining in her tired eyes.

"Yeah, I know what you're thinking, it's like the damn truck. Needs a heap of work done to it. But I can't manage all that myself now, not since..." Mrs. Clark began, her voice becoming distant as she exited the truck and disappeared around the back to let the tail down.

Shona cursed to herself. Taking her cap off, she again ran her hand through her greasy, matted hair and followed behind her.

"Hey, I didn't mean nothing by what I said. I meant it genuine. You got a nice place, Mrs. Clark. Yeah, it could do with a coat of paint here and there, but..." Shona rambled, scrunching her cap through her hands.

"Well, I try to keep on top of everything..." She paused, then waved a wrinkled old finger casually around the yard. "But I'm sixty-eight years old now and I can't get up ladders no more to see to those gutters."

"That's a shame," Shona replied, leaning on the truck and toeing the dirt. "Look, why don't you take the lighter bags in while I take a peek under the truck's hood. I can't promise I'll be able to do much but..."

Relief spread across the old lady's face, lighting it up. "Really? Well now, I surely would appreciate that." She climbed up the three steps, struggling to hold a bag under each arm.

"Don't you be lifting that coal bag, I got that one," Shona called after her, then turned back to the truck and sized up where to start.

~

It was almost lunchtime when Mrs. Clark looked through the tiny window by the side of the front door to see Shona tinkering under the hood of her truck, her shape distorted by the thin crack in the pane. She tottered down the porch steps and across to a patch of grass which now looked like an operating table. Bits of engine, springs, caps and covers were strewn around, with countless old rags showing how much diesel oil the poor battered engine had bled out. Shona emerged looking like a battlefield surgeon as the old lady approached, the contents of the glass mostly surviving the journey.

"How's it going? Am I calling the priest to give it its last rites?"

Shona shrugged. "Well, Mrs. Clark…"

The old lady waved her free hand and shook her head. "Call me Dorothy".

"OK." Shona smiled as she accepted the glass of tea. "Well, I think your engine's had it. When was the last time this thing had a service?"

Dorothy's smile evaporated. "Oh, well… I try to get it down to Harry's place in town to get the oil changed now and again. He tinkers with it until it runs smooth, but lately I've just let things around here slide a bit, I guess…" Her voice tailed off as she gazed at her house.

Shona sipped her tea and followed Dorothy's line of sight up to the gutters.

"Say, maybe you could take it down to Wreckers for me tomorrow? You probably know more about what it needs and what to ask for. Harry's a good man. He'll be fair with you."

"Tomorrow?" Shona repeated.

"Well, I just assumed that you'd care to stay here until then? You don't seem in a hurry to get over to your… um… family's place." Dorothy's eyes glinted in the sun.

"Um, yeah… I guess I should have said before when you

asked. I ain't got no family out here," Shona began. She drained her glass and offered it back to Dorothy who shook her head.

"Oh no. If you're staying, you can take that glass back in the house yourself. Leave it by the sink when you get washed up. Don't want you leaving oily handprints all over my countertops now." Dorothy headed back up to the front door.

❧

Shona looked around the yard, then bent down to pick up her jacket and satchel. After packing up the tools she'd borrowed from Dorothy's shed, she then headed along the cobblestone path and up the porch steps. Turning around at the top, Shona surveyed the land around her and smiled. *It'll do for the night at least. It'll be a nice change from a cold alleyway and a piece of cardboard to sleep on,* she thought.

In the hallway, Shona placed the toolbox on the floor, mindful not to scrape it too heavily on the wooden boards. They weren't up to much but the last job that Shona wanted to be given was to have to scrub oil patches off them. Dorothy was quite a salty old goat, but one who had offered her a warm place to sleep, and Shona was respectful enough to acknowledge that. Kindness was a rare commodity, not one she had encountered that often on her journey. The hostility she'd escaped from was more than enough for one lifetime.

Nervous, Shona stepped along the hallway, looking through the doorways to her left and right. Up ahead was a small kitchen, with a stove, tiny sink and a few worn-looking cupboards. On the right side of the hallway there was a small front room; the window looked out over the driveway. Perfect to notice visitors, Shona thought. The rickety staircase to the left of the hallway looked perilously steep, considering it led to the bedroom Dorothy must sleep in every night.

"You hungry?" a croaky voice called out from the kitchen.

"A little bit," Shona called back. "But, um, please don't go to any trouble for me, ma'am," she added.

Dorothy appeared in the doorway, her face blank. "I wasn't going to. And until you get those paws squeaky clean, you ain't getting a crumb."

Shona looked at her oily hands and flashed Dorothy a lopsided grin. "Oh, sorry," she replied, rubbing her elbow on the white doorframe to wipe off the smudge of oil she'd left.

Dorothy smiled back at Shona's efforts. "I think that's the least of my problems, don't you?" She waved her hand around in the air, pointing out the bits of wood missing from the paneling and the odd bit of bannister that was missing from the staircase. "Once you've washed up, I'll heat you up some stew. Made it this morning, my own special recipe. Got some biscuits too."

Following the old lady into the kitchen, Shona located the basin and ran the faucet. Shuddering when she felt the ice-cold water splash against her grubby hands, she persisted in scrubbing them as clean as she could with the welcome help of the scourer on the drying rack. She turned and held them up to Dorothy, who barely even registered a flicker of being impressed but motioned for Shona to take a seat at the table and placed a bowl of steaming hot stew in front of her. Dorothy popped a couple of biscuits on the side and sawed off a hunk of bread.

"There you go, eat up. Get some meat on those bones o'yours. I'll take you up to your room afterwards and you can get settled in." Dorothy passed Shona the lump of bread and started washing the pots and pans by the sink.

"Aren't you having anything?" Shona mumbled through a mouthful of bread.

"No. I'll have something later," the old lady replied, turning to face her.

Watching Shona polish off her dinner with huge hungry

mouthfuls, Dorothy leaned against the counter heavily with her eyes closed for a moment. After a few moments, the old lady's lips curled into a tight smile, her eyes narrowing slightly.

"You don't say much, do ya?"

"Not much to say," Shona replied, wiping her lips and mopping up the last of her gravy with her bread.

"Everybody's got a story," Dorothy said, her eyes glancing up towards a framed black and white photograph of a smiling young couple with their arms around each other. The young man was wearing an army issue uniform, complete with his World War One victory medal shining proudly on his lapel.

"Yeah. Well, maybe some don't need to be told," Shona replied, her tone clipped.

After finally being able to clean herself up with a warm bath, Shona now felt a lot more comfortable. She was wearing her less grubby pair of jeans and undershirt she had in her satchel and her hair was combed neatly, smelling fresher than it had for a long time.

"Here y'go, you should be snug as a bug in a rug tonight," Dorothy said as she handed Shona a pile of bedding comprised of a sheet, pillowcase and a thick wool blanket.

"Thank you," Shona replied, grateful that the bed Dorothy was showing her looked a lot more comfortable that the pile of folded boxes she'd slept on last night. Her still-aching back was a constant reminder to her how roughly she'd slept these last few weeks on her trek from Louisiana. If it wasn't a park bench, a storm drain or a drafty old barn, it was an alleyway with a cardboard mattress.

But as long as they didn't find her, it didn't matter.

"Here, let me take those. I got a pile to do tomorrow anyway." Dorothy reached out to take Shona's dirty clothes.

"You got any more in there?" she asked, pointing down to Shona's filthy satchel.

"No, really, don't worry, I can do them myself," Shona replied, clutching the clothes against her chest.

Dorothy nodded and backed off. She watched as Shona's eyes scanned the room, fixing especially on the tiny window at the far end. The bedroom was a little cramped and cold. It was obvious from the damp air that the old lady wasn't one for having guests very often, but somehow, despite this, the room still felt inviting. The bed was tucked away in the corner, with a small chest of drawers to the left of it and a tattered old red and green rug running alongside.

"Well, I'll leave you to it. I'm across the way there so just knock if you need anything, although I tend to sleep like the dead so—"

"I'll be fine." Shona interrupted, then smiled.

"Well... goodnight then. You can take the truck down to Harry first thing in the morning, if you don't mind?" Dorothy asked.

"Sure. Goodnight," Shona replied.

Closing the door behind her, Dorothy headed across the landing to her bedroom and clunked her door shut.

Once Shona had made up her bed, she climbed underneath the thick blanket and pulled it up to her chin. Shona smiled to herself.

For the first time in a long time, she felt safe.

It was the middle of the night when Shona woke with a jump. Her eyes darted around the dark room for some clue as to where she was. Bare walls and a chest of drawers reflecting the shard of moonlight blaring through the thin drapes were her only indications of where she could possibly be. She looked over the side of the bed to see her boots untied. Across the room, her pants were folded neatly on the little wooden armchair next to the bedside table, exactly where she'd left them, along with her coat and shirt. Peeking underneath her blanket, she found herself still wearing her cotton undershirt. She reached her trembling hand lower to see if everything else was as she'd left it too. It was.

Not like the last time she'd woken up in a panic. And the time before that. But all was well in this house. She was safe for now, it seemed.

Shona rubbed her eyes and shivered as she swung her legs out of bed. She pulled on her pants and crept to the bedroom door, jumping as she found the only floorboard between the bed and the door that squeaked without mercy.

"Goddamn it," she blurted out, mindful not to raise her voice too much. Turning the handle, she opened the door and poked her head into the corridor.

Nothing.

Seeing Dorothy's bedroom door closed, Shona breathed a sigh of relief that she hadn't disturbed her and tiptoed down the hallway to the bathroom. Clicking on the light, she squinted as her eyes adjusted. The bathroom was old and sparse, but it was clean. She walked up to the sink and turned on the faucet. Splashing her face with the ice-cold water, she brought herself completely into the here and now. Wiping her face with the towel that was draped over the rail, she looked at herself in the mirror.

"Jeez, girl, you really need some sleep. This ain't no good, moving from place to place. You need to settle."

She squeezed her eyes shut.

But they can't find you if you keep running, she thought.

Chapter 3

S unlight beamed through the bedroom drapes that Friday morning and landed square on Dorothy's sleeping face. Groaning, she winced as she opened her heavy eyelids. The welcome comfort of company had encouraged her to sleep in well past her normal waking-up time. She headed to the bathroom and, as she raised her head up from the sink, looked out of the window. Smiling, she dried herself off and headed downstairs, placing one careful foot after the other.

"You do know it's only 7:30 a.m., don't you?" Dorothy called out as she walked across the front garden towards a pair of boots poking out from underneath the truck. The hood had been unbolted and heaved off, with various tools strewn around on the pale green grass.

Shona slid out, her face smeared with axle grease and brake dust. "Huh? Oh. Well, I thought I'd just take another look at your truck."

"You must have been up at the crack of dawn to get those pesky bolts off that hood. That's a job and a half in itself."

"Yeah, I know, but I always get up early. I like the quiet," Shona replied as she felt the morning sunlight bathe her face in its glow. "Well, usually. There'd be no chance of sleeping in late with that goddamn rooster you got over there."

"Oh, you mean Buddy? Yeah, he's everybody's wakeup call around here. Regular as clockwork he is." Dorothy turned her head in the direction of the little chicken run by the side of her house. Three black chickens were clucking and bobbing in the dirt, with Buddy sitting proudly on the top of the henhouse holding court. "And before you say it, he ain't going in no pot-roast either." A mischievous grin crept across the old lady's wrinkled features as Shona opened her mouth to reply. "How's it going with the truck anyway? You found out what's wrong with it?"

"Yeah, think so. But it'll need some new parts and I don't think they're gonna be cheap. It needs quite a bit of work done to it too. I think you might need an expert." Shona's voice tailed off as she ducked her head down into the engine bay of the truck.

"Alright, then. Well, I guess you'd better take it down to Wreckers." Dorothy turned and headed back up the porch steps. "Now, I'll go make us some breakfast while you put that back on." She pointed at the hood lying on the grass. "How many eggs you want?"

"Um... just one," Shona replied, but her stomach protested loudly. "Maybe two?"

"Three it is then." Dorothy said, grinning. "You need filling out, you're too scrawny." She pointed a long fingernail at Shona, then trundled off into the house.

~

"So, when you get there, you ask for Harry, OK?" Dorothy instructed as she handed Shona a wad of dollar bills and the keys to the truck. "He never charges me full whack, but I want you to make sure he takes it this time."

Shona held the bunch of keys in one hand and the money in the other, her mind racing with the thought of how far she could get with a semi-working truck and thirty-five dollars.

"You remember where you're going, right?" Dorothy asked.

"Yeah, I think so. Back towards town, right?" she replied, pointing towards the tree-lined driveway and perimeter gate.

"Yep. Be as quick as you can, though, I could use a little help with those gutters. Buddy had to dodge a big chunk o'metal falling down the other day." Dorothy chuckled.

"I'll be back soon."

Shona walked over to the truck, started it up and roared off down the driveway.

"I hope so," Dorothy muttered to herself as she watched her beloved truck disappear into the distance.

As she bit her bottom lip, thoughts polluted Shona's brain. She stared down at the money burning a hole in her hand after pulling over about half a mile from Dorothy's ramshackle house. *Survival is survival,* she thought. But the idea of stealing from an old lady, who'd shown her nothing but kindness in the last twenty-four hours, disgusted her so much that it left her mind as quickly as it had entered. "No, Shona. That's not who you are," she chastised herself out loud, flooring the gas pedal as she did so.

After driving the mile back along the highway, Shona pulled up on the edge of Wreckers' parking lot. Several trucks were already lined up in various states of repair, with pieces of their vital parts being scrutinized by several mechanics wearing smart blue denim overalls. The air was thick with the smell of tailpipe emissions and petroleum gas, mixed with the sound of barely-in-tune singing to the wireless. Back slaps and tomfoolery between some of the younger mechanics added to the zip of the joint and Shona smiled briefly. Straightening her cap, she mentally composed the story she was about to tell Harry when she was finally introduced to him. Just then, she jumped in her seat as a figure loomed large at the side of the truck.

"How can we help you?" When the mechanic realized who was sitting in the driver's seat, his heart-shaped face broke out into a huge grin, his green eyes glowing. "Hey, it's you. Hi. We met the other day. I was the klutz who ruined your mornin'. Remember?" Jonny blushed as Shona stared at him.

"Not really," she replied after a few moments.

"Well, I guess Mrs. Clark found you in the end, seeing as though that's her truck you're sittin' in." Jonny paused, waiting for a reply, but Shona looked straight ahead. "You'll probably be lookin' for Harry, then?" His eyes dimmed noticeably until Shona looked at him to respond, causing the goofy grin to reappear on his handsome face.

"Yes. Please."

"Sure thing, ma'am, I'll go get him. Oh, and you might want this." Jonny reached down behind the truck and lifted up a piece of tailpipe that had fallen off. "If you pull the truck up on those ramps there, I can fix it back on if you like? No charge."

"If you could just get Harry for me, please, that'd be swell," Shona said. Jonny nodded and rushed off into the office at the far end of the garage, ducking underneath the car lifts and side-stepping the pneumatic drills.

Shona switched the engine off and climbed out of the truck. Three mechanics looked over, but rather than elbowing each other and letting out the low wolf-whistles she was used to getting in establishments like this, she was pleasantly surprised that all she received was a tip of their caps, then the sight of the tops of their heads as they inspected a Buick engine.

"How can I help you, young lady?" a deep, gravelly voice sounded out behind Shona. She spun around to face a tall, stocky, black-haired man wearing a set of navy-blue denim overalls. They were cleaned and pressed, the Wreckers logo stitched onto a badge next to a name tag.

"I brought Mrs. Clark's truck in. It ain't running so good."

Shona squinted in the glare of the morning sun as she looked up at him. Harry, sensing her discomfort, politely stepped into the path of the sunbeam. It was then that Shona saw his face properly. He looked to be in his late fifties. His face was a weather-beaten leathery-brown color, a testament to the amount of years he'd worked in the open air. His hands were bear-like, with a dent in the fingers of his right hand where a wrench had sat snugly all his working life.

"Well now, you pull it into the back there and I'll take a look at it. I know Mrs. Clark. She'll be madder than a wet hen if she finds out any other guy but me has been fixing up her precious truck." Harry nodded to Shona who then hopped back into the driver's seat.

"I think the fuel injectors could be clogged, maybe, or the head gasket could have blown?" Shona called back, leaning out of the window as she drove slowly into the garage.

"Well now, you sure know your terminology. You worked on these things before?" he asked, a smile forming at the corner of his mouth.

"Kinda. I used to fix tractor engines with my daddy back home in..." Shona stopped herself mid-sentence.

"In?" Harry pressed casually as he walked round to the front of the truck to begin unbolting the hood.

"Tennessee," Shona lied, clearing her dry throat.

"No kidding, really? Tennessee? I got a cousin out there. Lives up near the Stones River... in Rutherford. You know it?" Harry's voice muffled intermittently as he raised his head up and down every few moments.

"Um... yeah, I heard of it," Shona lied again. She rubbed her hand along the back of her neck, feeling the sweat beads starting to drip down between her shoulder blades. Harry seemed well-meaning enough, but her stomach turned at the thought of any more of his probing questions.

"Yeah, well, I got no clue why he wants to live there, so close to that old battlefield. Why he'd want a constant reminder of that loss is beyond me," Harry continued.

"I guess. So, about the truck?" Shona asked, nibbling her fingernail.

"Well, I'd say you were pretty spot on with your diagnosis, so it'll take a good few hours to fix up, I reckon. If you leave it with me, I can have it ready before we close up here. Come back, say, around four?" Harry replied.

Shona looked at the little clock on the wall behind him. It was only just after ten, but with little choice she nodded and looked around her to see what she could possibly do for the next seven hours or so to pass the time.

"Say, seeing as though you know a little bit about these things, why don't you stick around and help? We might get this done a whole lot quicker with two of us on the case." Harry's steel-gray eyes lingered on Shona as he waited for her reply. With little option other than hanging around in the diner across the street and making a cup of coffee last all day, she nodded.

At least I can stay out of sight, Shona thought. "OK. I don't know that much but I learn pretty quick," she said, picking up a spare wrench from the tool chest leaning against the wall.

As Harry and Shona got to work on the truck's engine, a loud holler rang out near the entrance to the garage.

"Uncle Harry."

The young man approaching the two of them was wearing a white t-shirt and stained blue jeans, ripped at the knee. His fitted black leather jacket completed his homage to James Dean. Harry looked up, his bright face noticeably changing.

"Frank. What are you doing here?" he replied, lowering his head.

"Well, ain't that nice. What's eatin' you?" Frank replied. "I just came over here to see how things are, there's no need to be ugly."

His stormy face softened when he spotted Shona. "Oh, it's you. I know you," he began, his finger outstretched towards her.

The color drained from Shona's face.

"Um... hang on, lemme think..." Frank clicked his fingers as he tried to recall. The wait was agony for Shona. "Oh yeah. You were with that old lady from outta town, outside the grocery store. She your grandma?" He pointed to the truck.

"Um. Yeah," Shona replied, scratching the back of her head.

Harry's eyes twitched, but whatever he was thinking at that moment, he chose to keep to himself. "Shona, why don't you check over that engine, see if the problem's what you think it is. I won't be a minute."

Harry led Frank to the other side of the garage and took out his wallet. Shona noticed him pass over a small wad of bills, then Frank slapped him on the shoulder and sauntered off.

Snapping her attention back to the truck, she continued to tinker away, searching for the problem.

"Any luck?" he asked, returning to her side.

"Definitely the head gasket. I think it's had it, judging by all that white smoke."

Harry smiled at her, his strong hands resting on his hips. "Say, you're not looking for a job, are you? I could use some fresh blood around here."

"A job? Here?" Shona asked, her heart pounding with uncertainty. If she could just keep her head down long enough to earn some decent money and get a new start, she could finally stop having to eat out of garbage cans and sleep on cardboard.

"Yeah. Come in on Monday morning for a trial. You can

meet the other guys too." He looked over to the group of mechanics who were wailing along to the song playing on the radio and laughed. "They can't carry a tune in a bucket, that's for damn sure, but they'll treat you right."

"Won't they be surprised to find a girl working with them, Harry?" Shona asked. "I ain't never found a place that would accept that. The most I ever got was a job out back cleaning tools." She looked at Harry, immediately regretting bringing his attention to how strange a notion it was for a woman to be fixing trucks.

Harry smiled. "If you ask me, any girl who knows a busted-up head gasket from the color smoke it blows out is good enough to earn a trial in my garage. The other guys here will be fine with it. They're not jerks like you find in other places. I wouldn't stand for it anyway. Marcie wouldn't let me even if I did." Harry smiled.

"Um... OK then. Thanks," Shona replied, shaking Harry's huge hand.

"Alright then. Well, let's see about fixing this heap of junk so you can get it back to Mrs. Clark." Harry walked over to the tool chest and picked up his trusty wrench, gripping its leather-wrapped handle. "You know, though, it's strange. I don't know Mrs. Clark that good, and I ain't never heard of her having any family to speak of but, well... you said she's your grandma, right?"

"Yeah?" Shona chipped in, her fingers wrapped around a rubber tube as she loosened the metal collar around it. She stopped dead when she realized she'd told yet another lie to this man who'd shown her nothing but respect. Looking up as Harry's questioning expression, she decided to come clean. "Well, Harry... Um... Well, she's not actually my grandma. I'm just staying with her. That guy Frank just assumed and, well..." Shona shrugged, rolling the wrench through her fingers.

"You know what, Shona? I appreciate your honesty. You'll do just fine here," Harry replied with a little wink.

~

Dorothy stared at the clock on her kitchen wall. It was getting late, well past six, and Shona had been gone for over eight hours now.

She feared the worst.

Knowing that Wreckers closed at 5 p.m. on the dot on a Friday, she knew it was pointless calling. Casting another look over the small carriage clock on the mantelpiece, she trundled over to the telephone, her loose gray bun bobbling on the top of her head, to make the call she didn't want to have to make.

After dialing the number for the operator and asking for her connection, Dorothy peeled back the edge of the drapes by the window facing out onto the driveway.

Still nothing.

A gruff voice on the other end of the call answered after three short rings. "Hello, sheriff's department. Hello? Hello?"

The man's voice echoed as Dorothy held the receiver away from her ear after suddenly hearing a familiar rumble catch the breeze and filter through the thin, single pane window. Slamming down the phone, she shuffled over to the front door. Yanking it open, she saw her freshly washed and waxed blue truck pull up on the driveway.

Shona flung open the truck door and jumped out, a huge grin of accomplishment draped over her oil-smudged face. "Sorry I'm so late, Mrs. Clark. It took longer than we thought to fix her up. You wouldn't believe what we had to strip back to get at the problem. You'll be as happy as a pig in mud when you see how good she runs now. We even gave it a wax and shine."

Dorothy watched Shona run her sleeve over the flecks of

brake dust and sand that had built up on the front fender during her journey back.

"Oh, and Harry said it would be an even thirty-two. I tried to give him the lot but he wouldn't hear of it. So here's your change." Shona delved into the top pocket of her jacket and handed over three crisp dollar bills.

"Well now... thank you." Dorothy held the bills for a moment before handing them back to Shona, whose eyes widened with surprise.

"Here, you keep this. For your trouble." Dorothy nodded, not taking no for an answer. Shona reached over and took the bills.

"Thank you, ma'am," she replied.

"So how was Harry?"

"He's fine. In fact..." Shona began, "he, um, he offered me a job."

Dorothy cocked her head to the side in surprise. "A job? At Wreckers? Doing what?"

"Fixing trucks. Harry said he'd teach me. I mean, I know the basics and I learn quick so..."

"Fixing trucks?" Dorothy repeated, openmouthed. "Well, I'll be damned. I ain't never heard of a girl doing that before. But I guess you're not the average girl, now are you?" she chuckled. "Harry musta seen potential in you. Alright then..." Dorothy paused, holding the silence between her and Shona for what felt like an age. "I guess you'll be looking for somewhere to stay for a while now then, won't you?"

Shona held her breath.

"Well..." Dorothy continued, "I can help you look if you like? There are always rooms going cheap above the grocery store in town. It's across the street from Wreckers so it'll be nice and convenient." She turned and headed back up to her porch steps.

"Oh, but..." Shona began, leaning forward, then rocking back on her heels.

"But what?" Dorothy turned to face her, then got the hint. "You wanna stay here? Why would you wanna do that? You got the whole of town to meet, girlie. You don't wanna spend your time with a doddery old codger like me, do you?" It pained her to say it, knowing how nice it felt last night to have company in the house, but she, like Shona, also felt the fear of rejection. She hadn't lived with anyone since her husband died over a decade ago.

"I wouldn't mind none, I like the peace and quiet around here. Well, apart from that dumb-ass rooster you got over there." Shona grinned as she pointed to the chicken pen. "If it's alright with you, I mean? I could help out, maybe do some repairs to those gutters up there? And I'd pay my way too, ma'am..." She stopped rambling when she saw the affection for her cross the old lady's features.

"I know, I know, you don't-do-charity." Dorothy chuckled, waving her hands. "Alright, you've sweet talked me into it. If you really wanna stay, you can stay."

~

The following Monday morning was Shona's first day at work. It was just a trial day, but she had every intention to prove to Harry—and the other mechanics there—that a mistake hadn't been made in trusting her.

As she was walking over to the truck, Dorothy called after her. Slinging her satchel through the truck door window, she turned back to face the old lady who was standing on the porch steps leaning on her stick.

"I need you to get me some groceries on your way home." She motioned for Shona to follow her back inside the house.

"How's your leg doing?" Shona asked, spotting the old lady's bandaged right knee.

"Let's just say I ain't gonna win any ass-kicking contests right now, that's for damn sure. Those stairs don't help none either," Dorothy replied. She reached up on to a shelf above the stove and pulled down a small metal canister. Tugging off the lid, she took out a few dollar bills and handed them to Shona. "Pick up some more cheese and bread too; I had the last of yours for lunch yesterday."

"No problem. You need anything else?"

"I got a list here." Dorothy reached into her pale green cardigan pocket and handed Shona the notepaper. "You should have enough, but if not, I'll give you some more tomorrow." She clamped the lid shut on the canister and reached up to put it back on the shelf. Struggling to balance on her one good leg, Dorothy yelped out in pain.

"Here, let me help." Shona jumped forward to steady the old lady on her feet.

Dorothy felt Shona's arms wrap themselves around her frail body and take the full weight of her as she wobbled. "Oh my, thank you, dear. I nearly fell on my ass then." She looked Shona dead in the eye. "You're a good girl. Now go, scoot. You'll be late for work." Slapping Shona on her back, she pushed her towards the door.

"Are you sure you'll be OK? I mean, I could call Harry..." Shona protested.

"No, don't you do that. I'll be fine. Now skedaddle."

Shona nodded, still unsure as to whether to leave the old lady alone. She turned and headed back outside, fired up the truck and sped off down the driveway.

~

"Well, hello again, ma'am," Jonny greeted, sweeping his cap off his head as Shona pulled up in the parking lot.

"Hi. Harry around?" she asked, jumping out of the truck.

"Oh yeah, he's just in the back. But he asked me to show you the ropes this mornin', get you all settled in."

"Oh, OK," Shona replied scanning the forecourt of Wreckers to get her bearings.

"I didn't really get the chance the other day to introduce myself properly. I'm Jonny. Jonny Pearson. That's Earl over there on the creepers. Don't let him get you talkin' about the World Series last year, he'll chew your ears off."

"Hey Pearson, I heard that," Earl retorted, scratching the back of his bald head.

"He's a Yankees fan so he wasn't too pleased about that result," Jonny whispered to Shona.

"I'll be sure to avoid that subject then," Shona replied, waving politely at Earl who slid underneath a truck, still muttering to himself.

"That's Kenny and Tom down in the pit," Jonny said, pointing to two short, stocky black-haired men who seemed to be in deep conversation as they scrutinized the underside of a Buick. "And that's Marcie over there by the office door." Jonny pointed to the far corner of the garage, just behind the vehicle lift and tool chests. "She's Harry's wife."

Marcie, holding a coffee mug, smiled and waved back. She was in her late forties and wore cat-eye glasses and a black-and-white spotted hair tie bandana in her dark brown shoulder-length hair. Her maroon blouse, loose-fitting black pleated skirt and black pumps completed her casual but smart look.

"What's his story?" Shona nodded over to another man at the opposite corner of the garage whose face looked a little less friendly at her arrival.

"Oh, him? Yeah, that's Doug. Don't take no notice of him, he's still got a little shrapnel in that brain o'his from Iwo Jima.

Harry took pity on him, gave him his old job back when he returned. Can't keep his hands steady, though, much anymore."

Jonny waved over to Doug, who eyeballed Shona with suspicion. They both watched as Doug chewed slowly on some tobacco, then spat out a blob into a bucket next to him. "What do you say we go over and introduce you to him, break the ice?" Jonny winked.

Turning away from the approaching figures of Jonny and Shona, Doug placed both hands on the edge of the tool chest in front of him and gritted his teeth.

"Hey Doug, this is Shona..."

"I know who she is, I was at the briefing this mornin', wasn't I?" Doug replied sullenly. "What I don't get is why Harry's got some broad workin' here. What does she know about trucks, huh?" Doug replied, not turning around.

"Oh, c'mon now Doug, that ain't no way to talk to a lady now, is it?" Jonny said. "Shona's shown Harry she knows her stuff, so he's agreed to do a trial for her. I think we should all give her a chance, yessir."

"Yeah? Well, there are enough guys comin' home from their posts abroad that need jobs, so as far as I'm concerned she's takin' up one of 'em."

Doug turned around and glared at Shona. He was in his early forties, with a face coated in days-old bumpy black stubble and a long, jagged scar running between his right eyebrow and his receding hairline.

"Is that right, Doug?" Harry appeared behind Jonny and Shona. "Well, considering you're one of 'those guys' who've benefited from a job here, I'd suggest you lay off the girl. I do the hiring around here." He fixed his stare on Doug. "And the firing."

"Yes, boss," Doug conceded, then picked up his wrench to start unbolting the hood of the car he was about to work on.

With Jonny and Harry talking over the day's delivery schedule, Shona looked back over to the struggling Doug, who couldn't quite keep his grip on the wrench, so much so that it kept slipping off the bolt he was trying to loosen.

"Here, try this one," she said, passing Doug another wrench from the tool chest. It fit around the head of the bolt perfectly and sure enough the reassuring squeak of a loosening bolt filled the silence between them.

"Don't think this makes us friends," Doug grunted under his breath.

"I don't," Shona replied, then set off back to her own first job of the day.

Chapter 4

Shona had been working at Wreckers for almost two weeks and all was going well, with the exception of the occasional run-in with Doug who seemed content to grunt every time Shona was near. She'd even been allowed to fix up Dorothy's truck when business was quiet, and these days it ran so smoothly that Harry barely even noticed it pull up behind him as he was unlocking the heavy wooden doors that Thursday morning.

"Well, g'morning Shona, five minutes early as usual," he joked, checking his watch. "How was your evening?

"Hey boss, it was good, thanks. Me and Dorothy watched that new game show," Shona replied, smiling.

"Now then, I can't be hearing this. A girl your age should be going out all gussied up to have some fun, not stuck indoors watching TV," Harry chastised, his bear-like hands resting on his hips. "Say, why don't you go over to the bar one night with the guys? They think of you as one of their own now, and Jonny... well, you must know by now that boy is head over heels in love with you. He's as happy as a puppy with two peckers every time he sets his eyes on you, girl."

Shona blushed as Harry jabbed his elbow into her side and

pointed over to another truck that had just pulled into the parking lot.

"Mornin' Harry," Jonny yelled, jumping out of the truck. Waving back, Harry turned to tease Shona again, but she had already disappeared into the back of the garage to start work.

~

"So, Shona, Harry tells me you're from Tennessee originally?"

Jonny tapped the edge of the Chrysler fender he was sitting on as he tried to make small talk with Shona, who was checking the air pressure in the tires.

"Um. Yeah," Shona replied, not looking up.

"Oh, that's so cool. Me, I'm just a country boy, Mississippi born and bred. I ain't seen none of the other states around, well, not really. Not unless I'm drivin' through on deliveries. Sometimes I get out to Arkansas, sometimes even over to Alabama. But it's just there and back, no time for sightseein'..."

Jonny rattled on for over five minutes before he paused and looked down at Shona, who hadn't responded to any of his open questions.

"Shona, I've been meaning to ask you somethin' these last few weeks..."

Shona pressed down hard on the valve of the tire, letting out a gush of pressurized air. Startled, Jonny almost fell of the fender.

"Oops, sorry Jonny. Kinda lost my grip on that." Shona smiled.

"It's OK, no harm done. Anyway, as I was sayin'..."

"Hey Jonny, you OK to drop these parts off to that guy in Birchfield?" Harry called out from the office.

"Sure thing, boss." Jonny jumped down from the fender and tipped his cap to Shona as he left.

"How's it going?" Harry asked, wandering over to her.

"Good, I think. Those two over there are all ready, and that one just needs a new headlamp, then it's good to go," Shona replied, pointing over to the trucks she'd fixed already that morning.

"Wow, you're on a roll, girl. Don't let me slow you down. Crack on." Harry slapped her on the shoulder and let out a deep booming laugh. "I'll go call Old Man Spooner and tell him his pride and joy is all ready to collect."

"OK, Harry, I'll get started on that headlamp."

As Shona strode over to her next job of the day, Harry hung his hands on his hips and smiled.

"You know what, girl?" he called over.

"What?" Shona replied.

"I think I may have just found my new secret weapon."

Secret? Shona thought. *That works for me.*

Jonny returned from his delivery run to see Shona lying on her back on a set of creepers, changing the oil on a Ford pick-up. Taking a deep breath to steady himself, he licked his hand and ran it through his light brown hair.

"Hi Shona, how's it goin'?" he asked after walking over as casually as he could make it look.

Shona slid out and looked up at him. "Hey Jonny, all good here. How was your morning?"

"Yeah, good too. Um..." He paused and licked his lips. "Say, I was wonderin' if you'd like to, um... Maybe come over to the bar later... With the rest of the guys, I mean, not just me." He let out a nervous laugh as Shona looked at him, making it even harder for him to get the sentence out without stumbling over every word. "I mean, they've all been askin' me to ask you to join us. You're one of us now." He grinned.

"I doubt everyone feels that way, Jonny," Shona replied,

motioning towards Doug who was staring at them both as he pumped the arm of a trolley jack wedged underneath a truck.

"He still givin' you the evil eye?" Jonny put his hands on his hips and narrowed his stare back at Doug.

"Nothing I can't handle. I'm used to it. A girl can't work in a place like this without getting a few stares now and again." Shona grinned and tipped her cap to Doug who shrank down to his creepers without responding.

"Yeah, well, not on my watch." Jonny began to march over to speak to Doug but just as he did so, Doug let out a cry of sheer agony. The arm of the jack had slipped out of its bracket, dropping the truck down and pinning him to the concrete. Only his legs were now visible underneath it.

"Help me! Oh God, help," he screamed, the two-ton truck crushing down on his chest and squeezing the life slowly out of him.

Shona ran to Jonny's side and while he tried to pull Doug out, she yanked the trolley jack handle back into place and began to pump it up and down, raising the truck just enough for Jonny to pull Doug out. Barely conscious, Doug gasped as his squashed lungs reinflated with precious air.

"Th-th-thank you," Doug croaked up to Jonny as he regained his senses.

"Wasn't just me, man. Shona was the one who got that truck off you," Jonny nodded over to an equally out of breath Shona.

After a moment or two, Doug reached out his shaking hand to Shona. "I misjudged you. I'm sorry," he spluttered, coughing.

"No sweat," Shona replied. "I get it all the time."

~

"Dorothy, I was thinking. Should we take a trip somewhere? I ain't had a day off work for four months now so I figure Harry owes me some time off. What do you say I ask him tomorrow?

It'll be nice to get out of town for a bit," Shona began, watching the old lady knitting. It was just after dinner on Friday evening.

"What's brought this on all of a sudden?" Dorothy asked, looking up.

"Oh, nothing. I was in the diner today and saw in a magazine that there's this place down in Gulfport. They got these beautiful beach houses down there. We could get a couple of rooms in one of those. Oh Dorothy, you should see them, they're just perfect. All white weatherboarding, blue-frame windows and their own private boardwalk down to the beach. I got a hankering for some ocean right now," Shona said, her keen eyes shining. "And I reckon we could both do with the fresh sea air, don't you?"

Dorothy clacked her needles together and lowered them into her lap. "And how do you suppose we can afford to stay in a place like that?" she said.

Shona sat up in her seat and leaned forward.

"Well now, see, I've managed to save a little bit here and there, my tips mostly... and I... Well, I might have already rung the number that was in the ad in the magazine and..." She grinned. "I've kinda already booked us a week there. Surprise."

Eventually, after seven long seconds of contemplation, Dorothy's pursed lips melted into a huge smile. "Well, alright. When do we leave?"

Chapter 5

Straightening the collar on his best red-and-black plaid shirt, Frank Smith wandered over as casually as he could make it look to a young brown-haired lady staring at the bus station timetable pinned to the wall. She was in her early twenties and wore a yellow summer dress and yellow-and-white ribbon in her hair.

"Well now, g'mornin', ma'am. May I be of some assistance to ya?" He drawled.

The woman turned around and smiled a smile that almost knocked Frank off his feet.

"Hello sir, do you know what time the next bus to Birchfield is? I need to get to my connection." She flipped her wavy shoulder-length hair out of her eyes and smiled again.

"Where, might I ask, are you headin'?" Frank leaned his shoulder against the wall.

"Oh, well, I start college in a week, so I need to get to my dorm, get settled in, you know?"

"OK. The name's Frank, by the way."

"I'm Lucy," the young woman replied, shaking his outstretched hand.

"Glad to meet ya, Lucy. But I'm sorry to say there ain't

another bus to Birchfield for at least another coupla hours. Sorry." He stood up straight and started to walk away.

"Oh, right. Are you sure? I was told they were every half hour…"

"No, they changed the schedule. Very recently." Frank stood with his back facing her, a smirk coating his face as his plan started to take shape.

"I see."

Lucy bit the corner of her bottom lip and looked around her to see what her options were for her wait.

"Say, I hope you don't mind me askin', but did you say you were *startin'* college?" Frank asked, confused.

Lucy laughed, then lowered her eyes. "I know. My friends all graduated this year but I," she paused, "took a little bit longer to get there. Creative mind, you see. It wanders sometimes. Took me a while to finish high school, but I made it in the end." She smiled and looked up at Frank who smiled back. "So, here I am, finally making my parents proud."

Frank noticed a slight bitterness in her last words. He folded his arms and sidled up next to her. "Well, if you've got no better plans for the next two hours, will you allow me to buy you a drink? That is, of course, if you're old enough to…"

"Don't worry, I'm twenty-one," she replied, putting his fears to rest. "Where?"

"I got a little bar in town. Chasers it's called. About five minutes' walk from here. I can help you with your bags if you like?"

"I should stay and wait really…" Lucy replied, looking around for any sign of the bus to Birchfield.

"Well, alright then. But it's one o'clock in the afternoon right now and that sun ain't gon' get any cooler in the next two hours. C'mon, just one drink?" Frank's charm was oozing out of him, bleeding into her resolve.

"Maybe I could use a glass of sweet tea. It is getting mighty hot out here."

Grinning, Frank swept back over to her and picked up the larger of her canvas bags while she swung her purse and smaller travel bag over her shoulder.

"So where are you from?" he asked.

"Monterey."

～

"Oh man, the first thing I'm gonna do when we get to Gulfport is jump straight into that ocean. Did you see the pictures, Dorothy? It's as clear as a... Well, I ain't seen nothing as clear as that water."

Shona could hardly contain her glee as she and Dorothy drove down the highway out of Riverside on the first day of their summer vacation together.

"Yeah, maybe a bit of that sea air will do my old bones good too," Dorothy replied, laughing at Shona's gusto and looking forward to the next two hundred miles in the presence of the young lady who'd turned her world completely upside down in the most wonderful way imaginable.

～

It was already six o'clock by the time Lucy remembered to check her watch.

"Oh Lord in heaven, look at the time. Frank, I've missed my bus..." She put down her third glass of tea onto the chipped mahogany bar top and reached down for her bags. "What time's the next one?"

"Well now, I think that's the only bus runnin' today. There won't be another one until tomorrow now." Frank raised his eyebrows, trying hard to sound concerned.

"You're kidding! What am I gonna do now?" Lucy mumbled into the air.

"You could always stay here tonight," Frank began, stopped in his tracks by a confused look from Lucy. "Oh, no, please don't misunderstand my intentions. It's a bar, there are lots of rooms for rent upstairs. I won't charge seein' as though it's my fault you missed your bus." Frank, sensing Lucy's growing feeling of uncertainty, began pointing people out in the bar. "That's Trish over there, by the restrooms. The one with the curly red hair. She's been here for years. And over by the juke-box, the old guy with the white hair, well that's Norm. He used to run this place before I took over five years ago when I turned twenny-one. My grandpappy left this place to me in his will and I swore I'd do the best job I could to make it the best bar in Mississippi."

Lucy scanned the tired-looking décor and chipped or torn furnishings. "Well, I guess I could stay for a bit, maybe the night? Then I can catch the first bus over to Birchfield in the morning."

Frank couldn't help the broad smile that spread across his handsome face.

"Well now, what's say we have a proper drink to celebrate then? Bourbon?"

Lucy giggled, then watched as Frank climbed around the bar and poured a double measure into two shot glasses.

The beach house was perfect. Whitewashed weatherboards glistened in the late afternoon sunshine, the window frames as blue as the ocean itself. Waves were crashing only yards away from a veranda that wove its way all around the perimeter of the house. There was a short boardwalk, which led down to the white sandy beach below, and there wasn't a soul to be spotted as far as the eye could see. It really was the most perfect place Shona had ever seen.

Shona walked over to Dorothy who was sitting on the veranda staring into the distance watching the ebb and flow of the waves.

"You know, you're the first person I've been on a vacation with since my husband passed," Dorothy said. She passed Shona a wallet-sized photograph. "I had a copy made of the picture that's hanging up on my kitchen wall. You remember the one?"

"Yeah, I see it every time we sit down to dinner. He was a pretty handsome guy," Shona replied, sitting down next to the old lady. She smiled at the picture of a much younger Dorothy standing next to her husband, their arms linked and eyes radiant with adoration for each other. Careful not to bend the crisp edges of the photograph, Shona handed it back to Dorothy.

"Sure was. He didn't seem to mind that I was quite a few years older than him when we met. Walter and I were married only a year before the American Expeditionary Force took him away to France just after Christmas, 1917. He managed to survive. Just about. Came back with shrapnel stuck in his leg and his lungs full of gas but I had him home and that's all I cared about. That's him there, a couple of years after he got back. He wanted to wait until he got his Victory Medal first before we had that done." Dorothy pointed down at the picture.

"You must have been so proud of him. It looks like a real special medal," Shona remarked.

Dorothy smiled. "It was. Those boys had to wait a while for it but eventually everyone got theirs in '21. After that we started our life together properly. We wanted to start a family but after the amount of time Walt had spent exposed to all that mustard gas, he just wasn't able to... Well, we tried but it never happened for us."

Shona saw the tears prick the corners of the old lady's wrinkly eyes, but before she could say anything to comfort her, Dorothy took a deep breath.

"Then, after spending the most wonderful years of my life making a home here with Walt, it all blew up over there in Europe again, didn't it? One day he got a call from the Department of War. They'd found his service record and requested his help with the strategy plans for Omaha. They promised him he wouldn't be doing no more fighting, not now he was in his late forties. Couldn't have even if he wanted to, not with his leg the way it was. Said he'd be kept at a safe distance from all of that." She paused again, her handkerchief screwed up in her fist. "He agreed to go over to Normandy in '44 with the navy and he never came back. Telegram said his ship had been blown completely out of the water. Well, you only get so much luck in your life. After a while, it runs out." Her eyes glazed over as she stared down at the thin gold band on her finger.

A few moments of silence fell between them.

"I'm so sorry, Dorothy. So you've been on your own at the house since?"

"Yep, but I'm like you. I prefer the quiet. I talk to him sometimes, only inside the house though. If I do that in the street, they'll be locking me up." She chuckled.

"I would've liked to have met him," Shona said.

"He would've liked you. You got that same glint in your eye, that same thirst for seeing the big wide world. Maybe that's why you travel around as much as you do." Dorothy lingered her gaze on Shona for a moment before smiling.

"I wouldn't really call it traveling," Shona whispered.

"What would you call it?"

"Running."

There was a long pause.

"Running from what?" she asked.

"Something happened... Back in Louisiana. Something bad."

Seeing her struggle, Dorothy laid a hand on Shona's knee. "It's OK. Just take you time. You don't have to tell me, but it might help to confide in someone. You can trust me, I swear."

Another age passed before Shona was finally able to swallow the lump in her throat. She squeezed the pink pebble on the pendant that hung around her neck.

"It's my fault my momma died."

~

Dorothy listened in silence to every word of Shona's story. Clearly the events of that night seven years ago still haunted her, but it certainly wasn't the time for Dorothy to begin passing judgment on her.

"What about your father?" Dorothy asked.

"He'll be hunting me down after what happened that night."

Dorothy put her arm around Shona and pulled her body into her own. "After what you've just told me, I think we'd better keep you safe from that ever happening. Thank you for telling me, Shona."

"That's OK," Shona replied, sniffing. "Thank you for telling me about Walter."

"You're welcome."

~

"Dorothy, look!" Shona exclaimed. They were standing in the small gift shop at the end of the Gulfport boardwalk. It was packed with handmade shell bracelets, beach toys and souvenirs. In the distance they could hear the waves crashing and children laughing as they played on the white sand only feet away. The smell of frying donuts and cinnamon filled the air.

Dorothy trundled over to find her holding a postcard, with a picture identical to their beach house. "They're selling them for a nickel. I think we should get one each." Shona's eyes were as bright as the mid-morning sun as she spoke.

"I think so too. A little memento of our trip for us to keep forever," Dorothy replied, fishing into her purse for the coins.

"It's the best trip I've ever been on, Dorothy, I swear it."

She wrapped the old lady up in a tight hug, then tucked the postcards away safe and sound in her top pocket.

"Me too," Dorothy replied.

Chapter 6

Shona came downstairs that morning, her first Monday back at work after their vacation, to see a khaki green army-issue lunch box resting on the counter in the kitchen. Curious, she walked up to it, then spotted the note.

Don't lose this.

Picking up the lunch box, Shona smiled when she noticed one word engraved on the front:

WALT.

~

"Where you going, Frank?" Lucy asked as she leaned over the side of the bed and picked up the bedside clock. It was just after 9 a.m.

"I need to see my uncle," Frank mumbled as he pulled his jeans on and fastened his belt. "Don't you worry 'bout what I'm doin'. You need to be gettin' yourself to that bus. You don't wanna be late for your first day at college."

"Classes don't start this morning until ten, so I got time.

What time are you opening up the bar later? I thought I could make us a nice dinner before you go."

"Not sure yet." Frank slipped his white t-shirt over his head, then leaned down to plant a wet kiss on her lips. "I'll see you later. Have a good day at college." Frank slammed the door behind him, and the sound of his boots on the staircase eventually tailed off.

Getting up out of bed, Lucy wrapped the sheet around her shoulders and sauntered over to the window. She'd spent her first night in Riverside staying in a room at the end of the hallway above the bar and since then spent every day with Frank, listening to his stories of how he was going to make the bar thrive. Towards the end of the week, Lucy had completely fallen for Frank and forfeited her dorm room to another student, deciding to bus it into college each day instead.

Pulling back the drapes, Lucy squinted as her eyes adjusted to the morning sunlight. She looked down to see Frank standing with his hands on his hips as Harry reached into his pocket for his wallet. Drifting her eyes across the scene, something else caught her attention. A tall, slender young woman wearing fitted overalls emerged from a side door of the garage and, feeling the heat of the morning sunshine, removed her cap to reveal a mop of short blonde hair. Lifting her face to the sky, she poured a canteen of water over it, wiping off the excess by running a tanned hand over her cheeks.

"Well, that I did not expect," Lucy whispered.

Quickly, she put on a peach summer dress and headed down the outside steps of the apartment and across to the garage parking lot. "Morning, Harry. Who's your new mechanic?" she asked, walking up behind Frank and linking arms with him.

"Hi Lucy," Harry replied. "You mean Shona? Been here the past five months now, one of the best I got."

"I been in this town a week now and ain't seen her before." Lucy tilted her head to try and get a glimpse of Shona who was at that moment unbolting the hood of a Buick.

"That's 'cos this ain't the place for a lady to be seen now, is it? You've got your college work to concentrate on with it bein' your first day today and all, right honey?" Frank chimed in, gripping her around her tiny waist.

"What?" Lucy's eyes were fixed on the back of the truck. "Oh, yeah," she replied, her voice trailing off.

Shona dropped the wrench she'd been holding. Cursing her clumsiness, she stood up to find Lucy's smiling face greeting her.

"Hi," Lucy said, wiggling free of Frank's cloying grip and walking over to the far corner of the truck where Shona was standing.

"Hi," Shona replied. Sensing Lucy's presence drawing nearer, she walked around to the front of the truck and leaned over the open engine. Frank watched Lucy for a moment, then turned his attention back to his uncle. Their conversation ended in the usual way, with Harry now ten dollars lighter.

"So what's wrong with the truck? Looks pretty complicated in there. How do you know what to tighten and what to loosen?" Lucy asked. She edged closer and closer to Shona, whose attention remained fixed on the engine manifold cover, counting every one of its screws as she removed them one by one. As she leaned on a thick black tube, Shona's greasy hand slipped.

"Shit!" Shona exclaimed, to which Lucy raised an eyebrow.

Feeling a sudden spray of oil flick up at her face, Shona recoiled, catching a droplet near her eye. Another one landed on Lucy.

"Gosh, darn it," Lucy gasped, looking down to where the droplet had landed just above the thin belt that pulled in her perfectly fitting dress.

"You should stand back a bit," Shona said as she squinted and wiped away the oil on her cheekbone with the back of her shirt cuff.

"And you should roll your sleeves up. Oil ain't easy to get out, you know," Lucy countered, rubbing at the stain.

Shona tried hard to stifle the smile that crept across her face and, taking Lucy's advice, rolled her sleeves over her wrists.

"My name's Lucy, by the way. I'm staying just across the street at the moment. Above the bar. There, you see?" Lucy leaned in closer to Shona, encouraging her to follow her pointing finger. Sensing how close Lucy had moved towards her, Shona took a step to the side. "So where are you from, Shona? Who you staying with?"

"You know Mrs. Clark? She owns the truck over there. I came in to get it fixed for her, then Harry said he'd give me a trial here so..." Shona began, looking everywhere but at Lucy's inquisitive face.

"Wow. I ain't never come across a girl working on truck engines before. You must be pretty darn good at it." Lucy twirled a lock of hair around her fingers as she leaned against the truck's fender. "So, where you from originally?"

The hairs on the back of Shona's neck prickled as she thought of the same lie she'd told Harry five months ago. *Don't matter what you tell 'em, as long as you tell 'em all the same thing,* she thought. *They can't catch you out then.* Before she had the chance to answer, Frank called her over after finishing his rant at Harry.

"Well, I'd better run along. It was nice to meet you... *Shauna,* was it?" Lucy hesitated as she waited for confirmation.

The first word Shona uttered was inaudible until she cleared her throat and tried again. "Shona," she repeated, swallowing hard as her stomach began to twitch.

"Never heard that one before today," Lucy giggled, her eyes fixed on Shona, who looked away and gave her full attention to the sprocket she was attempting to wrap her wrench around. "Well... I guess I'll see you around then... *Shona*." Lucy's smile faded as she received no reply but instead a pull on her elbow from an impatient Frank who led her away back across the street towards the bus stop.

Harry walked over to Shona. "You OK?"

"Yeah. I'm just... just not that good around new people," she mumbled, taking in several slow deep breaths. "S'why I like to keep myself out back here. Keeps things real simple for me."

"Well, Lucy seems like a good kid. Poor choice in men, though, even if her new boyfriend is my own kin." Harry shook his head and smiled. "You should get to know her, Shona. She's only just got into town so could do with a friend to show her around. She's a long way from home too."

Twisting her cap over in her oily hands, Shona watched as Frank left Lucy to wait for her bus to college, then headed back over to his bar. She looked away when she saw Lucy turn her head back.

"Say, you wanna help me on a delivery? It'll get you out of town for a few hours."

Shona smiled. She had really begun to like Harry.

Lucy found herself daydreaming as she sat in her classroom. Her thoughts drifted back to Shona and the blue denim overalls that looked so comfortable on her, so natural. They weren't in the slightest bit feminine, but they fit her slim, toned frame perfectly. Shona intrigued her. Even underneath all the engine oil and grease from Wreckers, she was stunningly beautiful, her baby blonde hair cut short at the back, her long bangs swept at an angle over her heart-shaped face. Her eyes were the color of the Pacific Ocean, something Lucy had long stared at as she was growing up on the West Coast. Her spirit had captured Lucy's attention, her aura infectious. There was something about Shona that was completely refreshing and new.

Chapter 7

"Hi Shona," Lucy greeted after wandering into the diner that Thursday afternoon. It was late September and it had become a regular thing now to see Shona in there with a few other guys from the garage, including Jonny.

"Hi. How was college today?"

"Real good. I'm a bit of a slow starter when it comes to books and writing and stuff, but I think I'm getting the hang of it." She twirled a lock of hair around her fingers as the guys around the table elbowed each other. Just then one of the younger guys, Tom, cleared his throat and began speaking.

"Um... Miss Lucy? I was just wondering if I could buy you a soda. That's if you'd care to stay with us for a bit?"

Lucy looked at Tom, his large blue eyes hopeful, then at the other guys and then finally at Shona who shrugged.

"Well, thank you Tom, that would be swell. If nobody else minds me crashing the party? Shona?"

"I don't mind," she replied, budging up to let Lucy sit down after nods from the other guys to do so.

~

It took less than twenty minutes for Lucy to completely win over the group of mechanics she'd been sharing stories with. Each man gazed at her longingly with every word she spoke.

"So, I was saying to Shona the other day, we should do something fun on the weekend. Why don't we go down to the river for a swim on Saturday? It's so hot at the moment, it'll be so nice to cool off in that water." She looked at the faces around the table. Each man, apart from Jonny and Shona, declined, with them having families. Jonny's eyes lit up.

"Well, I guess that means it's us three chickens," he grinned, looking between Shona and Lucy.

"What do you say, Shona? You wanna come?"

"Sure, why not," Shona replied, to huge grins from Jonny and Lucy.

"So when I was twelve years old, just after my daddy passed, I started to work for Harry. Oh, not doin' much, just runnin' around fetchin' him the right screwdrivers and wrenches and stuff. As soon as I was tall enough to reach inside the engines, he had me workin' on them. That man taught me everythin' I know and I'm grateful for that. Treated me like his own son, he did. Well, the son he and Marcie were never able to have, that is."

Jonny, staring into the distance, leaned against a tree stump at the edge of the water as he and Lucy traded stories one after the other. All along the bank, as far as he could see, there were cattails in the water and huge cypress trees looming large over their heads, following the curve of the river.

Only one story was left to be heard.

"So Shona, tell me about home. You got a ma and pa back in Tennessee?" Lucy began, chewing on the end of a blade of grass.

"Um. Well, I don't really like to talk about that. It's complicated, you know." Shona stood up and brushed her pants clean of the grit from the riverbank.

Jonny jumped up and grabbed three flat pebbles from the edge of the riverbank. "Say, I'll bet I can skip a stone better than either one of you two. You up for the challenge?"

Smiling, the two women each took a stone from Jonny.

"You're about to lose that bet, Jonny boy," Lucy grinned.

"Well, we'll just see about that," Shona chimed in, walking up to the edge of the water.

Shona's stone flew through the air, bouncing on the surface of the water at least seven times before sinking.

Laughing, Jonny and Lucy both held their hands in the air, conceding defeat.

Chapter 8

Christmas of 1956 was fast approaching and Lucy had already made plans for how she was spending it. Unfortunately for Frank, they didn't include him.

"Honey, of course I'd want you to come back with me, but I still need to tell them about you. I ain't found the right moment yet and the last thing I want is for them to think you're distracting me from my studies. I promise I'll tell them when I get back. And I'll only be away for a week or so, just 'til after New Year's. You'll be so busy here over the holidays, you'll hardly even notice I'm gone."

Lucy had spent the last twenty minutes pleading her case to Frank who sat in his armchair, staring up at the bus ticket to Monterey that had been placed partly behind a photo frame on the mantelpiece. The only sound from him was the drumming of his fingers on the armrest.

"How can you leave me now? Did you not see the flyer on the church notice board? The last of the men are comin' home from Korea over the next few weeks. You know how long I've waited to see him return and now you're sayin' you won't be here for it?" Frank said, his voice eerily calm.

"There ain't been a bus for two weeks now, Frank. The next

one's not due until after the New Year and I'll be back by then, OK?" Lucy replied.

Frank's hand clenched around the armrest. "It's our busiest time of year, Lucy. I need you here with me. We already talked about this. A few shifts behind the bar, maybe a bit of dancin', just to bring the guys in. You promised you'd think about it." Frank stared up at her.

"I have, and I will. Just as soon as I get back, I'm all yours. OK? I'll go to college in the daytime and work in the bar at night."

"Promise?"

"Cross my heart." Lucy kneeled down in front of him and kissed his cheek. "Now, I better go pack. I'll go straight to the bus station after my last day on Friday. Don't worry, Frank. When I get back, I'll do whatever you want me to do to make this place the best bar in all of Mississippi."

"Merry Christmas, Dorothy!" Shona cheered as she appeared at the old lady's door on Christmas morning holding a breakfast tray.

"Now then, what's all this?" Dorothy sat herself up in bed.

"Well, I ain't no cook but I can fry an egg or two. And we deserve a treat. Breakfast in bed." Shona reached over to the plate piled high with toast and grabbed a slice. "Merry Christmas," she spluttered after taking a huge bite.

"Merry Christmas, Shona," Dorothy replied, sipping her coffee. "You want your present now?"

Shona stopped chewing. "You got me something?" Her blue eyes widened.

"Of course. Everyone should get a present on Christmas day." She looked at Shona who suddenly looked downcast. "You feel bad 'cos you didn't get me anything, don't you?" she asked. Shona nodded. "Don't you feel bad. I've been on my own for more than ten Christmases now. You being here and sharing this one with me is the best present I could ask for."

"Really?"

"Really. Now, reach under my bed, will ya, feel for a little box." Dorothy winked.

Shona obeyed, found the box and plonked it on the bed. It had a little red bow tied around the handle.

"Go on, open it," Dorothy prompted.

Shona pulled at the ribbon, then lifted up the little catch on the lid. Inside was a small set of screwdrivers and two wrenches of different sizes. All the tools had a thick strip of brown leather wrapped around them and looked very familiar.

"I asked Jonny to help me. He was happy to oblige, bless his heart. They are the same type Harry uses, apparently. The best you can get."

Seeing Shona stare at them with her mouth open, not saying a word, Dorothy wrinkled her brow. "You like 'em?"

Shona looked up at the old lady with tears in her eyes. "Dorothy, I love them. They're perfect. Thank you so much." She reached over the bed to hug Dorothy, almost knocking the cups over on the breakfast tray.

"You're welcome. Now, let's go get things prepared for dinner. I got a turkey the size of Texas downstairs."

Chapter 9

Perched on the edge of a bench, the same spot he'd waited each time, Frank frowned as he checked his wristwatch again, then fixed his eyes back on the distance ahead of him. It was early January and had just gone ten o'clock that Wednesday morning.

"Military time, my ass," he cursed under his breath, his lips pinching the edge of a cigarette. Seconds later, about twenty yards away from him, a group of women, some old some young, emerged from the diner across the street. Heading over to the bus stop, they broke into squeals of excitement at the sight of the long-awaited army bus finally appearing on the horizon.

Grinning, Frank felt his heart thump. He stubbed his cigarette out on the armrest of the bench and jumped up, straightening his perfectly pressed checked shirt as he did so and tucking it into the waistband of his best pair of Levis. He took out a comb from his leather jacket and ran it through his oiled black hair. Striding over, he smiled at the happy chirps from the children in the crowd.

"Mom, is Pa really coming home? Like *really* this time?" one little girl said to her equally excited mother.

"Yes, honey, he ain't goin' off anywhere else this time. He's comin' home specially to spend your birthday with you and he can't wait to give you his present." She squeezed the hand of her nine-year-old daughter. Frank felt himself smile again, the anticipation for his own reunion fizzing within him.

Cheers sounded as the bus groaned to a halt and one by one the returning heroes gingerly disembarked, in various physical states. The campaign in Korea had ended over three and a half years previously and taken over a hundred and fifty able-bodied men from Riverside, only to return most of them as incomplete, broken shells. Endless redeployment for those not wounded or made prisoners of war had also taken its toll on their morale, but, at long last, they were being discharged and returned to their homes.

Hugs and kisses were exchanged at the bus stop, with children being held aloft by tearful fathers. After a few minutes the crowd began to dissipate, leaving Frank standing on the sidewalk, his expectant smile fading just like his vision of the bus.

"Hey mister, why you sad?" The same little girl from before appeared at Frank's side. She looked up at him, her innocent blue eyes unblinking.

Through glassy eyes, Frank opened his mouth to respond just as her mother wrenched her away.

"No, Jessie, we don't talk to criminals," the little girl's mother scolded, flashing Frank a disgusted look.

Feeling the judging eyes of the crowd bearing down on him, Frank flung out his boot at the garbage can next to the bus stop, sending its contents flying.

"What the hell you lot starin' at, huh? You mind your manners," he snarled, stomping off across the road towards the bar he owned. Seeing his bar manager wiping tables outside, Frank halted.

"Norm! For God's sake, when are you gon' get those damn windows cleaned? This place is starting to look like shit. What the hell am I payin' you for?"

Before Norm could respond, Frank had stormed off.

~

"Hello, Dr. Adamson's residence. This is Mrs. Adamson?"

Lucy had picked up and put down the receiver several times. This time, though, she'd finally plucked up enough courage to ask the operator to dial the number she knew by heart. Each unanswered ring gave her another chance to hang up, but at the same moment she was about to do so, a bright feminine voice answered.

Lucy blinked away the tears, squeezing her eyes shut when she heard her mother's voice. As she ran a pale-skinned hand through her shoulder-length chestnut brown hair, she gritted her teeth, then made herself sound as breezy as she could.

"Hey Mom, it's Lucy. How are you?"

The voice at the end of the line became animated as Mrs. Adamson gushed with pleasure at hearing her only child's precious voice. "Oh, my dear, it's so nice to hear from you. How's your first week back been?"

Lucy swallowed hard. "Yeah, Mom, everything's fine. My tutor told me that the local school said they'd love to have me come in to teach a couple of classes this semester to help me with my training." The story she'd carefully crafted over the last week just seemed to flow out of her effortlessly. Lucy's eyes, however, were as dull as the ache in her guilty heart. "How's Daddy?" Lucy continued.

"Oh, he's fine. Well, he had a patient die on his operating table last week, but he did all he could. You know your father, he's such a perfectionist. It really hurt him that he couldn't save that young lady. Apparently, she'd gotten into prostitution, drink and drugs... her heart gave out in the end. He was furious, said it was such a waste of a life. He couldn't believe how the parents could let that happen to her. He wanted to report them for neglect and, well... Anyway, I don't wanna dwell on *that*, honey. Tell me all about what you've been up to. When can we come down to visit you?"

Chewing the nail on her index finger, a commotion on the street below caught her attention. As she began making up another reason why 'now wasn't a good time' to have visitors, Lucy pinched open the blinds to see Frank lashing out at anything remotely in his path. Counting his stomps up the fire escape at the side of the bar beneath the apartment, Lucy knew she had to hurry.

"Look, Mom, I gotta go. I'm sorry I can't talk longer but ... um... my... um... study period is over and I gotta go back to class. But... can you ask Daddy if it's OK for him to put a little bit more money in my checking account this week? I need some more... books and stuff. Please?" She bit down on the corner of her mouth, hating every word she was forcing through it. Her stomach flipped as she heard Frank's key slide into the lock, his keychain clanking against the wooden door.

"Of course, honey, I'll ask him to do it this evening on his way home from the hospital. But I wish you would just let him send you a check, it's much easier for us. We know the college's address but we really need to know what dormitory you're in so it gets to you OK. Or maybe instead we could bring it when we visit—"

"Sorry, Mom, I gotta go. Tell Daddy thank you for the money. I love you, Mom."

Lucy hung up the phone halfway through her mother's goodbye and just as the door swung open. Frank stood there, his face like thunder, the creases on his contorted face glistening with sweat.

"Who was that?" he asked, catching Lucy's hand moving off the receiver.

"Just my mom. Dad's good for the money, he'll put it in my account tonight. I didn't want her to hear your voice and start asking questions," she replied, sweeping a strand of hair off her damp brow. "It'll help us, right?"

Frank nodded and walked over to the refrigerator, taking out a bottle of beer.

"Was he not there again?" Lucy asked, her soft voice normally enough to calm Frank when he was riled. "Oh honey, I'm sure he's just been delayed or something. He'll be waiting on his papers, that's all. You just gotta be patient. He'll be on the next bus, I just know it." She slunk over and wrapped her arms around his waist but, in no mood to be soothed, Frank twisted himself away from her arms, the stubborn cap on his bottle tipping his frustration over the edge.

"What the goddamn hell do you know about it, huh? You ain't got no right to promise me anythin', the amount of lies you told this week just 'cos you don't feel like goin' to college."

"Frank, why would you say that to me? I only wanna make you feel better."

"Well, you know what'd make me feel better? You gettin' off your ass and ready for work tonight. Clearly you ain't thinkin' of goin' into college today, you been sittin' around this place all mornin'. You wanna do somethin' useful, you can help me out again tonight. This ain't no hotel I'm runnin', you know."

"But Frank, I don't feel so good. My head hurts and I've been feeling dizzy all morning. What did you make me take last night?" Lucy mumbled, reaching for the glass of water she'd left on the sideboard.

"Nothin' much, just somethin' to help you relax. Gary's a good customer, but he wasn't happy with the one-way conversation he was havin' with you at the bar last night. He expects better from my servers, so you need to loosen up, girl." Frank walked over to her and took the glass out of her shaking hands. Placing it back on the sideboard, he pressed his face into hers. "Look, when I met you at that bus station all those months ago, lookin' all lost and alone, I offered you a place to stay and now I ask you to help me now and again in the bar you start losin' your head. You got to get your shit together with the customers and start helpin' me bring some money in." He paused to take a long slurp of his beer.

"I'm sorry, Frank. I'll try harder, I promise," Lucy sobbed.

"And another thing, you not goin' to college at *all* was not part of the deal either, Lucy. How long do you think you're gonna get away with it for? I know you hate it there, but you gotta go in at least a few days a week." He pinched her chin and pressed his face into hers. "That college ain't stupid, they're gonna start askin' questions and then they'll ring your father. Do you want him to stop your allowance? Because he will. You need to keep things sweet with them, honey. We need that money, otherwise we're both screwed. You promised me before Christmas that you'd help. All I'm askin' is you paint a smile on that pretty lil' face when you're servin' the drinks and maybe do a little dance for the guys every now and again. It's not too much to ask, is it, honey? You're my savior, you know that. I can't lose that bar, Lucy. It's all I got." Frank's dark eyes blazed with raw emotion.

"I know, Frank. I'll go tomorrow. I'm just so tired after working late last night," Lucy murmured.

"Well, you see that you do. Otherwise that college'll be rattin' on you to your parents before you can spit. And I don't need anybody snoopin' round here asking questions either." Frank drained his bottle and slammed it down on the coffee table, then slumped into his armchair. Rubbing his eyes, he looked up at Lucy who was now leaning against the mantel-piece sobbing. Sighing, he beckoned her over and sat her on his lap. "Honey, don't cry. I'm sorry I upset you. You know I hate the idea of you schmoozin' those guys across the bar, but it keeps 'em comin' back in. We both gotta do what we gotta do. It won't be long now and if we work hard enough, we'll make Chasers the best this town's ever seen it. I'm gonna make my father proud of me, I swear it. You believe me, right?"

Lucy sniffed and wiped her nose on the back of her hand. "Of course I do."

"Good. Now go get ready. Show me how beautiful you look in that red dress I got you."

Lucy left Frank slouched in his armchair, his red-rimmed eyes fixed on the framed picture of a black-haired young boy, no more than eight years old, sitting on the shoulders of a smiling man in uniform that was taking pride of place on the dusty mantelpiece.

To everyone else in Riverside, apart from Frank, Chasers had become the seediest joint in town in the five years since he'd inherited it from his grandfather. The Christmas festivities had filled the register with dollar bills, but Frank had emptied it just as quickly hoping that one night at the poker table his luck would change.

It hadn't. Not once for the last three games since New Year's that he'd played. And lost. Now time was running out.

In one of the windows that faced the street, a huge bright pink neon sign spelled out its name. Inside, the mahogany wood of the bar top was mottled, with sticky wet mats draped over it and a bored looking bartender standing behind it, cleaning glasses with a grubby tea towel. After a couple of wipes, he held a glass up to the light to see if he had gotten most of the stains and lipstick off. He placed the towel it on the shelf below the bar just as Frank swaggered through the entrance.

"Whiskey. Neat."

Norm hesitated for a moment too long, before the wrath of Frank came his way for the second time that day. Draping his tea towel over his shoulder, he grunted, then reached behind him for a bottle of Jack Daniels and poured his boss the drink. As Norm went to take the bottle back, Frank gripped his hand.

"Leave it... You ain't been in charge here for the last five years, Norm, so come down off your high horse there." He smirked as the bartender released his grip on the bottle. "I own everythin' behind that bar anyway." Frank turned to walk away, the bottle tucked under his arm. Seating himself in a booth in the corner, he spotted Chuck at the other end of the bar, holding a tray balancing four bottles of beer on it. With a sense of dread, he watched Chuck make his way to his table of friends, the bottles wobbling precariously. Three steps from reaching the table safely, Chuck's hands twitched, sending the bottles crashing over each other on the tray and spilling the amber liquid all over his friends at the table.

"For fuck's sake, Chuck, I just had these shoes shined," one friend exclaimed as he scrabbled his hands across the soaking tray to salvage what he could from the half-empty bottles.

"Sorry, guys, I'll send some more over," Chuck assured, putting down the tray and gesturing over to Norm. Walking over to Frank's booth, Chuck's shoulders dropped. He slumped down in his seat, hardly able to look his best friend in the eye. "I'm sorry, Frank, I'm such a klutz."

"I saw, Chuck. God damn. What the hell am I gon' do with you, huh? You're as useless as tits on a boarhog. I gave you a job behind the bar 'cos no one else in this town'll hire you, but you can't add up for shit. Then we try you out as a server and look what happens." He shook his head in dismay. "And people in this town still ask why the military wouldn't let you enlist either. That damn brain damage of yours alone would be enough of a reason. Why, I wouldn't trust you with a squirt gun now."

"I'm sorry, boss," Chuck said, his dirty fingernail gouging lumps out of the cardboard coaster on Frank's table. "I ain't been right since that day at the grocery store." Chuck held one hand out to show Frank. "See? Can't keep the damn thing still anymore."

Seeing his friend's contrition, Frank softened. "Well, you were never gon' be no brain surgeon now, were you?" Frank said, half smiling. "And anyways, why you draggin' all that up again? I wanna forget that now. Ain't it enough that this damn town won't let us forget what we did? It was almost ten goddamn years ago. I've taken their shit for long enough and so have you."

Chuck watched as Frank poured a shot for them both. "It's not as if we killed the guy now, was it? He gave as good as he got, waving that damn bat around like Mickey Mantle. He socked me a good'un," Chuck said, rubbing the jagged scar running across the top of his skull, very much noticeable these days on his bald head.

"Yeah, well, Jake has always been one to hold a grudge." Sensing his oldest friend's discomfort, Frank slapped him on his broad shoulder. "Don't worry, once my father gets back we'll clean up around here. He'll know what to do to make this place the best damn joint for miles. I got big plans for this place and together we're gon' rule this town. Ain't nobody gon' stand in our way this time." Frank grinned as he swigged another shot and scanned the crowded bar.

"And I'm gonna be your deputy, yessir," Chuck whooped, banging his bear-like fist into the table and almost sending Frank's bottle flying. Grabbing it, Frank flashed him an exasperated grin.

"If we can find you a job you can't possibly fuck up. But I guess even a blind squirrel finds a nut every now and again. First, we gotta think up some ideas of bringin' more money into this place. I want my father to be proud of what I've built up while he's been gone. The man's a goddamn hero, it's the least I can do." Frank's smile faded to a look of determination. He sipped his next shot much slower this time.

"Well, the girls are all ready for tonight's show." Chuck pointed over to the door to the side of the bar that led backstage.

"Lucy here?" Frank asked, his eyes drilling holes in Chuck's pudgy red face.

"Yeah."

"She look good?"

"Oh yeah," Chuck replied, a thin trickle of spit rolling out of his open mouth. His eyes glazed over for a moment as he pictured her, until Frank punched him hard on the arm to snap him out of it. As he did so, the boisterous crowd hurried to take their seats to watch the show. A hush fell across the room as the red spotlights flicked on and all eyes turned towards the stage.

The clicking of stiletto heels on the stripped wood floorboards caught everyone's attention as the silence became gasps of anticipation. Behind the bar, Norm reached his hand up to the main light switch and flicked it down completely. A long shadow then fell across the jukebox in the far corner, the room now only lit by one overhead red spotlight.

Lucy leaned forward against the jukebox, both palms pressed against its yellow frame, seductively mulling over which song to play. But it was all part of the act; she knew exactly which song she wanted.

With all eyes completely hypnotized by her presence, she dropped in a dime and punched in the number, her long red nail keeping the button from connecting flush with her fingertip. As Dinah Washington's smooth seductive voice filled the air, Lucy's body swayed gently, then, as she found her rhythm, her shiny red lips began mouthing the words to *Big Long Slidin' Thing*. After thirty seconds or so, she turned to face her audience who were all seated around tables that were cluttering up the dancefloor. Frank liked to pack them in on nights she was performing.

Catching the eye of a middle-aged businessman loosely holding a dollar bill, Lucy sashayed her way through the tables, then, almost reaching her target, cocked her eyes to the left to Frank who nodded his encouragement, his keen eyes also drifting over that dollar. Chuck wiped the drool escaping the corner of his mouth.

Leaning back in his booth, Frank fixed his stare back onto Lucy, who was still miming along to the song and dancing slowly around the businessman. *Damn, she's good at this*, he thought, his arms draped over the back of the booth as he blew his cheeks out in awe of her performance. Chuck leaned forward, his hands below the table.

As Lucy was reaching the end of her performance, she began emphasizing the sexier words to the businessman who couldn't take his eyes off her for the whole duration. The innuendo contained within the lyrics wasn't lost on him one bit. Transfixed, he reached into his pocket and pulled out another dollar bill, then looked over to Frank, clearly wanting more for his money. Frank grinned and nodded again to Lucy who then slipped the front zipper on her dress down to show the merest glance of her cleavage.

As the song built to its crescendo, she leaned forward, now only a foot away from the businessman, then inch by inch pulled her zipper down further. Licking his lips, he took out another dollar bill, to the increasingly loud cheers from his party. When the song finally ended, she placed one stilettoed foot on the arm of the man's seat and hitched up her sequined dress to reveal a scarlet-edged lacy garter. Hooking her long finger underneath it, she lifted it away from her silky-smooth skin, leaving just enough of a gap for him to slide the money in there. He did so without hesitation but lingered his hand there just a moment too long. Stroking her inside leg, he grinned at her then over at Frank, who raised his glass to agree the deal. Lucy lowered her leg back to the sticky bar floor and strode away as confidently as she'd entered.

Standing at the bar, two of Frank's girls were waiting for their next customer. As Lucy passed them on her way to the restroom, they noticed something in her demeanor that the rest of the bar had missed.

"What the hell's up with Lucy? She gets access to all the high cotton that come into this bar every night just 'cos she's new, and still looks so darn miserable," one girl drawled to the other, then sipped her drink through a straw so as not to ruin her thickly applied bright red lipstick.

"Frank'll be spittin' fire at her later too unless she gets at least twenny bucks out of that guy tonight... And when Frank's not happy, we all suffer," the other girl replied, rolling her eyes, then glaring at the restroom door.

"Back in a minute, Joanie. Watch my drink and if my seven o'clock comes in, come get me."

"Where's Lucy?" Frank hissed at Joanie, suddenly appearing behind her. She pointed to the restroom door, then turned her attention back to the cute young hustler who'd just approached holding two whiskey sours.

Frank stood for a few moments listening to the young man's opening lines. Unimpressed, he then turned back to Joanie, who was now draining her drink and laughing as the young man did the same. Leaning over, he grabbed her by the elbow and started to lead her away. The young man's cocky smile dropped. He slammed the empty glasses on the bar and caught up to Frank.

"Hey, come on Frank, I was only talking to her," he protested.

"Oh yeah?" Frank spun around, almost nose-to-nose with him. "Well, look at you. Pretty boy Bobby, star of the football field, gettin' too big for his britches. I'd shut your yapper if I were you. Put your lil' boy hand deeper in your pocket and find me at least a Lincoln greenback before you talk to one of *my* girls again." He tapped Bobby's clean-shaven cheek. Knowing only too well that it wasn't wise to protest, Bobby backed off. Straightening his smart plaid button down shirt, he grabbed his jacket and stormed off.

Frank tightened his grip around Joanie's thin, white arm and led her over to a group of rowdy older men sitting at the booth in the corner, empty glasses and bottles of bourbon littering their table.

"Who the hell gave you permission to pick your own customers? You do as I say, you got me?" he growled in her ear as they crossed the floor to the booth.

Joanie creased her face at the drunken cheers that greeted her. Faking a smile, she smoothed down the sequins on her skirt and glared at Frank's back as he marched over to the restroom door.

"I wish he wouldn't talk to you like that, really gets my goat," Norm whispered in Joanie's ear through gritted teeth as he laid another tray of drinks down on the table for the group.

"Yeah, I know, but he's the boss around here. But thank you for always lookin' out for me, Norm. It's nice to know there's at least one gentleman around here," she whispered back.

Lucy sat on the toilet holding her spinning head in her hands as she bent forward, then raked her long red fingernails through her backcombed hair. Staring down at the small pool of toilet water that had collected around the leaking cistern, she sat on the cracked edge of the seat. Floating within the puddle was the latest chip of ceramic from the grimy toilet bowl. Lucy's hopes for a bright future seemed to be drifting further away from her with every sordid dance she gave. She was snatched from her daydream by a pounding on the stall door.

"Hey girl, you in there? Lucy?"

Lucy opened the door to see Trish leaning against the frame half-smiling at her. Her bouncy red curls were pinned on one side of her head by a silver hair clip, her mouth bright red from thickly applied lipstick.

"Hey Trish, I'm sorry, I just needed a minute to set myself right. I'm not used to all o'this yet," Lucy said, blowing out her cheeks. She walked past Trish and over to the sink and leaned her slender body against the wall, cooling her flushed skin on the cold tiles. "It's busy out there, ain't it?"

Trish stood with her arms folded. "Look, what the hell is wrong with you? Me and the rest of the girls are getting a little bored of your 'poor little rich girl' drama. You've had all the good gigs since you started to work for Frank and you're still getting all uppity about it. Do you know how much we all wish that Frank protected us in the same way he did you?" she said, keeping her voice low.

"Good gigs? Trish, we've *all* been getting an equal share of the shit that walks into this place. I could be so much more than..." Lucy stopped mid-sentence when she saw Trish's face darken.

"Go on, finish what you're going to say," Trish said. "You really *do* think your shit don't stink, don't you? Well, not all of us were lucky enough to grow up with a rich mommy and daddy. You had everything back home, then you choose to leave and come here. Why the hell did you do that, huh? Are you crazy or something?" She stared at Lucy in disbelief. "You roll into town and fall in love with a guy you meet at a bus station, then let him sell you some two-bit dream that you'd make a million dollars with this place one day. Are you kidding me? The only thing you'll make here is a few dollars stuffed up your skirt and whole load of bad choices." She walked over to Lucy, pointing her finger at her. "You go around this place wanting us to feel sorry for you, but the only folks I feel sorry for are your parents. *You* chose to feed them some bullshit story about how well you're doing at college. Your first week back after the holidays and you've been, what, once this week? If that. And it's already Wednesday. Just so they don't rat you out to mommy and daddy. So why don't you do us all a favor, paint a smile on that pretty lil' face of yours and stop pretending you're so much better than all of us out there." Trish pressed her face into Lucy's.

Lucy flung herself forward and grabbed her. "You're such a bitch, Trish. You're just jealous that Frank loves me now instead of you," she yelled, yanking on clumps of Trish's hair and causing the clip to clatter to the ground.

"Get your mitts off me!" Trish shrieked, wriggling in Lucy's tight grasp.

The restroom door burst open and a pair of strong, grubby hands grabbed Lucy's wrists and slammed her up against the tiled wall.

"What in the goddamn hell are you doin'?" Frank's eyes flashed with rage as his fingernails dug into her delicate skin. Seeing him distracted, Trish slipped past them both. She was inches from the doorway when Frank turned to face her.

"And *you*. How many times have I told you, I don't want to hear my girls arguin', even in private? It tightens you up and those guys out there are payin' good money for a hassle-free night. Now, get the fuck out there and make me some money."

Trish nodded.

"Oh, and if I see you upsettin' my girl again, I'll snap your goddamn neck, y'hear me?" Frank hissed.

Swallowing hard, Trish lowered her eyes.

"Trish, I'm sorry," Lucy whispered, her wrists still being held above her head.

"Don't sweat it, girl. We all got a cross to bear." Trish

smoothed down her messed up hair, bent down to pick up her clip and slipped through the door which closed behind her.

Frank let go of Lucy's wrists. "You wanna tell me what that was all about?"

"I was just powdering my nose. I wasn't meaning to get in a fight with Trish. Please, Frank, don't be angry with me." Lucy felt the tears fill her eyes once again as she rubbed her chafed wrists.

"OK. Look, I'm sorry I grabbed you. I thought she was gon' hurt you. I can't have that happen." He ran his hand through his thick black hair. "I just want you to clean yourself up and make yourself look worth the money those high-rollers out there are gon' pay for you to entertain them," he whispered, stroking her face with the back of his index finger.

"Whatever you say, Frank."

"That's my girl. You know that, don't you? You're my girl, my best girl." Frank kissed her on the cheek. "Now, go freshen up. I got a good one waitin' out by the bar to talk to you. Real smart guy, real high-flyer. Just make sure you loosen up this time. I don't want any more complaints about how you ain't laughin' at his jokes or nothin'." He waited to see her nod, then walked towards the restroom door. "Say, how 'bouts I give you a little somethin' later, just to steady your nerves? Would you like that, honey?"

Lucy nodded.

"Well, alright then. Be out in five minutes, OK?" Frank pushed open the restroom door and disappeared from Lucy's sight.

Wiping her face on a threadbare, stained towel, Lucy stared at her reflection in the mirror. She was only supposed to dance. That was the agreement. But now, Frank was pushing her into doing more. With no words to describe the hollow shell of the person staring back, she splashed her cheeks with cold water, reapplied her lipstick and heaved a huge intake of breath into her lungs.

~

"Honey, come sit with me over here," Frank said as Lucy wandered into the apartment they shared above the bar. Sitting on the sofa next to him was the guy she'd been chatted up by downstairs earlier.

"I think I'm gonna go lie down, Frank, my head don't feel too good. Feels a little fuzzy again," Lucy slurred.

Frank got up and moved across the room to where Lucy was standing then gently led her back to the sofa. "Baby, Don just wants to chat with you. He wants to know more about what it's like goin' to college." He leaned into her and whispered in her ear, "You'll be OK. Just relax. Act like I showed you, OK? Do it for me?"

"Yeah, sweetheart, I'm thinkin' of goin' myself. Frank here said you could give me some advice on how to apply," Don added, licking his lips and watching her carefully. He was in his late thirties, round in the middle and wearing a bottle green button-down shirt and black slacks.

"Alright," Lucy said and swayed over to the sofa.

"Well, I'll leave you college nerds to it. I got a bit of business to see to. Take as long as you need," Frank said. As he pulled open the door, he looked over at Don and winked.

Halfway down the internal staircase to the bar area, Frank passed Chuck on his way up.

"Keep an eye on her, Chuck. It's her first one," he whispered in the big man's ear.

"Sure thing, boss," Chuck agreed and carried on up the staircase.

~

There were thirty-nine star patterns in total on the dirty gray strips of peeling wallpaper in the room above the bar, thirty-nine and a half if you counted the ripped one in the corner by the air vent. It was difficult to tell as they were all in and out of her focus.

It couldn't be long now; he'd been hammering away at it for ages.

Every few seconds or so, Lucy flashed a half-smile to Don, who grinned back as he thrust himself deeper into her. Finally, he flopped his sweaty, spent body down on top of her, breathing heavily into her ear as he regaled her with how amazing she was. Lucy nodded and tapped him on the shoulder, hinting to him that it was time to go. Grinning, he stood up and dressed as quickly as he'd torn his clothes off, then reached into his wallet to settle up.

"Here you go. And here's another $5 for the other stuff you let me do. Frank was right about you." His voice sounded like Lucy was hearing his words through water, his smirk unmistakable as he dropped the cash on the bedside table and closed the door behind him.

The sound of his hacking cough had kept Trish awake for most of the five hours she'd been home since returning from her shift at the bar at 3 a.m. The tiny snuffle that came after every bout broke her heart. Then came the five minutes of wheezing and crying until the gurgling finally cleared. Her son's lungs were only four years old, but they sounded like they belonged to someone from the trenches who'd barely survived a mustard gas attack.

"It's OK, baby, Momma's been reading about this new treatment they're trying out. I just gotta get a bit more money together and then, as long as the Lord is willing and the creek don't rise, we'll go get those lungs all cleaned out and you'll be all better for a little bit. It won't be long, but for now Momma's gotta do it her way, OK?"

Trish sat by her son's bedside and pulled him up close to her, lying him face down on her chest. Slapping him on his back, she fought back the tears as he flinched from the impact, but she knew it was the only way to clear the mucus. After several slaps and one big gurgly cough, Tommy sat back and wiped the tears from his own eyes with the back of his tiny hand. Breathing deeply for a few moments, he smiled.

"Don't cry, Momma, it's OK now," he croaked.

"You're right. Silly me getting all upset. We got this, you and me. We can fight anything, right?" She leaned over him and kissed his clammy forehead, then tucked his arms underneath his blanket and patted his chest. "Are you high enough?" she asked, reaching up to his top pillow and adjusting it.

"Yes, Momma." He snuffled again, wiped his wet nose and closed his eyes.

"I just wish... Well, never mind that now. You go to sleep, baby."

Trish kissed her son's forehead again and listened for a few moments as his ragged breathing became steady and calm. Lifting her weary body from his little bed, she dragged her feet to his door and looked back at him one last time before clicking his light off.

"He alright?" a gravelly voice sounded in the half-light of the hallway.

"He is now," Trish said to her mom, running her palm over her tired eyes.

"I heard him while you were asleep. I gave him the... inhaler thing, and it seemed to settle him, but he started again." Her watery eyes struggled to meet her daughter's.

"I told you before, you gotta clear the fluid as well. Like I showed you? The inhaler only works for a lil' bit—"

"You know I ain't got the strength no more to do that. I do the best I can," she interrupted, pausing to lick her dry lips. She swept a lock of lank brown hair away from her damp brow. "While you're out at work until God knows what hour."

"I'm doing the best I can too, Mom... but business has slowed down a little since the holiday season ended. Some of the girls ain't working as *hard* as they could be either and it's causing issues. I had a word with Lucy tonight and I think it'll get better." Trish watched her mother's eyes closely as they struggled to focus on her as she was speaking.

"I wish I was well enough to work instead of you. Your place is here with Tommy. You know how that makes me feel to know you work in a... *bar*?" Her voice trailed off as she ran out of breath.

Trish stared at her mother. "You had a drink today?" she whispered, leaning in to her.

"No, I have not. You know I wouldn't now, not with the boy in the house. You need to speak to that no-good father of his. It's too much for you to do on your own. I won't be around forever." She stomped off down the hallway and into her bedroom, slamming the door behind her.

Squeezing her eyes shut, Trish looked up at the peeling plaster on the ceiling. Frustrated, she let out a long exhale of breath. After two or three minutes of listening to her son's gentle snoring, she made her way to her own bedroom and sank onto her bed in exhaustion.

"I'll get the best doctor for you, Tommy. I promise the Lord I will," she whispered into the darkness.

Chapter 10

Lucy stood in front of the mirror that sat on her dressing table, trying to refocus her eyes on the mess that was staring back at her. Her eyes stung as she stroked the brush ineffectually over her tangled brown hair.

"I know you'll never forgive me now. For what I've done," she whispered to the photograph that was snugly tucked inside the frame. A well-dressed middle-aged couple stared back at her, their perfect smiles frozen in time. Behind her, the door burst open and in walked Frank, large as life and grinning from ear to ear. Sloping up behind her, he grabbed Lucy around the waist and kissed her neck, his wet lips leaving trails of spit on her pale skin.

"G'mornin' beautiful. I just got off the phone to Don. He said he loved spendin' time with you last night and you really cheered him up. Reckons he'd like to see you again. This is gonna help us out so much, darlin'. You are my angel." Frank embraced her and nuzzled her neck. "God, I love how you smell after a night makin' us lots of money. Really turns me on."

"No, Frank, I need to wash up. And I'm a little sore after last night—"

"Don't worry, I'll be real gentle," Frank interrupted. He clasped his tight grip around her hand and led her to the bed.

～

Gathering up a small pile of envelopes and wrapping the same old piece of yellow ribbon around them, Gloria Smith exhaled as she sat at her bureau leaning back in her wooden chair. Deep in thought, she pulled open the drawer and dropped the letters inside, then lingered a freshly manicured maroon fingernail on the little brass handle. She was in her early fifties, tall with thick bleached blonde hair.

"Morning. I didn't hear you get up. You OK, honey?" George asked, yawning and pulling his navy blue robe around himself as he walked into the living room. He was in his mid-fifties with dark brown hair already neatly combed in a parting to the side of his head. He looked down over the top of his horn-rimmed glasses at the inside of the open bureau drawer. "What are those? Love letters? Should I be worried?"

Gloria looked up at her boyfriend and smiled, holding his attention as she closed the drawer. "Of course not, they're just some old bills. You're more than enough for me, darlin'."

"For a minute there I thought you'd finally had a letter from that husband of yours," George replied.

Gloria swept a strand of blonde hair away from her forehead and wiped her brow. "*Ex*-husband. Oh, we may not be divorced properly yet, but you're my man now in all but name," she replied, scratching the end of her nose. "It's pretty much impossible to divorce a man who's overseas. Especially when I ain't heard from him in years. No, it's Frank who receives the letters. His father's always spinnin' him some line about how it'll 'definitely be the next bus' he'll be on. Well, when his father can be bothered to write back to him, that is. Poor Frank junior

83

falls for it every time." She turned the little key in the lock of the drawer and pocketed it.

"Can't help but feel sorry for Junior. Not easy to grow up without his father around all this time," George said as Gloria nodded her agreement.

"I know. I'll never forget seein' Junior wait by the front window every day after we got the news that the war in Europe was finally over in '45. Every time a car pulled up, he'd run to the door, big smile on his face." Gloria rose up out of her chair and walked over to the liquor cabinet. She poured herself a large bourbon from the decanter. "I had to watch that disappointment flash over his face every day. It was the worst pain a mother could feel, seein' their son so upset. I wish I could have given him some hope that his father hadn't just decided to stay with his military platoon rather than come home, which is exactly what he'd done. He was never much of a family man anyway. Not like you, honey." Gloria paused and smiled at George. "But then one day Frank junior himself finally had enough of waitin' around and he just changed." She took a huge swig from her glass. "He became bitter. Got himself a shotgun and went to rob the grocery store with that imbecile friend of his. Heaven knows why. He was just angry with the world that day, I think." She drained her glass. "I just wish you'd come along sooner, honey. Your influence on him when he was younger might have made the difference."

George perched his weight on the edge of the couch. "I remember you telling me about that robbery. He was sixteen years old, honey. There was no way the judge was going to be lenient with him after what they did to Jake," George reflected. "He and Chuck were lucky to only get four years' jail. It should have been a lot longer."

"Broke his heart, though, when the military didn't want him because of it," Gloria replied. "That was more punishment to him. He couldn't be like his 'hero' father. Still, he had the bar his grandpappy left him. As soon as Junior turned twenty-one, I signed it over to him. Old Norm Taylor wasn't too happy, but he couldn't have expected to have been my bar manager forever. Not after Frank junior came of age. I was hopin' that place would straighten him out, give him a purpose. But..."

"You know I've tried to be a father figure to him. I even tried to teach him about bookkeeping once, thinking it would help him with the business, but he doesn't wanna know." George looked down at his navy blue slippers and took in a deep breath. "Honey, I need to know. If he ever did come back... where would that leave us?"

Gloria put her glass down on the cabinet and stared at the bureau drawer before walking over to throw her arms around her boyfriend.

"Trust me. He's not comin' back," she asserted. She softened her expression. "But if he did, I would tell him that the last two years of my life, since you came along, have never been happier. Now, you go get dressed. I've ironed your favorite shirt. It's hangin' up on the dresser. I'll go see what I can fix us for breakfast." She smiled, kissed him on the cheek and headed into the kitchen.

"You got any of that bacon left?" George called after her, turning his head back to the locked bureau drawer.

Chapter 11

Lucy stood up and unhooked her red-and-black sequined dress from the hanger. Pulling it over her legs carefully so as not to snag her silk stockings, she fed the straps over her thin shoulders, then looked back at herself in the mirror. Hating what she saw, she put one final coat of bright red lipstick on and slipped on her stiletto heels. As she passed the window looking out onto the garage parking lot, she sneaked another glance to see Shona chatting to a group of mechanics, laughing heartily as one of them made a joke. She watched as Shona had an oily rag thrown at her by Jonny, then gave him a menacing look before grinning and throwing it back. Lucy, swallowing the lump in her throat, let the drape fall back into place and turned to leave the room, wishing for one tiny ounce of the freedom that Shona was enjoying that same moment.

"Harry, I've been thinking," Marcie began as she strode up behind her husband, who was lying on a set of creepers tinkering away at a tailpipe. Hearing the clump of her heels on the concrete, he rolled out from underneath the truck.

"Let me guess, you've been trying to decide who you're running off with, Marlon Brando or James Dean?" He paused to wave his wrench at her. "I'd go for Brando, Jimmy drives way too fast."

"Oh honey, I'd pick you every time." She smiled down then added with a wink, "If we broke down, you'd know how to fix the car. I'm smart, you see."

"That's my girl," Harry chuckled.

"I know." Marcie straightened her cat-eye glasses. "Listen, I was thinking about how hard the guys are working for us and the other day I saw how little food Kenny had in his tin..." She paused as Harry sat upright. "I don't feel they're eating a proper meal at lunch, Harry."

"What's your plan? 'Cos I know there'll be a plan. There always is with you, darling," Harry said, narrowing his eyes and pointing at her with his wrench.

"Well..." she began. "You know that branch of Howard Johnson's that's just opened up in Birchfield? Well, I called them up and asked them if there was any way we could arrange for them to bring hot food into a workplace. They said they could arrange a lunch delivery if I give them a few hours' notice each morning. It's only a couple of miles away so..."

Harry's bushy eyebrows arched. "What is it, some kinda hot dog cart they got?"

"Not quite a 'hot dog cart', but... the point is, they can get a nutritious hot meal to keep them going all day, instead of sand-wiches. I had a look at the menu and they do chowder bowls, buttermilk chicken, collard greens, you name it." Marcie tapped her notepad with the end of her pencil. "I worked it out, and we can afford it. And think of the morale boost it'll give everyone."

"OK, we'll give it a try. You're right, they deserve it; they work damn hard for us." Harry nodded as he spoke.

Marcie bent down to kiss her husband on the cheek.

"Mom, I gotta get to work. You sure you don't need anything else before I go?" Trish called up to the ceiling, then tasted the soup she was heating up for her mother's supper. Nodding, she replaced the lid on the pot, then reached across the counter to collect her purse. As she did so, her eyes drifted over the cupboards and units around the small kitchen and, knowing that *not* looking through them would play on her mind all evening, she opened each door and rifled through them, reaching as far as she could towards the back. To her relief, all she found in the glass bottles was drain cleaner.

"I may move as slow as molasses, but I can manage a few hours without you, y'know. I'm a big girl." Doria shuffled into the kitchen, then stopped in her tracks, looking down at her daughter's startled face. "If I was back on the drink, I'd have found a smarter place to hide it than behind the bottles of poison," she said.

"I'm sorry, Mom. It's not that I don't trust you—"

"I've given Tommy his bath. I think the steam has done him some good tonight. He don't sound as bad. I put a few lavender oil drops in the water. He's all tucked in and ready for his story," her mother interrupted.

"Thank you. I really do apprec—"

"I know. I can't blame you for thinking the way you do about me. Now get up there and kiss your son goodnight. Oh, he said he wanted *Harold and the Purple Crayon* for his story tonight."

"Again?" She chuckled.

"Again. He's only had it a week, but I think he knows it by heart now. I swear one day there will be drawings all over these walls."

"Thanks, Mom. You know I love you, don't you?" Trish whispered as she climbed the stairs.

"Just remember to do the voices. He won't go to sleep until you do the voices," her mother said, ladling out a portion of soup and sitting at the kitchen table.

Tapping on Tommy's bedroom door, Trish walked in to find him propped up with three pillows behind his tiny torso.

"Hey Momma. I smell like flowers."

"Hey baby, I know. You smell like a meadow in June." She giggled and perched on the edge of the bed as her son passed his reading book to her.

"You have to do the voices."

"So I'm told," Trish replied. "On one condition. You look after Grandma for me, OK? You pick up that phone, like I taught you, if anything happens. You promise?" Her eyes widened as she implored her five-year-old son.

"I promise, Momma."

"Right. Well now, let's get started."

Trish opened the already worn cover of her son's new favorite book and began to read until his eyes became too heavy to keep open. She closed the book and rose off the bed, praying it wouldn't creak.

"Why don't I have a daddy?" Tommy's tiny voice piped up just as Trish managed to make it to the doorway. She paused, her finger poised on the light switch.

"You do. But... well, it's *his* loss. Now, go to sleep, honey. Mommy loves you. Goodnight."

"How was it today?" Dorothy asked as Shona returned home later than usual. It was just after eight o'clock. Smiling, she set a large bag of groceries down on the kitchen counter.

"It was good. Harry took me out on some deliveries this morning, then afterwards taught me how to fix a starter motor.

Seems pretty easy, just pull a few wires, flick a few switches," Shona replied, unpacking the groceries.

"That's good. You eaten?" Dorothy asked as she busied herself putting tin cans in the cupboard above the little stove.

"Yeah, me and Harry went across the street to the diner for dinner with him, Jonny and Marcie. The catfish is delicious. Oh, but not as good as your pie, ma'am. I'm sure I could force down a slice or two," Shona added, seeing Dorothy's stern eyes narrow. She handed Dorothy the few coins from her top pocket to change the subject.

"Here's your change. Jake gave me two-for-one on the Tide. We're going through it fast me coming home covered in oil every night, I think he took pity on me. I never washed my clothes so much in my damn life," Shona joked, leaning on the counter.

"I've told you before; I don't mind doing them in the daytime when I do my own, while you're out at work. You pay more than your way around here," Dorothy replied, putting the change in her canister on the shelf.

"Now, Dorothy, we've already had this conversation. We're a team, you and me. We help each other. But I'd never expect you to clean my clothes as well as cooking for me and giving me a bed. I can do that myself, have done all my life. Well, since my momma passed." Shona stopped talking when she saw the look of sympathy on Dorothy's kindly features. "I really like it here," she continued, gazing out of the kitchen window. "It's so quiet and out of the way. But I guess that's why you like it here too, huh?" she asked, turning to face Dorothy.

"Yeah. Most days I just sit out there on the porch swing just listening to the birdsong. I can't be bothered with all the drama that goes on in town. Oh, that reminds me, I nearly forgot. I gotta go vote soon, the election's coming up, so I'll need you to take me into town one day next week."

"Who you gon' vote for?" Shona asked, only vaguely knowing who the candidates were.

"Not sure. They're probably all criminals. I know there's one guy from outta state trying his luck, but people in this town aren't too trusting of outsiders even if they are flashing the greenbacks to buy their way into office," Dorothy replied.

Shona half-smiled at Dorothy's all too close to home opinion on strangers in town. It had been six months since she came to Riverside, but the questions about her background still rattled around Wreckers on a daily basis.

"But I heard that this one guy," Dorothy said, "Max something or other, is really keen to do something about that monstrosity of a bar. It's an eyesore. I might not go into town that often, but I still care what happens down there. He wants to 'clean up this town' so he's got my vote."

"Mine too, I guess. Not so keen on strangers coming to town myself. For obvious reasons." She looked at Dorothy, who responded with a knowing smile. "I've only just gotten used to the faces I see there already." Shona grinned and started laying the cutlery on the table for dinner as Dorothy paused from lighting the stove and stared at her.

"Shona, your father? And those other people, back in Louisiana? Well, I can't be sure but I reckon they will have stopped looking for you by now..."

"Ouch. Goddamn," Shona exclaimed, her bleeding thumb dropping red dots on the white tablecloth. The knife she'd run over her skin without realizing it clattered to the floor.

"What happened?" Dorothy asked as she left the stove and scuttled over with a wet dishcloth. She dabbed the wound gently and looked up at Shona, whose face was now pale.

"Nothing. It's fine. Listen, I gotta go. I'll be back later. Sorry," she mumbled, wriggling clear of Dorothy's grip on her bleeding thumb.

"You'll need a Band-Aid for that..." Dorothy called after her, but it was too late. Shona had already slammed the front door, almost off its hinges, behind her.

It didn't feel right to take the truck. Shona hadn't meant to run out on Dorothy, but the thought of being found by her father cut deeper into her than the knife had to her still-bleeding thumb. Pressing it to her lips, she sucked the blood away and carried on walking along the edge of the field next to the highway.

Before long, she reached town. Not really feeling like company, she found a bench at the end of the street outside Wreckers and sat cross-legged on the seat. Some the mechanics had chosen to return to their families for dinner and bedtime stories, but some had opted to take a liquid meal in the bar instead. Watching people go about their business was a favorite pastime of hers but always from a distance. She'd often wondered where they were going, what their lives were like. Who they were going home to? Were they in love? Did they have a dream? People fascinated and terrified her in equal measure.

At the opposite end of the street to the bar, a dark green Toyota pulled over under a streetlight and the passenger side door opened. Moments later, Lucy swung her long legs clear, stood up and straightened her black-and-red sequined dress. Smoothing her hair down on one side, she stuffed a folded wad of dollar bills in her purse. Not even saying goodbye to her ride, she slammed the door and watched as the car pulled away. Her face was expressionless, her demeanor vacant.

Looking up, Lucy saw a familiar face watching her from the

bench outside Wreckers. Feeling the fizz of panic race through her veins, she put her head down and desperately tried to avoid being recognized. In her urgency, Lucy's heel caught on the grid by the curb, sending her crashing to the ground and landing in a shiny sequined heap. Shona jumped up from the bench and raced over.

"You alright?" she asked, crouching down. She put her arms around Lucy's shoulders and helped her to her feet.

"Got my damn heel caught. Thanks," Lucy mumbled, trying not to let Shona see her properly, but the streetlight above her was enough for Shona to notice the tears that had left their mascara-stained streaks down Lucy's face.

"Where are you heading?" Shona asked.

"Home. I'll be alright now, you can go," Lucy insisted, still trying to wriggle free of Shona's embrace.

"OK. But you might wanna take those shoes off before you tackle that fire escape. That's a helluva height to fall from," Shona replied, half smiling as Lucy swayed away from her.

"I don't need you telling me what to do," Lucy snapped.

Looking up at the steps and realizing Shona was most probably right, she bent down to slip off her heels, holding them limply at the end of her index finger.

"Well, alright then. I'll leave you to it," Shona said, flicking her hand to wave goodbye.

"How many of those damn things did you take? They were only supposed to make you relax, goddamn it. You'd better not have fucked this up for me. Did you do what he wanted?"

Frank's questions all went unanswered as he waved the bottle of smelling salts underneath Lucy's nose until she snapped back into the here and now. It was way after nine o'clock.

"Wha-aa-at?" she croaked, her mouth dry.

"You heard. I got a lot ridin' on this so you'd better not have let me down, girl," he mumbled as he began searching through Lucy's purse. He pulled out the wad of money and began counting it. Smiling, he bent over the bed and kissed her on the cheek. "Good girl, you must have really satisfied him. I only expected $20; there's $25 here. Say, why don't you take the night off? I can't have you walkin' around the bar in that state. Sleep it off, will ya." He wrapped the bedsheet around her messily and stroked her hair. "You're my best girl, you remember that. You know I love you, don't you? I just want you to have the best ones. Not the pieces of shit I give the other girls. You're different, Lucy. You're special." He watched her for a moment as she appeared to fall fast asleep, then left to head back down to the bar.

As soon as she heard his footsteps become fainter, Lucy dragged her heavy body up from the bed and headed to the shower.

She had an apology to make.

"Who is it?" the old lady called from behind the door.

"It's Lucy, Mrs. Clark. Could I please talk to Shona?"

The door opened a crack. Spotting the old lady's wrinkly blue eyes, Lucy implored her silently to let her in.

"Alright, hold on a minute. You stay there," Dorothy ordered, leaving Lucy standing on the porch.

Moments later, after hearing hushed tones, then silence, Shona appeared. "Hi," she said, half hidden by the door. "Shit, you OK?" she added, noticing Lucy swaying slightly, her forehead clammy.

"Hi. Look, I needed to tell you I'm sorry. I was rude to you before and all you were trying to do was help me... I've been working for Frank lately and... well, I don't usually dress like this and, well, I was just embarrassed."

Lucy wrapped her trembling fingers around a loose lock of hair, desperate to see Shona's hard stare soften. The calm blue eyes she'd gotten used to seeing these past few months of their friendship somehow didn't look right being so cold.

"It's fine. You don't need to explain yourself to me, Lucy," Shona replied.

Lucy smiled. "So... am I forgiven?" She leaned against the doorframe.

"Nothing to forgive."

"Alright. Well, that's good then." Lucy exhaled. "I guess I'd better get back. But thank you, Shona."

"For what?"

"For not slamming the door in my face." Lucy smiled again as she attempted the joke. It worked. She saw the merest glimpse of softness spread across Shona's beautiful face.

"It *was* tempting. But I already busted it a little, slamming it myself earlier."

Lucy looked down at the door hinge nearest the ground, seeing that the old wood had splintered. The lock had also come away from the frame.

Admitting defeat at not being asked in, she sighed. "I'd better go, Frank will be home soon, but I just wanted to apologize. G'night, Shona."

"Wait...I'll run you home." Shona grabbed her jacket and led Lucy to the truck, encouraged by a nod of permission from a just-as-worried Dorothy.

Chapter 12

Frank prowled around his mother's kitchen, the beer bottle in his hand belying the early hour. Pacing up and down, he finally settled in a dining chair, his eyes fixed on the wall clock as it ticked to 8:30 a.m.

"What the hell are you doin' here so early?" Gloria recoiled, her satin pink nightgown billowing behind her as she stopped dead in her tracks.

"Dad's comin' home. Another bus's due in town at twelve today, and another one due tomorrow, so the flyer said. That's two in a week, so he's gotta be on one of them," Frank replied, his lip curling as he reached into his jeans pocket to pull out his lighter as his mother held her long black cigarette holder out.

Gloria breathed in a lungful of smoke, face unreadable underneath the thick layer of make-up. Her bright pink lipstick stained the end of her cigarette holder as she pulled it out of her mouth and leaned against the counter.

"Honey. We've talked about this. Your father..." She paused, trying, not for the first time, to broach the subject delicately with her son. "He's not interested in comin' back here."

"I got a letter yesterday," he replied, smirking. "Yeah, that's right. Said he can't wait to see how I've made a success of

96

myself. He remembered everythin' I'd told him about the bar. I knew he would," he rambled on, hardly noticing his mother's demeanor change.

"Frank, are you *sure* that's what the letter said?" Gloria asked, wiping her brow as she took another long drag on her cigarette.

Frank looked at her. "Well, not those exact words. It just said he wanted me to get on and make somethin' of my life. But he meant so he had somethin' to come back for. I just know it."

Gloria blew out a large plume of smoke and shook her head. "It's been nearly four years now since Korea, Frank. Buses are comin' back all the time and he's not on any of them." She paused. "I think he meant what he said in your letter, son. He wants you to stop waitin' around thinkin' he's gonna walk back through that door. He's not, Frank."

"Well, at least I ain't given up on him." He snarled. "Look at you all dolled up like Marilyn Monroe. Tryin' to prove you can do better, huh?" He rose up out of his seat after catching a glimpse of George coming down the hallway and into the kitchen. Striding out of the kitchen, Frank eyeballed George as he barged past him and slammed the door.

"He ain't a child no more. 'Bout time he grew up and acted like a man." George, dressed in his smartest gray flannel suit, straightened his tie and smoothed down the front of his crisp white shirt.

"You're right, honey. I know you're right. But the only one around here that gets the vaguest amount of respect out of Frank is his Uncle Harry. But I think even he's gettin' sick of him now." Gloria stubbed her cigarette out and set the holder down on the counter. Pouring two cups of coffee, she turned to face George, who waved away the cup.

"I gotta run, those shipping accounts won't do themselves." He straightened his belt and leaned over to Gloria, who smiled and turned her cheek towards him to receive her usual kiss goodbye.

~

Frank almost kicked down the door of the bar as he unlocked it at 11 a.m. On the mat inside was a pile of letters, one standing out more than the others. After opening it, he read the first five lines, then crumpled it in his fist.

"What's the matter with you?" Lucy asked, appearing behind him.

"Nothin'. How comes you ain't at college?" Frank replied, frowning.

"Study day," Lucy said. "Who's that from?"

"It's a warnin' letter from the council. We've had some complaints. Says it's been lookin' a mess since New Year's and that we need to clean up the joint," he replied.

"Or what?"

"I'll deal with it. You don't need to worry. And don't you go telling the other girls either. I don't want them flippin' out and goin' elsewhere for jobs. We need them bringin' the customers in." Softening his glare at her when he noticed the fear in her eyes, he leaned in to kiss her. "I got some things to do here. Why don't you go treat yourself to a chocolate shake and some pie or somethin'," he said, reaching into his jeans pocket and pulling out a dollar coin.

"OK. If you're sure?" Lucy said, taking it from him.

As Lucy left the bar, she looked across the street to Wreckers where Shona was leaning over a Ford pick-up. Smiling, she headed over.

~

"What's eating you?"

Shona was rubbing a towel over her just-washed hands, staring at Lucy, who had wandered into Wreckers an hour earlier and sat on a tire the whole time hardly uttering a word.

"Huh?" Lucy's face hardly even registered the question as she turned to look at Shona.

"You've been staring at that same poster for ten minutes now, and even I don't find brake fluid that interesting." She laughed as she threw the towel into the tiny sink in the corner of the workshop.

"Oh, was I? I was just thinking. Shona, do you know we only have twenty-five thousand days of life on this planet? If we're lucky to make it to seventy, that is." Lucy's eyes shimmered.

Shona grinned. "When did you work that one out?"

"Last night. I'm over seven thousand days into my quota and I've done nothing with my life."

"Well... what do you wanna do with it?" Shona asked, folding her arms.

"I don't know. That's the worst part of it. All I know is I ain't happy with the math." Lucy blew her cheeks out as she looked around the spotlessly tidy garage.

"Listen, I gotta run over to the store now and get some groceries, then take them back to Dorothy's house. You wanna come with me? I mean, unless you gotta be around for Frank?"

"Sure," Lucy interrupted, jumping up from the tire.

Stubbing out his cigarette and cursing the families who were hugging their loved ones as they hobbled off the bus, Frank seethed.

Casting his glance across the street, his frustration doubled when he saw his laughing girlfriend step out of the grocery store and walk over to a blue truck with Shona.

Lighting another cigarette, he jumped into his own truck, letting Shona drive to the end of the street before he set off.

~

"Where shall I put these?" Lucy asked as they arrived back at Dorothy's house laden with two grocery bags each.

"On the counter, please," Shona replied, resting her own bags by the sink. Dropping a bag of wood in its usual place by the stove, she crossed the kitchen back to where Lucy was standing. "Sorry, could I just..."

"Oh, sorry." Lucy maneuvered her body to let Shona reach up over her to the shelf and pull the canister down. She watched as Shona took off the lid and popped Dorothy's change inside. Realizing how close they were now standing to each other, Lucy took another awkward step aside.

"Damn, I always seem to be in your way, don't I?" Lucy blushed as Shona lowered her arm from replacing the canister on the shelf.

"No problem," Shona smiled back. "I'm making coffee. You want one?" she offered as she held the kettle underneath the thin trickle of water from the faucet.

"Yeah, if you got time?"

"Cream and sugar?" asked Shona, pulling out two of Dorothy's best mugs from the cupboard.

"Both. Dorothy not here?"

"Yeah, she'll be upstairs. She normally takes a nap around lunchtime."

Shona passed Lucy her coffee mug and watched as she blew the steam off it.

"It's good. Thank you," she said after taking a sip.

"You're welcome. So how was Frank today?"

"Oh, he went out early this morning to his mom's. Came back in a real ugly mood. He did give me a dollar to go get some breakfast, though, but I didn't want to sit on my own so that's why I came to bug you." Lucy grinned.

"He won't be happy with that. Then again, is that guy ever happy lately? He's given Harry earache for something pretty much every day since Christmas. What's the story with them anyway?"

"Frank doesn't like the fact that in his mind the wrong brother went off to war and now he's missing out on what he should have had from his father. Thinks Harry owes him some-how. Frank don't seem to get that it's not his uncle's fault he busted his leg years back. And anyhow, he was too old to enlist, but that's not a good enough reason for Frank either."

A loud holler rang out from upstairs. "I'd better go see if she needs anything." She put her cup down and ran up the stairs two at a time, holding onto the bannister as they shook with her movement.

Lucy smiled in admiration of Shona's kind heart. Her fingernail tapped the rim of her coffee mug as her eyes floated across the layout of the kitchen. She noticed the tiny spots of oil on the towel that, no matter how hard Shona had scrubbed on the washboard, just would not come out. Including the two mugs Shona had used for their coffees, there were two cups, two dishes and two sets of cutlery all washed up on the drainer, ready for dinner later.

Lucy's gaze travelled upwards over the shelf and landed on the canister. Before she processed what she was doing, she reached up, twisted off the lid and took a few of the bills from inside, stuffing them in her pocket. Hearing Shona's footsteps returning, she replaced the lid, her fumbling fingers struggling as she popped the canister back on the shelf. With one huge step, Lucy moved to the other side of the kitchen and leaned against the counter, only seconds to spare before Shona's blonde hair appeared around the doorframe.

"Forgot to get something from town. But I can get it after work. You all set?"

"Yeah, let's go," Lucy replied, feeling a bead of sweat drip down the back of her neck.

Jumping back in the truck, Lucy swallowed hard as she leaned against the inside of the door and felt the bulge of the bills in her pocket, already regretting her decision.

~

Standing on the other side of the bushes outside Dorothy's house, Frank glared at the blue truck.

"You're spendin' way too much time with that girl, Lucy," he muttered to himself as he docked the third cigarette he'd smoked in the half hour he'd been watching the house.

~

Returning home that Monday evening after work, Shona felt an icy coolness in the usually cozy house. It was just after 6:30 p.m. when she found Dorothy sitting quietly in the kitchen, the canister open in front of her.

"Hi, you get some rest this afternoon? I got the cream you asked for. Drugstore guy said it'll sooth that redness on your knee, but said to try and not wear that bandage too much. I don't see as it helps none anyway, just stops the air getting to it. Oh my, you'll never believe what happened at work this afternoon. Harry had this guy in who said his truck was making this clunking noise, so I offered to take a look, 'cos my hands are smaller and what did we find in there? Damn raccoon asleep on the radiator. Jumped like his ass was on fire when he saw us." Shona continued her tale as she busied herself around the kitchen, finding her and Lucy's coffee mugs already washed and on the drainer.

"Shona, I need to ask you something… but I want you to tell me the truth," the old lady began.

"OK," Shona replied, sitting down in the chair opposite and placing her hands on her knees.

"I had seven dollars in bills and some change in this canister this morning. Then I took out two to give you for the groceries. Now all I have left in here are three quarters, a few dimes, and a button I thought I'd lost," Dorothy began. She stared at Shona. "Five dollars missing."

The moments that passed between them felt like hours.

"You sure? I don't remember seeing that much in there." Shona shook her head and looked down at the table, before the same thought struck her that had struck Dorothy when she'd opened the canister an hour earlier.

"Yes, I'm sure. I put a little in there each day from my other hiding place. I got a call this afternoon from an old friend saying that her sister had passed so I was going to get some flowers for her. To save myself from having to go back upstairs, I knew I had enough in here." She tapped the canister with the tip of her fingernail. "But not so, it would seem."

Shona swallowed. *Would she?* Her memory drifted back to the brief five minutes she'd left Lucy alone in the kitchen. *Or was Dorothy mistaken?* Thoughts spilled over themselves in Shona's muddled head.

"I didn't take it, Dorothy, I swear. I wouldn't do that. Not to you," Shona blurted out, rising from her chair, frowning with confusion.

"Almost a year you've been living here, and I've enjoyed every minute of your company. But this? Well, I never thought you'd ever steal from me. Why would you do that?"

"I didn't take it, on my life, Dorothy," Shona protested, tears in her eyes.

"Then who did?"

The silence between them was deafening.

"Lucy."

"Lucy?" Dorothy repeated, creasing her forehead.

"She wasn't thinking straight. When you called me to come up the stairs, she must have taken it. It's my fault, I shouldn't have let her see me put your change away. I'm sorry..." Shona wiped her eyes with the palm of her hand.

"Why was Lucy in my house?" the old lady asked, her tone even.

"I asked her to come with me to help get the groceries. She seemed upset about something and I wanted to help her, be someone she could talk to, you know? I didn't know she would steal from you. I would have never brought her here if I thought she'd do that."

"You know how I feel about that girl. She associates with trouble. You remember me telling you what her reprobate boyfriend did to Jake, don't you? If you know what's good for you, you'll stay away from her and that Frank Smith." Dorothy took out her handkerchief and wiped her nose.

"Here, take this." Shona held out a crisp dollar bill. "I got a tip today for being early finishing a job. Harry let me keep it. I'll give you the rest of what's missing at the end of the week when I get paid. Please, Dorothy, take it."

Dorothy put a hand on either side of her chair and pushed her aged body up slowly. "I don't want your money," she said, walking past Shona's outstretched hand.

"Please, tell me how to make this right," Shona begged.

Taking a pot down from the shelf, Dorothy opened, then poured two cans of soup into it. Looking square at Shona, she pointed her long, bony finger at her. "You tell that girl to come over here and apologize to me in person. I want *her* to give me my money back. Not you."

Shona nodded.

"Well, you gon' stand there all evening? It's mushroom,"

Dorothy barked as she set two bowls down on the table and returned to the stove.

Shona slipped into her seat at the table, her hands resting on her knees. "Does that mean you're not angry with me?"

The old lady lifted the pot from the stove and filled the bowls. "You didn't lie to me, Shona. You chose to tell me the truth even though it meant admitting you'd made a mistake. I respect that." She poured the last remaining drops into Shona's already-full bowl and sat down at the table.

Shona breathed a sigh of relief.

Chapter 13

"Goddamn it," Shona cursed as the wrench careened across the stone floor of the garage, flung clean away from her grasp as she battled with the stubborn engine cover.

"Hey, what's got your goat?" Harry called out as he crossed over to her.

Shona kicked at the ground in pain as she shook her stinging fingers. "Damn bolt won't shift," she mumbled, sucking away a thin trickle of blood on her knuckle.

"Well, here... let me try. You got that wrench?" Harry said, holding his hand out as Shona bent down to pick it up. As she did so, her eyes fell upon a pair of yellow sandals approaching. As she lifted her eyes upwards, her stare hardened.

"Morning, Shona," Lucy chirped.

"Harry, I'm gonna get a Band-Aid for this." Shona looked through Lucy and waved her knuckle at her boss.

Lucy hovered for a moment and looked at Harry, who shrugged and returned to his tool chest. She followed Shona into the office and watched as she lifted the first aid tin down from the shelf and opened it up, taking out a small Band-Aid.

"Here, let me help you," she whispered, edging closer.

"I'm fine, I can do it," Shona snapped back, struggling to free her fingers from the adhesive.

Lucy stepped in and peeled the Band-Aid off Shona's good hand, screwing it up and throwing it in the trash. Unwrapping a fresh one, she pulled out Shona's damaged finger from the fist she'd made and fixed the new Band-Aid in place.

"There you go. Now, what's the matter with you? Why are you angry with me?"

"Dorothy had some money taken from the canister on her shelf. She was real mad at me," Shona snapped, watching her reaction.

Lucy's face blanched. "What? She thought *you* took it?"

"Of course she did. I'm the only other person who lives there. She ain't no flake, she's as sharp as a tack. She knows exactly how much she had in there." Shona clamped her teeth together so hard they almost squeezed through her cheeks.

"Oh my God, I'm so sorry... I only needed to borrow it. I was gon' give it back," Lucy blurted out, the tears beginning to roll down her pale face.

"Why? Why'd you take it? If you'd only asked first, I could have tried to help." Shona struggled to contain her rage.

"I needed it. I'm sorry..." Lucy sobbed.

"Did you think she wouldn't notice? She may be old, but she notices everything. Believe me." Shona stopped. "Needed it for what?"

Lucy looked up at her through tear-filled eyes. "I just needed it. I don't think I wanna be around Frank anymore. I shoulda gone to live at college, like I was supposed to in the first place, but I gave away my dorm room when I first started, thinking I wouldn't need it now I was with Frank. But it was a big mistake. Frank takes all the money I get from my parents and now he's got me working in the bar and..." Lucy paused to look at Shona. "I don't think I'm in love with him after all, Shona. I know we've only been together a few months but he's got a nasty side, and he's three sheets to the wind most days. Oh, I know he tries to be all charming to the other ladies in town but he's jealous and bitter with me. Terrified I'm gon' leave him, like his father did. I guess deep down he loves me, and I thought I *did* love him when we first met. But I just don't feel... the same... anymore." Lucy hesitated on the last sentence.

Refocusing her eyes on Shona, who looked just as mad as she did before, she continued, "I just wanted to get some money together. To give me some options. I've done too many bad things these last few weeks to go home. I just thought maybe... Maybe I could start over, like you have? I'm so sorry, Shona. Please let me explain to Dorothy that it wasn't you... I owe you that much at least."

"Listen, I of all people understand the desire to make a fresh start, but I just can't believe you would come into an old lady's house and steal from her. You must have known that she'd blame me. I thought we were friends?"

"What the hell is goin' on in here?" Frank asked, looking furious as he stormed into the office.

Shona backed off and looked down at the concrete, her hands thrust deep in her overall pockets.

"Frank... where you been all morning? I didn't hear you leave," Lucy blurted out, wiping her eyes before casting them up over his newly polished boots, smart slacks and button-down shirt. His normally scuffed leather jacket also looked as if he'd had it cleaned. "You look real smart. Where you been?"

"It's Tuesday. Another bus was due to get in today. Don't you remember me sayin'?" Frank glared at Lucy. Getting no flicker of recognition from her, he threw his hands in the air in frustration. "Why don't you ever remember *anythin'* that's important to me, huh? Look, never mind that now, I wanna know what's goin' on in here." He chewed his gum, switching his glance between his weeping girlfriend and an angry-looking Shona.

"We just... had a disagreement. I had a tough morning," Shona said.

"Well now, that don't give you cause to go upsettin' my girl-friend, now does it? How about I tell my uncle... your boss, about how you speak to people? He don't need staff like that," Frank snarled, stepping closer to Shona.

"Frank, come on, let's go. I gotta get ready for work tonight," Lucy whispered, pulling on the cuff of his jacket.

"You think about what I said. You speak to my girl with a bit more respect next time," Frank warned.

Shona opened her mouth to respond but at the last second thought better of it. She'd already nearly lost the trust and respect of her best friend; she really didn't want to risk her job too. All because of Lucy's dishonesty. But there was just something about the look on Lucy's face when Frank led her away. Lucy's whole body seemed to freeze.

Shona knew that feeling only too well.

"What were you and that Shona arguin' about, earlier today?" Frank asked, as he leaned against the bedroom doorframe watching Lucy get ready.

"What?" Lucy froze. "Oh, nothing. She just asked to, um... borrow some, um... money from me. I said no, but she didn't like it so got upset," she added, trying to make her lie sound convincing.

"Oh, right," Frank replied. He ran the tip of his finger over the rim of his beer bottle. "Mighty rude to get angry about that, don't you think?"

"Mmmm... I guess." Lucy looked at his reflection in her mirror, the hairs on the back of her neck prickling as the atmosphere between them began to thicken. "I mean, it's not even as if we've been friends for years now, is it?" she said, letting out a nervous laugh.

"See, that's what I don't get." He walked up behind Lucy. Putting his bottle down on her dressing table, he began massaging her shoulders. "You say you don't know her that well, but you went back to her house yesterday. Didn't you?" His fingertips pressed into her collarbones.

Lucy spun around to face him. "What? How did you... Have you been following me?"

"I'm just curious to know why you felt the need to lie to me," he replied.

"I just wanted to talk with her. I'm allowed to have friends, Frank." She turned back to face the mirror.

Frank stood up straight, grabbed his bottle and took a step back. "You don't need anyone but me. I don't want you hangin' around that garage anymore. It's not the place for a lady of mine. You need to be concentratin' on your job now, not gettin' covered in oil and grease like that girl in there."

"But Frank, I really like talking to her. That so bad?"

"Really? Hmmm... well, maybe I should put her on the payroll too? I got a couple of guys who'd just *love* to help her out with her cash flow problems." He sniggered as he drained the last drops from his bottle.

"Don't you dare, Frank." Lucy whipped around and threw her hairbrush in his direction. Ducking as it clattered against the bedroom wall, Frank stared at her in surprise.

"Jeez... you're really taken by her, ain't ya?" he exclaimed, covering his mouth as beer dribbled down his chin. He shook his head as he left her to get ready.

Chapter 14

"Where is it?"

Lucy woke up with a jolt that Wednesday morning to find Frank leaning over her.

"What?" she slurred, burying her head in her pillow. "Where's what?"

"The money. From last night? He did pay you, right?" Frank snapped as he rifled through her panty drawer.

"Of course he paid me. You think he'd get past Chuck?" Lucy squinted as she opened her exhausted eyes. "I put the money in the same place I always put it."

Frank strode over to the mantelpiece and reached behind the clock. "It's not here. Did you lock the door when you came back down to the bar?" Frank's sweaty face was turning redder by the second.

"Of course I did," Lucy said. Her head had been fuzzy from the pills Frank had given her last night. Suddenly she remembered that, in her haste to get her customer out and herself into the shower, she'd completely forgotten to flick the snip on the lock. Realizing her mistake, she sat bolt upright.

"Is it all gone?" she whispered to Frank who was standing with his hands on his hips.

"I told you, there's nothin' here. You ain't stashed it anywhere else, have you? You don't think too straight when you're on those pills."

"No. If it ain't here, I've been robbed." Snapping her head upwards, she glared at Frank. "Do you think it could have been Chuck?"

Frank creased his face. "Chuck? That knucklehead couldn't find his ass with both hands, you think he'd have the balls to come in here and steal from you? Knowin' what I'd do to him if I found out?" His expression changed. "How do I know *you* ain't got a little secret stash somewhere? Are you stealin' from me now? Or is it your friend Shona who's rippin' me off?"

Lucy froze. With every ounce of composure she could muster, she rose out of bed and stroked Frank's arm.

"Could you please ask Chuck if he *borrowed* it? He might have thought he was doing me a favor by taking the money straight to you. He might still have it?" Her eyes implored him to alter his own line of inquiry.

Frank paused for a moment. "OK, I'll ask him," he said, walking towards the door.

Lucy's smile faded as the door closed behind him. Her heart panged as she thought again about the missing money and the five dollars of it that she *really* needed back.

~

Groaning with exertion, Harry heard the welcome squeak of the bolt as it gave up its resistance after almost ten minutes of battling with it.

"Hey, you finally won your fight then?" Marcie joked, passing her husband a mug of coffee. "Maybe I should have brought you out a cold sweet tea instead, honey, you're sweating like a sinner in church."

Harry smiled at his wife. "This'll do just fine. Thank you."

"Your protégé has been a bit quiet this morning," Marcie remarked, perching on the edge of the tool chest as she pointed over to where Shona was cleaning some engine parts. "She OK?"

"Yeah, she's fine. She's been a breath of fresh air these last ten months. Picked up things quicker than I can teach her." Harry paused.

"But?" Marcie cocked her head forward.

"Well... I just worry about the amount of time Frank spends hanging around here. That bar of his was struggling before Christmas and now it seems to have gone downhill again judging by the state of the outside of it, even though he had a good few weeks of earnings over New Year's. Knowing Frank, though, that's probably all gone by now. I can't help but have the feeling he's starting to eye Shona to be one of his dancing girls. Or worse..." Harry stopped, noticing the concerned look on his wife's face. "Maybe I should try and put a stop to that. Ain't no way I'd wanna encourage her to go over there after work if that *is* what's in Frank's plans."

"She is a pretty one, that's for sure. I think you should have a word with Frank. Let him know that Shona's got more than enough work to keep her occupied here?" Marcie paused. "That is, unless Shona *wants* to do that sort of thing? Maybe that's why Lucy has started to hang around her so much? Maybe Frank has asked her to butter Shona up?" She raised her eyebrow as she leaned over to take Harry's empty mug from him.

"Maybe. Or maybe it's just because Lucy needs a friend? I know Frank's blood but he's not the nicest person to live with. And since Christmas he's just got worse. Beats me what she ever saw in him in the first place. Leopards don't change their spots. Oh, that reminds me, I need to talk to him anyway. His damn mother's been on the phone to me this morning again, bellyaching about his behavior. I gotta try and 'pull him into line', apparently."

"When you gon' speak to him?"

"When he's calmed down," Harry replied. "Senior wasn't on that bus again."

"OK. Well, I'd best get back to work, and you've got more bolts to fight with." Marcie kissed the tips of her fingers and pressed them to her husband's tanned forehead.

Watching her walk away, Harry reached into his overalls pocket and pulled out his handkerchief. As he ran it over his face and the back of his neck, the last sentence that Gloria had said to him on the phone echoed through his brain.

"He just wants his father back, Harry."

~

"Harry, c'mon, you know I'm good for it. It's only five dollars!" Frank exclaimed, eyes widened at his uncle's reluctance to open his wallet yet again later that Wednesday morning.

"You say 'only' every time, Frank. I'm getting a little tired of you coming over here whenever you're short," Harry replied, putting his hands on his hips.

"I really need it this time."

"Well, alright. But I got my own business to look after here too, you know. I can't keep bailing you out." Harry took his wallet from his back pocket and slipped out the bills to give to his eager-faced nephew. "No gambling. OK?" he said, then released his grip.

Frank grinned and pocketed the money, then headed back over to the bar.

"Why do you do that?" Shona asked as she walked up behind Harry.

"I owe him."

"Why?" she asked.

"Long story."

~

"Hey Shona," Lucy greeted as she strolled over at lunchtime to where Shona had seated herself on a tire to eat her sandwiches.

"Hi," Shona replied.

"Can I sit?"

"If you want."

Shona shifted her body over enough to let Lucy sit next to her. They sat there for a few awkward moments before Shona's hostility waned.

"You hungry?" Shona asked, gesturing down to the lunch box on the ground in front of her.

"Oh, no. I ain't gon' eat your lunch. But thanks for the offer." Lucy smiled as her eyes lowered to Shona's sandwiches. "Nice box."

"Thanks."

"Doesn't Harry get hot meals delivered here now? Why you eating sandwiches?" Lucy chuckled as they both watched the just-arrived lunch delivery being demolished by the other hungry mechanics.

"Dorothy likes to make them for me. I don't mind. She cuts the crusts off, just how I like it." Shona grinned and took another huge hungry bite.

"Did you tell Dorothy it was me who took the money?" Lucy's tone became more serious.

"Yeah," Shona replied. "She wants it back. I offered to give her it from my wages, but she wants you to be the one to give it her."

Lucy frowned as she bit the corner of her lip. "That could be a problem."

"How come? You ain't spent it already, have you?"

"I got robbed. Someone came into my apartment while I was…" She paused. "I shoulda hidden it better."

"Does Frank know?" Shona asked.

"Yeah, he had a fit when he found out. Called me an idiot for not locking the door. But I ain't had anyone let themselves in to my place the whole time I've been there. Probably some stranger from outta town."

They paused for a moment in thought. Shona put her sandwich down on her knee and reached into her top pocket.

"I tried to give the only dollar I had on me to Dorothy the other night, but she blew a gasket at me. This morning I got a couple of nice tips. But… Well, here." Shona pulled out five one-dollar bills and handed them to Lucy. "Maybe Dorothy will accept it if she thinks it's from you? And before you get all stubborn like her, it's only a loan. You can pay me back when you get paid next, OK?"

Lucy looked down at the money, then back up to Shona's calm blue eyes. "Are you sure? Why would you do that for me?"

"You're my friend. And we all need to catch a break now and again."

"Thank you, Shona," Lucy whispered.

"No problem. I'll take you over there after I finish up here, if that's OK with you?" Shona stood up from the tire and brushed the crumbs off her overalls, then reached her hand down to help Lucy up.

"It's fine. I'm working later on, but I can go over with you, say around five?"

"Good. I'll keep hold of this for safekeeping until then. Just in case, you know?" Shona put the five dollars back in her top pocket and turned to walk back over to the bar.

~

George returned from work that evening holding the biggest bunch of flowers Gloria had seen in a long time.

"Well, my goodness, what on Earth have I done to deserve such a grand gesture?" she joked, taking them from him and receiving her usual kiss on the cheek.

"Can't a man buy his angel flowers when he feels like it?"

"Honey, you can buy me roses every day of the week and I'd still appreciate it. You spoil me, George Wilson."

"Well, I saved a client a lot of money today on his tax return. I got a nice lil' bonus so we're going out tonight. You're gon' have the biggest catfish they can find in the whole of the Gulf of Mexico." He picked her up around the waist and swirled her.

"I can't wait. I'll go get ready. I just wish you could find some way of savin' Frank a bit of money." Gloria's tone became more somber. "It's runnin' dry, that place, and I don't mean the liquor."

"I know, honey. I'm good at my job, but I'll be honest with you, that place ain't gon' survive. I heard at lunch today that an inspector has had a tip-off about it. They're planning a surprise visit soon."

∾

"What the hell game you playin'? You only left yourself half an hour to get ready!" Frank roared as he stormed into the apartment.

"What?" Lucy replied, shocked at his approach.

"I asked you to be home by five tonight, not past six."

"I went for a walk, that's all. I am allowed to, you know. You don't own me, Frank, I'm my own person," Lucy asserted.

"Well, if you don't up your game and start lookin' like you can actually be bothered to make yourself look worth it, we ain't gonna make anythin' out of these guys. And if that happens, then I'm gon' have no choice but to get rid of some of the other girls. I won't be able to afford to keep you all on."

Lucy spun around in her seat. "Frank, you can't do that. Some of those girls got nothing else keeping the roof over their heads. And you know Trish has got a sick son. What's she gon' do if you let her go?" She stared at him in horror.

"Why the hell should I give a shit? What's that to me? If you care so much, then start performin'. It's on you, Lucy. One more complaint about you and I'll fire someone, I goddamn swear it." Frank pointed his dirty fingernail at her, then stormed out.

Chapter 15

"Morning, Trish, how was your night?" Lucy asked as she walked into the bar that Thursday morning.

"OK. Yours?" she replied without looking up.

"Same. What you doing here so early anyway?"

"Frank offered me some extra shifts cleaning up. Need every nickel I can earn at the moment." She looked up from the floor she was sweeping and leaned on the broom handle. "Tommy's not getting any better. The medicine he needs every month ain't cheap."

"How's your mom doing? How many days has it been now?" Lucy asked.

"Thirty-seven dry. But I'm worried that the more I leave her alone, the more likely she'll be tempted again." Trish wiped a tear from her eye and carried on sweeping the floor, with more vigor this time.

"I wish I could help," Lucy said.

"Well, you know what, you actually can." Trish's expression hardened as she looked up at Lucy. "I heard you and Frank arguing last night. He needs you to try more. I can't lose my job, Lucy. I just know I'd be the first one he kicks out. You need to get your shit together for all our sakes. So if you really wanna help, then that's how." Trish clattered the broom against the wall and stomped off into the back room.

～

"There you go, Mrs. Crawford. Your tailpipe's all fixed up and as shiny as a new penny now. It shouldn't give you any more trouble," Harry announced as he walked out of his office. Keys outstretched, he handed them to her and watched as she reached into her wallet for the fee.

"No charge," he said, waving away the bills she was holding out to him. "It was only a small job. Least I could do after..." He watched as she put the bills back in her wallet and placed it back inside her purse. She took out a handkerchief and dabbed her moist eyes.

"Thank you, Harry. I sure do appreciate it. Money's gon' be tight from now on," Mrs. Crawford said, her trembling voice trailing off as she blew her nose.

"I'm so sorry, Richard didn't come home. I was hoping I'd see him step off that bus one day, but..." Harry stumbled over his words.

"Well... he'd appreciate your kindness, as do I." Mrs. Crawford looked over as Marcie approached them from her desk in the office.

"Hi Mary. I'm real sorry about your husband. He was a wonderful man."

"Thank you, Marcie. Gosh, you're so lucky to have Harry," Mrs. Crawford replied, smiling through her sadness. She took her keys from Harry, nodded her goodbyes to the two of them, then drove away.

"What's up, honey?" Marcie asked. She linked her arm with her husband's.

"Just wish I could do more to help folks like Mary."

120

Marcie looked at Harry. "Now, don't you go feeling bad. You're the best mechanic in Mississippi. That's how you help them. It's not your fault that out of the three wars this country has fought this century, one you were two young to fight and the other two you were too old to fight. The Lord above timed you just right and I for one am mighty grateful for that stroke of good fortune. Your place is here. With me." She put her arms around his neck and pulled him into her. "What about this as an idea? Why don't you give the boys Friday afternoons off? We don't get much business then anyway and you could do some good by sending them home to their families at noon. Howard Johnson's won't need to bring in food that day so instead we could use that money to keep the guys' pay the same. Think of the morale it will generate in town. What do you think? We could try it?" Marcie smiled up at her husband who appeared to be mulling over the idea.

"You think we can afford to do that?" he replied.

"I do the books, remember? If you stop giving Frank your money all the time, we'd be able to do it," Marcie said with a smile.

"Yeah, I know. Well, if you think it'll work, I'll call a meeting this afternoon and tell the boys the good news."

Harry kissed his wife on the cheek and strolled back to his workbench. Marcie watched as he carried his weight mainly on his good leg and reminded herself just how lucky she was not to have to contemplate a similar future to what poor Mrs. Crawford was now forced to do.

～

"What's the matter with you? You've hardly said a word since dinner." Dorothy had stopped darning a sock and looked up at Shona who was staring at the TV.

"Huh? Oh, nothing. It's just... Well, the guys invited me over to the bar again tonight but..." Shona began.

"But what? Oh, I know that place is a dive, Shona, but you're twenty-two years old. You should be out having fun. Maybe you could keep an eye on your new friend while you're there?"

"Maybe. It's just all the questions that come with socializing, Dorothy." Shona exhaled and shook her head. "I don't know what it is but folks in small towns just always seem to wanna know your life story. I've already told them the basics, but they always wanna dig a little further down. More than I wanna go into, you know?"

Dorothy nodded.

"And anything they don't like, they hold against you for the rest of your days. That's why I try to keep myself to myself. But it's getting harder each day." Shona's voice trailed off as she leaned on her hand.

Dorothy placed the sock down on her lap and turned to face her.

"Now you listen here. I am sixty-eight years old and have lived in this small town my whole life. I go there to do my grocery shopping, pay my bills and mail my letters. Then I come home. Do you know how many times I've been asked questions about my life over the years? Hundreds. It's what folks do. Some want to pass the time, some just want the latest gossip, but you know what else, Shona?"

"What?"

"Some people actually just want to get to know you because they think you're an interesting person." Dorothy jabbed her finger at Shona, then picked her sock and needle up again. "So you go out with your friends tonight, Shona. That's an order. And if any of them ask questions you don't wanna answer, you don't. OK? No one can force you to tell them your life story."

"OK." Shona rose out of her chair and kissed the old lady

on the cheek. As she reached the front room door, she turned back. "Dorothy?"

"Yeah?" she replied, inspecting the sock.

"Thank you. I won't be late."

"Hey. Haven't seen you in here for a while." Lucy grinned and put down the cloth she was wiping the bar with.

"I know," Shona replied as she sat down in front of her.

"Well, it's real good to see you. What can I get you to drink?" Lucy watched Shona pick at the edges of a coaster and scan the room.

"Oh, um… just a soda, please."

"You wan' ice? And maybe a bourbon shot in there too?" Lucy asked.

"Ice, please. I'll take a raincheck on the bourbon," Shona replied, mirroring Lucy's smile.

Lucy passed Shona her drink, and Shona reached into her pocket to pay. "On the house."

Shona put the dime away. "Thanks."

"So how was your day?" Lucy asked, leaning forwards on the bar.

Before Shona could answer, a man's gravelly voice bellowed across the bar. "Hey! Lucy! It's you, isn't it? Loose Lucy. The guys have been tellin' me 'bout you. They say you're the best in the business. What time you workin' tonight?" he slurred. Before he could say another word, the giant hulking figure of Chuck wrapped his arm around the man's neck and dragged him out of the bar.

"Time you took a walk, pal," he hissed. He looked over to the bar. "Sorry about him, Lucy."

Lucy nodded her thanks to Chuck. Unable to hide her red

face, she turned her back on Shona and began wiping down the bottles on the shelf behind the bar.

"Who was that?" Shona asked after a few moments of staring at the back of her head. "Lucy? Why'd he say all that?"

"I don't know. Back in a minute." Lucy lifted the bar hatch and scurried out of sight.

"Wait." Shona jumped up off her stool, then looked at Norm, who shrugged as he picked up the cloth Lucy had dropped and began wiping a glass.

"Hey Shona, you wanna shoot some pool? I got a dollar says you can't beat me. Not once," Jonny called over to her, snapping her out of her bewilderment at Lucy's sudden departure.

"Yeah, OK then, Jonny. Might as well," Shona replied.

Jonny passed her the cue he'd been holding out for her, his optimistic smile glowing. "You can go first."

"You might regret that," Shona joked, sinking two balls straight off her first shot. "You ready to lose that dollar?"

~

"What's up with you?" Frank asked, seeing his girlfriend standing by the restroom door.

"Nothing. Some guy being a jerk. It's OK, Chuck threw him out, like always. What's got you so giddy?" Lucy asked, noticing his wide grin.

"These magic hands, my darlin', have just won us a lot of money. I can finally get that kitchen sorted and I'm gon' treat you too." He reached down and pulled her into him by her wrists. Twirling her around him, he kissed her messily on the cheek. "I'm gon' get a drink, go upstairs and you... you make yourself all pretty. No work for you tonight, I want you all to myself. I've earned it."

Lucy freed herself from his sweaty grip and smiled, strangely grateful that it was only Frank she was entertaining tonight rather than a complete stranger. The words that had been shouted to her in the bar were still playing in her mind.

The worse part, though, was that Shona had heard them too.

$$\sim$$

"You have a nice time?" Dorothy called out, hearing Shona close the front door with a thud a few hours later.

"Kinda," Shona replied. "Oh, I'm gon' fix that door properly this weekend. It's been coming off its hinges again since the other night," she added.

"Yeah. Slamming it in a temper tantrum'll do that," Dorothy said, the corners of her mouth turning upwards into a tiny smile as she looked back down at her newspaper. "Why only kinda?"

"Oh, nothing. I think I might head on up. You need me to help you?" She walked over to the high-backed chair Dorothy was seated in and held out her arm.

"Yes please. You're a good girl, Shona. Always looking after me." Gripping on to Shona's arm, Dorothy pushed her body up out of the chair with her other hand.

"Well, you're good to me too. Those sandwiches were delicious. Thank you for making them for me."

"You're welcome. I never had my own children to do it for."

Reaching the top of the stairs, Shona gave Dorothy a hug goodnight, then watched the old lady disappear into her bedroom. Walking into her own room, Shona sighed with exhaustion. Sitting on the edge of her bed, she removed her boots, then stood up to take her nightshirt out of her drawer. Lying it on the bed, she began to undress.

"Oh, I forgot to ask—" Dorothy pushed open Shona's bedroom door, just as she was lifting her undershirt over her head. Wrenching it down as quickly as she could, Shona felt sheer horror at the look on Dorothy's face. "Never mind… It can wait till morning. Goodnight." As quickly as she'd burst in, Dorothy disappeared, closing the door behind her.

Shona's shaking fingers held on to the hem of her under-shirt as she stared at the closed door. But it was too late. Dorothy had already seen the scars.

Chapter 16

Breakfast was the quietest it had been the whole time Shona had lived there. Dorothy had served the bacon, Shona had said thank you, then Dorothy had set a plateful of toast down in the middle of the table.

After several minutes of polite smiles and awkward silence, Dorothy swallowed the mouthful of toast she'd been chewing.

"Those marks. How did you get them?"

"I don't wanna talk about it right now," Shona murmured.

"You know, when we were in Gulfport, I tried to make it clear that you could tell me anything and I wouldn't judge." Dorothy paused. "And you did. You told me all about your past. But you never mentioned... This." Her gaze was fixed on Shona's trembling face.

"I should get to work."

Rising out of her seat, Shona pushed her chair under the table. She walked out of the kitchen and tugged on the front door, closing it quietly behind her.

~

"Penny for your thoughts," Marcie said, walking up behind Shona with a small envelope of wages in her outstretched hand. "Say, you've been quiet all morning. Everything OK?"

"Yeah. Just had a lot of jobs to get done," Shona replied, smiling her thanks and placing the brown envelope in her top pocket.

"So I see. You've been doing great here since you started. Harry's so pleased with you. You've picked stuff up real quick. I'll be honest, the guys didn't know how it'd be having a woman working with them, especially Doug. But even he's now taken a shine to you after his accident n'all. And young Jonny over there, well, you don't need me to tell you how giddy you got him over you." Marcie waved over to the floppy-haired mechanic who waved back, then smoothed his hair down. "He's been working with Harry since he was knee-high to a grasshopper, but in all that time I ain't never seen him gush over a girl like he has you. He's a sweet boy. Like the son we never had." Marcie's eyes misted over for a second before refocusing on Shona's reactions.

"I went over to the bar last night. Ended up playing pool with him," Shona replied, turning her wrench over in her palm.

"And...?" Marcie leaned in and playfully shoved Shona. "Why, he's as cute as a button. You could do a lot worse, you know. Most of the guys around here look like they've been hit by the ugly stick. Apart from my Harry, of course," she added, staring over at him and smiling.

"I normally keep work separate, ma'am. Hope that's OK with everyone?"

"Of course. Jonny will just have to work a little harder on you." She winked.

Shona smiled, rubbing her hand over the back of her neck.

"Oh, well now, where are my manners. There's me matchmaking and I haven't even asked you if you're already courting." Marcie hung her hands on her hips, her eyebrows raised as she waited for a response. Just as the silence between them began to lengthen, Lucy hollered Shona's name from across the street.

"Well, you're all finished up for the week. Off you go." Marcie reached over to pat Shona on the arm then said her goodbyes and walked back into her office. Shona, after putting all of her tools away in the correct slots in the chest headed over to the front door of Chasers where Lucy was waiting.

"Hey. You all done for the day?" Lucy asked.

"Yeah. You finish early on a Friday too?"

"Umm... Well, no actually. I wasn't feeling too good this morning so I didn't make it in," Lucy said, her cheeks burning. "I've been a little down lately and... Well, now, listen to me bellyaching. I haven't even offered you a drink yet. You wanna come inside?" Lucy brushed a lock of lank hair out of her dull, tired eyes.

"Won't that boyfriend of yours be annoyed if he catches me hanging around you?"

"That man ain't the boss o'me. I do as I please." With her hands clamped on her hips, Lucy stared Shona dead in the eye. "And you know what? I think it's high time we had a little fun around here for a change, you and me. Cheer us both up. Life can't all be about work, especially as we both have the whole afternoon off. So, apart from beating me and Jonny in every game we play, what other kinds of things do you like to do, Shona?"

"Nothing really. Back home though I used to like to ride. Give me a wild horse and I'll break him in a day," Shona replied, her eyes gazing out into the distance.

"Well, I ain't got no stallion hidden away down that alley over there, but why don't we go for a drive or something? Get out of this town. Or go sit by the river maybe?"

"Another time. I should get back to Dorothy. But how 'bout I come over here later? I'll be just another paying customer so Frank can't get all uppity about it."

Lucy blushed.

"Who was that guy yesterday? He called you 'Loose Lucy' or something?" Shona's brow wrinkled.

Lucy froze for a second. "No one. He... has a stutter that's all. Couldn't quite get my name out right," she said, wiping a strand of hair away from her left eye. "I'd better go back in. I'll see you later, yeah?"

"Yeah," Shona replied to the back of Lucy's head as the door of the bar closed behind her.

~

"Hey Norm, is Lucy around?" Shona asked as she walked up behind the bartender. It was just after five o'clock that Friday afternoon.

"In the basement. You can go down if you want."

Shona headed over to the far corner of the bar, passing Chuck who was drinking on his own. He watched closely as she descended the steps.

"Hey." Shona's voice echoed as she walked into the damp, cold basement. "What happened over there?" she said, pointing to a wet patch of wall.

"Oh, hi. Yeah, I think we got a leak from the restroom faucet. I gotta move these before we have any more stock damaged. Frank says he's sorting it out, but..."

As Lucy moved a barrel away from the wall, Shona leaped towards her.

"Look out," she yelled, grabbing Lucy and twisting her away from the large chunk of masonry that had fallen away from the wall.

"That was close," Lucy gasped, still wrapped in Shona's arms. Letting her go gently, Shona brushed the flakes of plaster out of her own clothes, then cleared her throat as she pointed to a little bit stuck in Lucy's hair. Picking it out, Lucy noticed the wall was now letting in a steady trickle of water.

"That's all we need. Frank's gonna be pissed," Lucy huffed as she searched for something to plug up the hole.

"It wasn't your fault. It would have come down anyways at some point," Shona reasoned, picking up an old hessian sack and ramming it into the gap. "There. Should hold it for a bit." She smiled and dried her hands on her pants.

As they headed back up the basement steps, relieved at their near miss, they passed Chuck who was working his way through the bottle of Jack Daniel's he'd taken from the bar. He glared at Shona.

"Why is it you don't drink, Shona? Come on, do a shot with me. It's Friday night, damnit," Lucy encouraged, placing two bourbons down in front of them.

"No thanks. I might not be working tomorrow but I still gotta drive home, remember," Shona replied, sipping her soda instead.

"Your loss." Lucy reached over the bar and took both glasses, downing them one after the other. She gasped, screwing up her face. "Goddamn. Why do people drink this stuff?"

"Lucy, why do you put up with Frank, if he pisses you off so much? You've done nothing but bellyache about him for fifteen minutes now," Shona asked.

"Wanna know a secret?" Lucy whispered, the bourbon loosening her tongue. "I'm thinking of taking a little time away from him. Head up to Tennessee, spring break maybe? I've got an aunt up there so I thought I might spend some time with her. I need some time to think about what I want. What I really want to do with my life." She rolled the empty glass between her index finger and thumb. "And she's a little less square than my parents. She won't be as mad as my mom and dad'll be about me skipping classes."

"How come you ain't been going to college lately? I thought you liked it there?" Shona asked.

"I thought going there was what I wanted. Thought it would finally make my parents proud of me. You see, Shona, they are the height of social climbing. But I made so many mistakes while growing up. I've always been a disappointment to them."

"They politicians or something?"

"Not quite. Mom's a school principal and Dad's a surgeon. They've done so well for themselves and I am proud of them. I always thought I wanted to teach, you know? One day. But..." Lucy trailed off.

"What?" Shona pressed.

"Oh, nothing. You know what, Shona? I envy you."

"Why's that?"

"Because you're so free. You don't answer to no man, have nothing holding you back, no textbooks to smother you. Why, you're like the birds out there. You can move around any time you want," Lucy replied, refilling her glass.

"So can you. You're not a tree," Shona retorted, raising her eyebrow. "Nothing to stop you travelling around for a bit, then maybe after a while try college in Tennessee when you go and stay with your aunt? Just tell your parents it didn't work out here. I'm sure they wouldn't be too disappointed."

"That's not why they'd be disappointed, believe me. I've done far worse lately." Lucy held the glass in front of her mouth for a moment of contemplation, then downed the shot. Just as Shona opened her mouth to speak, Lucy's eyes refocused on her. "Say, didn't you say you were from Tennessee?" she said, her half-drunken mind regaining its sharpness.

"Um... Yeah. Born and raised," Shona said, taking a sip from her drink, hoping, unlike Harry, that Lucy wouldn't pry too much for specifics about the state she'd only visited once in her life.

"Really? You know, it's funny, you don't sound like my aunt does. Your accent is more… Louisiana."

Shona almost dropped her glass.

Chapter 17

"It's all over the news again today, Harry. Damn election ain't even for weeks yet," Marcie said, looking over the top of her cat-eye glasses to Harry as she flicked through the paper the following Monday morning.

"Who's running again?" Harry asked.

"Um... Max Whitfield and some guy from outta town, Dennis Compton his name is. I ain't never heard o'him." She closed the paper and took off her glasses, laying them both on the table next to her plate.

"Max'll be good," Harry mumbled through a mouthful of toast. "I heard he wants to invest in this town. Gets my vote."

"Mine too. I can't bear the sight of Frank's bar falling apart like it is lately. It was such a nice place to go when Norm was running it, but since Gloria signed it over to Frank, it's gone to Hell in a handbasket. That damn window on the front has been broken for weeks now." She paused for breath and took a sip of her coffee. "At least if Max gets elected, we might get a little help around this town to smarten everywhere up, starting with that bar. And it won't have to keep coming out of our pocket, like usual." Marcie leveled her eyes at her husband as she emphasized the final two words of her rant.

"I know I can't put it off any longer. Me and his mother need to talk. Frank can't keep drifting from day to day, not knowing if his father's ever coming home. It's high time that boy knows the truth."

～

"Gloria? It's Harry. Yeah, look, I'm sorry I ain't called you back sooner but... I know we need to tell him. I know he's gone too far with the drinking and gambling these last few weeks... Hey, I said *I know*. Quit yelling at me about it. I agree with you, OK? We should tell him. Today? OK. I'll meet you over at his place, say 4 p.m.? I can ask one of my guys to lock up. We gotta catch him before he goes downstairs to the bar, otherwise we'll never get any sense out of him once he starts drinking. OK, bye."

Harry replaced the receiver and looked over at Marcie who smiled to show her support.

～

Leaving Shona to lock up the garage, Harry made his way across the street to meet Gloria, who was already waiting at the foot of the fire escape.

"You ready for this?" she asked, dropping her cigarette and squashing it underneath the heel of her pump.

"He needs to know," Harry replied, gripping the handrail.

Gloria headed up first, then waited the few moments it took for Harry to join her. She watched him limp heavily on his bad leg, and then banged her knuckles on the heavy wooden door.

"Yeah?" yelled the voice inside.

"It's your mother. Open up."

Frank's annoyed face emerged as the door opened.

"What's with the rough talk? Georgie-boy not puttin' out?"

He cackled at his own crass joke, draping his arm upwards against the edge of the doorframe.

"You watch your mouth," Harry retorted, pushing Frank's arm out of his way and striding into the apartment.

"Come in, why don't you," Frank muttered as his mother glared at him as she passed. Closing the door behind them, he drained the last of his beer and plonked it down on the coffee table. "This gon' take long?"

"Sit down, Frank. We need to talk. Your poker game can wait," Gloria said.

Lucy stepped out of the bedroom.

"Frank, do you have the... Oh, hi Harry... Gloria, what are you both doing here?"

"You've heard somethin', ain't you? He's comin' home." Frank's face erupted with a smile as he stared at his mother.

As if she hadn't noticed the happiness glaze across his face, Gloria planted her hands on her hips, then looked at her son. "Oh, grow up, Frank. Stop actin' like a baby. It's time to let go." Gloria hated herself for being so cold, but it needed to be said. "Harry has somethin' else he needs to tell you. Sit down."

All eyes turned on Harry, who licked his dry lips. "Frank, um... we've come over to talk to you about your, um... problem." Harry looked at Gloria who rolled her eyes at him backing out once again and changing the subject. "There's the election coming up and if you act smart you can really put that bar on the map. Max Whitfield wants to invest, and yours could be the first place he goes."

"I know all about that election. It's a no-brainer. Whitfield'll get in, not the other guy. They won't vote for an out-of-towner."

"For God's sake, boy, you can't just sit on your ass and *hope* that happens. You gotta clean that place up so it impresses him. The gambling, the drinking, the state of the building? It's gotten out of hand, son. You need—"

Frank, as if in slow motion, lifted up his booted foot and

struck the beer bottle he'd left on the coffee table, sending it careening into the wall less than six inches above Lucy. Ducking as it smashed into pieces, she covered her head with her shaking hands and stared in silent disbelief at Frank.

"Frank... my *God*," Gloria gasped.

"Now you listen here, you ignorant son of a bitch. This is serious. You will lose that bar if you don't start growing up. You gotta face facts, son!" Harry bellowed.

"What the *goddamn* hell gives you the right to tell me what to do, huh? I'll clean up that place in my *own* time, you hear? And I ain't your son. You ain't fit to tie my father's bootstraps." Frank squared up to Harry, who didn't back down. As both of them stood red-faced and toe-to-toe, Gloria suddenly noticed something that everyone else, including Lucy, had completely missed.

"Oh, my. Honey... you're bleedin'."

She rushed over to Lucy, who stood motionless by the fireplace, staring down at the remnants of the broken bottle. Raising a hand to her forehead, Lucy pulled it back to see dark red blood coating her trembling fingers.

"Let me see that..." Gloria held Lucy's face in her hands as she inspected the cut just above her left eye. She turned to Frank, giving him a look that he'd never seen before. He was used to disappointment, disgust, even pity from his mother, but this was one of pure contempt.

"Harry, we need to get this lil' girl down to the doctor. She's gon' need a stitch or two, I'd say. And *you*, boy? Lose the business, see if I care. But don't you come cryin' to me when it's all gone."

Gloria, clamping her handkerchief to Lucy's eyebrow, walked her to the door and carefully down the fire escape.

"I'm fine, really, Mrs. Smith. I really don't think I—" Lucy began, stumbling.

"Nonsense. You're gon' need that seein' to. And if I had my

druthers, you'd be headin' to the bus station straight afterwards. That son of mine is no good. You should get yourself as far away from him as possible. He'll drag you down with him."

~

Frank looked out of the window and watched his mother walk inside the doctor's office with his girlfriend's bleeding head pressed against her palm. With tears in his eyes, he turned back to Harry and stared at him.

"You need to sort it out, kid. Double time," Harry said in a low voice, before stepping past Frank and closing the door quietly behind him.

Sinking down into his armchair, Frank buried his face in his hands and broke down in pitiful sobs, stopping momentarily to look up at the picture of him sitting on his father's shoulders, the precious letter he'd received now splattered with the dregs of his beer. Shattered dark brown glass from the bottle lay strewn around it.

"Where the hell are you?" he whispered.

~

"What in the blue blazes happened to you?" Shona gasped as she opened the door to a patched-up Lucy.

"Long story. Can I come in?" she replied.

"Um... best not, Dorothy's got the doctor round. Her leg's bad again. Wanna go for a walk?"

"Sure. Not sure I wanna see the doc twice in one day anyway." Lucy grimaced.

"Looks painful. How many'd you get put in there?"

"Just three. Wasn't that deep. I was lucky it missed the eyeball." Lucy smiled, then winced.

"*It?*" Shona repeated, reaching behind the door to get her jacket and a lantern flashlight.

"I'll tell you on the way."

With the lantern beam illuminating the way, they walked to the edge of the driveway and then hopped over the fence into the field opposite, which led down to the river. Shona felt most at peace when she was by the water, and judging by the snippets of information she was getting from Lucy, it was a safe bet that peace was what she needed too.

"It don't have to be this way, you know. Why can't you just leave him if you've had enough?" Shona asked, staring at Lucy's profile as she gazed into the distance.

"Shona... can I ask you something?"

"Depends what it is," Shona replied, feeling a familiar prickle of dread.

"Have you ever done a thing so bad, so unforgivable, that you don't know how to make it right?" Shona stared at her. "You ever felt so trapped in your head that you can't catch your breath? Like the walls are closing in on you and you just don't know what to do." She turned to face Shona, the tears pooling in her bloodshot eyes. "I can't go home. My parents would never forgive me after what I've done."

"What can you have done that was so bad?" Shona asked, shaking her head. It would have been the easiest thing in the world for her to put her arm around her friend, but her instinct was telling her not to. Instead, Shona looked out over the moonlit water.

"You know," she began, "when I was about ten years old, back home, I once took a filly out for a ride. She was from the farm up the road. Wasn't even our horse. She was beautiful, though, the most gorgeous horse I ever laid eyes on. I just wanted to take her down to the river, see how fast she could go. I felt like I was flying." Shona paused, as Lucy had now stopped crying and was lying back on the cool grass, her eyes closed as she listened to her story. "But once my momma realized I was gone, and the farmer found the stable empty, they sent out a search party for me. They were so mad when they found me by the river asleep, the horse tied to the tree next to me. Wanted me arrested for horse rustling." Shona laughed. "I was only ten." Her smile faded. "But when my momma turned up at the river, she'd been so worried that I'd fallen in or been thrown off that she ran over and scooped me up in her arms. I told her I was sorry for worrying her. You know what she said back?" Shona paused and looked down at Lucy, who opened her eyes and turned her head to meet Shona's gaze.

"No, what'd she say?" Lucy whispered.

"She said, 'I wasn't worried by you leaving. I was terrified you wouldn't come back.' Then she hugged me so tight. My momma was the only one who ever truly understood me. She knew who I was inside."

"She sounds amazing. Where is she now?" Lucy murmured.

Shona stood up and wiped the tears from her eyes with the palms of her hands. "Heaven. Seven years ago."

"Oh. I'm sorry."

"What I'm trying to say is... what can be so bad that someone like you can't go home? Your mom will be OK, you just gotta tell her you're sorry." Shona held her hand out to help Lucy off the ground.

"Not about this," she mumbled. "What happened after your mom passed, Shona? You live with your daddy?"

Shona swallowed hard. "So, what got Frank so mad anyway? Why did he lose his shit and kick that bottle?" Shona asked. She pulled out a huge clump of long grass, picking it apart as she walked a few paces ahead of Lucy.

"What?" Lucy replied, catching up to Shona. "Oh, lots of reasons. His father mainly... and he's probably just worried about this election coming up, in case that Max fella don't get in. He's gon' be the one investing a whole heap o' money into the town, but if this other guy gets in then..."

"Who's the other guy?" Shona asked, chewing on the end of a strand of grass.

"Um... I can't remember his name, Frank just calls him D.C. or something. God knows why when he's actually from Louisiana." Lucy's guffaw at her own joke meant that she completely missed the look of pure terror on Shona's face as she turned around. Almost choking on the grass, Shona shot her arm out and grabbed Lucy's elbow.

"What's his name, Lucy? D.C. what? What does D.C. stand for?" She yelled at a bemused Lucy.

"I don't know... All I know is that he's some rich guy from Louisiana, who thinks he can make even more money for himself by investing in businesses in this town. But it won't matter, Shona, 'cos he won't get in. People won't vote for him. Shona? *Shona*."

Shona was already striding away from her. A few yards away, she broke out in a run.

"What on earth's the matter with you? You're behaving like you got the devil in you," Dorothy exclaimed as Shona ran past her and into the kitchen. Running the faucet and filling a glass, Shona gulped down the water.

"Dorothy... what's the name of the man from out of town who's running for mayor?" she asked, panting between gulps.

"Hold your horses now. What?" Dorothy replied.

"D.C.," Shona yelled.

"His name is..." The old lady, in her bemusement at Shona's frayed temper, stumbled over her words.

"What? What's his name?"

Dorothy stared in disbelief at this new person in front of

her. She shuffled into the front room and picked up the newspaper. Reaching down to the glasses that were hanging round her neck, she fumbled trying to put them on straight. After what felt like an eternity, she eventually located the story and read out his name.

"Compton. Dennis Compton," Dorothy confirmed. She removed her glasses and stared at Shona, who had slumped against the doorframe.

"Calm down, Shona, it's not *him*."

~

"Hi, Mrs. Clark. Is Shona there, please?"

Lucy had gone straight back over to Dorothy's house, unable to keep pace with Shona who'd run from her side like a scalded cat.

"She's upstairs lying down. That my lantern?" Dorothy opened the door enough for Lucy to pass it to her.

"Yeah, Shona left in such a hurry she dropped it. I hope it ain't broke or nothing."

"It'll be fine. Best leave Shona tonight. See her tomorrow."

Dorothy closed the door with a clunk, leaving Lucy bewildered on the step. Seconds later the door opened.

"So, I guess you'll be wanting a ride back to town?" she asked, her eyebrow raised.

"Yes. Please. Thank you, Mrs. Clark."

"It's no less than what Shona would do for you."

After begrudgingly letting Lucy help her into the truck, Dorothy drove back down the highway into town. The air inside the truck was thick with silence as the truck rumbled along the road, until after ten long minutes Lucy finally plucked up the courage to speak. "Mrs. Clark, may I ask you please if, well, is..."

"Spit it out, girl," Dorothy chastised

"Well, is Shona OK? She seemed pretty upset before and I'm not sure why. I seem to be putting my foot in it a lot lately. I don't mean to. We've become real close since I came here and, well, I don't mean to pry but..."

"Shona is fine. I'm looking after her," Dorothy interjected. "And she don't want people asking questions about her all the time, OK?"

"OK," Lucy whispered back.

Chapter 18

George walked into the almost-dark living room, lit only by the desk lamp on the bureau, to see Gloria seated there surrounded by the same letters and envelopes he'd seen before.

"What are you doing?" he asked after a minute or two of silently watching her.

"Oh my... George. I didn't hear you come in. I thought you were out late tonight?" She scrabbled to collect the letters and slip them back into their envelopes before George could reach her side.

"Client cancelled. I thought you said they were old bills?" he asked. Gloria looked back at him. "Let me see that." George reached out to take the letter Gloria was still holding and began reading it. His expression hardened as he reached the bottom of the page.

"Please don't tell him, honey, it'll break his heart," Gloria whispered.

George looked down at his girlfriend.

"He needs to be told, Gloria. You've got to tell Junior the truth."

"You heard anythin' more from him yet? There was another bus in last week but…"

Chuck sat down next to Frank, who was pushing an empty shot glass around the bar top.

"No. But he'll come. Mom and Uncle Harry don't know shit. And when he does, I want this place shipshape. People in town have been complainin' that the paint's lookin' shabby and the door needs the dents taken out of it." He turned to Chuck. "You still got that paint you used to do up ol' man Marley's place last summer?"

"Um… yeah, but it wasn't great stuff. Needed three coats in the end, it was so thin."

"Don't matter. Bring it over tomorrow, will ya? I got a job for ya. Even *you* can't mess this up."

Just as Chuck was about to protest, a loud shriek echoed out over the noise from the jukebox. Before he'd even registered what he was doing, Chuck strode over to a table occupied by three truckers, one of whom was pawing at Lucy as she was finishing her dance.

"Hey, get your hands off her. No touchin', you know the rules." Chuck wrapped his huge hand around the rowdy trucker's shirt collar, lifted him out of his seat and threw him on the floor.

"Chuck, it's OK. I can handle it," Lucy protested, smoothing her dress down.

"He ain't allowed to touch, Lucy. He's got damn nerve puttin' his hands on you." He pointed at Lucy's skirt, his face sweaty.

The trucker picked himself off the sticky floor, brushed himself down and fronted up to Chuck. "You think you've got a chance with her, you son'bitch? As if she'd look twice at a guy who fell outta the ugly tree and hit every branch on the way down."

Chuck's head twitched as he bristled in rage at the cheering from the men seated around the trucker's table.

Frank stormed over and looked at the trucker. "What the hell is goin' on over here, Barney?"

"I was just about to take my business upstairs with your girl here, Frank. Then this meathead turned up and started throwin' his weight around."

"He was gettin' too familiar with Lucy, boss," Chuck replied through gritted teeth.

"Well, that ain't for you to decide now, is it? I pay the wages around here. Lucy, take this gentleman upstairs." Frank nodded at her and leaned into Barney. "Anythin' you want, OK?"

Barney smirked as he passed Chuck, looking up into his scarlet face. With his teeth grinding a hole in his jaw, Chuck watched as Lucy took Barney by the hand and led him away.

"Now you listen to me. Lucy is *my* girlfriend, you got that? I can't have you in here losin' me business. OK?" Frank warned. "So you just go up there and do your job. And let me know where Lucy puts the money afterwards, you got that? Too much of my money is going missin' lately. Unless you know anythin' about that, huh?" Frank watched his friend's reactions carefully.

Chuck's attention snapped back as he processed the question Frank was asking. He was speechless for a moment before he responded. "'Course not. Why would I take money off her?" He looked at Frank in disbelief.

"Look, I know I don't pay you much, and I'm sure you needed it for somethin' real bad, but that's no reason to steal off your best buddy. You understand?" Frank raised himself up to his full height to squeeze his hand just a little bit too firmly around the back of Chuck's thick neck.

"I didn't take any money," he repeated.

"Just promise me you won't do it again?" Frank whispered in his ear, not believing one word.

Chuck ripped his body away from Frank's grasp. "*I didn't take her money, goddamn it!* I wouldn't do that to Lucy."

"OK, settle down." Frank held his palms up in front of him.

In a rage that Frank had only seen a handful of times in the years he'd known him, Chuck stormed towards the exit, throwing the door wide open. A small table full of empty glasses behind it crashed to the floor, causing all of the patrons in the bar to look up from their drinks. Frank swept his arms out wide and tried to defuse the tension.

"You can all go back to your drinks, everythin's fine," he said, raising his glass to the onlooking crowd who slowly but surely went back to their conversations.

~

"Hey Chuck, what you doing out here all by yourself?" Lucy asked as she edged towards him sitting on a bench outside the diner a few hours later.

"Nothin'. Just thinkin'," he replied, his hands clamped together between his knees. Rocking back and forth, he lifted his sad eyes. "Miss Lucy, you don't really think I'd steal your money, do you? I'd hate it if you thought badly of me in that way."

"What? No, of course not," Lucy lied. It made no sense to tell him the truth of how she felt right now, not with him in such a state. She looked down at his hands and gasped. "What you gone and done there, huh?"

Chuck thrust his pudgy hands in his jeans pockets and looked away. Lucy grabbed his wrists and pulled them out. His hands were covered in scrapes and blotches, the skin on his white knuckles worn away in places. She took a handkerchief out of her skirt pocket and began to wrap it around the more wounded-looking hand.

"There. All better now," she murmured.

"Thank you. I'm sorry about before. Just can't stand the thought of guys thinkin' they can put their dirty mitts all over you. I saw that Barney guy leavin' your place before, smirkin' and high fivin' his pals. You're too good for that, Lucy." Chuck's anger was beginning to brim again, his heavy boots clumping on the ground. Sensing this, Lucy put a soft hand on his forearm to try to ease him.

"Listen, I'm a big girl. Frank don't make me do anything I don't wanna do, OK? That guy ain't worth you worrying."

Chuck smiled at her words of comfort as he fiddled with the delicate lace at the corners of her makeshift bandage on his hand. Lucy stood up to leave and flashed her perfect smile at him.

"But, for what it's worth? I'm real glad I got you looking out for me. And you know what? You got my full permission to sock it to anyone trying it on with me who shouldn't be, right?"

"You got it, Miss Lucy," Chuck replied, blushing.

His timid smile evaporated, however, the second she walked out of sight. He stared down at the dark red flecks speckling his right boot, remembering the noise Barney's head had made when it crunched underneath it. Removing the lace from his damaged hand, he picked at a scab, not entirely sure if it was formed of his own blood or Barney's.

Chapter 19

It was Friday, April 5ᵗʰ, the day of the election, and the whole town had congregated in the town square by the church. All around the sidewalks were hot dog carts and lemonade stands, with children squealing to their mothers that they wanted an ice-cold drink to quench their thirst in the cloying spring humidity. All of the noise and excitement, though, just added to the slowly building atmosphere.

The five candidates, including the favorite, Max Whitfield, and Dennis Compton, stood side by side waving at their supporters in the crowd as the emcee held his hands out to quiet everyone down. Whitfield was in his mid-forties, tall, square-jawed, with light sandy brown hair and keen blue eyes. Dressed in his finest three-piece navy suit adorned with his impressive array of war medals, he straightened his tie and leaned on his silver-topped cane as he looked to the side and nodded politely to Compton, who returned the gesture. Compton, much smaller and older than Whitfield, and more plainly dressed in a well-tailored gray flannel suit and fedora, clasped his thin hands together and focused his gray eyes on the emcee as they all waited to hear the announcement. Standing in the crowd, Shona and Dorothy moved closer to the makeshift stage area as the crowd hushed to hear the result.

"Ladies and gentlemen, it is my honor and privilege to announce that the new Mayor of Riverside is..."

There was a long, drawn-out pause for effect from the emcee, until he read aloud the name of the winner just as the crowd was becoming restless.

"Max Whitfield!" he roared, turning to slap him on the back.

Whitfield raised his cane aloft in triumph and then shook the hands of the other candidates as they consoled each other with back slaps and offers to buy each other a drink. Compton declined the handshake from Whitfield, choosing to storm off the stage instead.

"Well, that's a relief... for Frank," Marcie whispered to Harry as they watched on from a distance.

"For all of us," he murmured back. "Hopefully Whitfield will wanna clean up that eyesore over there properly." He nodded his head in the direction of the bar. It had received the third coat of paint in as many weeks, but the cheapness of the emulsion Chuck had used was obvious from the amount of peeling already happening around the window frames.

Marcie elbowed Harry who turned back towards the stage. "Shh... I think our new mayor is about to speak."

Whitfield waited for the cheers to subside before beginning his victory speech. "Thank you, thank you all. It is my honor to be chosen as your new mayor. I will work hard every day of my life to make businesses thrive. It's no secret I come from a long line of successful businessmen and I wanna assure you fine fellows that I fully intend to put this town on the map. I'll have investors from Louisiana to Alabama coming here with their money, you see if I don't." His rousing words had everyone cheering every time he paused.

Shona's blood froze. *People from out of town?* she thought. She looked at Dorothy, who gave her a reassuring nod.

"It'll be alright. Don't worry, you're safe here with me. It'll be fine," Dorothy whispered sideways to her, staring straight ahead as the new mayor finished off his speech and began shaking hands with all those who approached him, including Frank and Lucy.

"Can we go home now? I don't feel so good," Shona whispered back, looking around her as she felt a swirl in her stomach.

"Alright," Dorothy replied, without questioning her reasons.

Shona passed Dorothy a glass of sweet tea and sat down on the porch swing next to her.

"It ain't been the same between me and you since... Since I told you how I got the scars," Shona said, staring at the side of the old lady's head. After a minute or two of silence, Shona took a deep breath. "Maybe I should move on, away from here."

Dorothy lifted the glass to her parched lips and took a long drink. "I just needed time to come to terms with it myself. What happened to you... Well, that wasn't easy to hear. Especially on top of what you told me in Gulfport about... Well, you know." Her eyes remained fixed on the horizon.

"I know," Shona replied, picking at a splinter on the armrest. "I'm sorry I didn't tell you the full story sooner, but I just didn't know how to. I've trusted people before, and it's not worked out so good for me. And I really like it here. You're as close as I got to family these days and I just didn't wanna ruin things I guess."

Another few moments of silence passed between them.

"Shona, you've lived with me over a year now and I've enjoyed every day of having you here. But I need to know something. After all the horrors that you've told me about from your past..." Dorothy hesitated, then turned to face Shona. "Can you guarantee me that what happened in Louisiana is all over now? That you are absolutely sure nobody's gonna turn up on my doorstep here looking for you? I don't want no trouble in this house, y'hear?"

Shona looked at her and shook her head. "That's the last thing I'd ever wan' do. But no. I can't guarantee someone won't show up here one day looking for me. I'm sorry."

Dorothy clamped her eyes shut.

Lying on her bed and staring up at the postcards she'd collected and pinned to the wall, including the one of the beautiful beach house, Shona wondered what to do for the best now. Dorothy hadn't actually told her to go but Shona couldn't assure her that they would be safe in the long term. Sitting upright, Shona came to the decision that Dorothy deserved better than to live in fear. She picked up her satchel, packed her possessions and took one last look around her bedroom before closing the door tight.

As she was halfway down the stairs, she heard a crash and then a dull thud.

"Oh no," Shona whispered to herself as she flew down the rest of the stairs and flung open the front door. "Shit, *no*. Not like this."

At the bottom of the three steps leading up to the door, Dorothy's crumpled body lay motionless. Beside her were broken pieces of her glass and one of the black chickens that had escaped from its run.

"Dorothy. Wake up. Please... *no*. I can't lose someone like this again. *No!*" Shona kneeled down and scooped up the frail old lady in her arms, desperately trying to rouse her. Flattening her palm to Dorothy's chest, Shona closed her eyes and prayed. After what felt like the longest seven seconds of her life, she felt a heartbeat and saw Dorothy's eyes flutter.

"Come on, wake up. Please," Shona begged as she rocked her.

"Wha... what happened?" Dorothy murmured.

"Chicken got out. You musta tripped over it," Shona replied, lifting Dorothy up.

"Huh? Oh, right, I remember. Felt my damn leg give way." She rubbed her knee, then attempted to get up, leaning heavily on Shona.

"I'll get you up to bed, then I'll call the doctor. No arguments," Shona ordered.

Chapter 20

Lucy placed a plateful of Frank's favorite dinner in front of him that Tuesday evening. It was her last day of college tomorrow before spring break, and she had a question to ask him.

"Must be important if I get fried chicken," he replied, digging in. Seeing her serious face, he put his wing down and stopped chewing. "What is it?"

"Well, you know it's my last day of college tomorrow? I was thinking I could maybe go visit my aunt for a few days." She paused. "Stay for the week, maybe? It's been ages since I last saw her and..." She leaned against the kitchen counter.

"Why now all of a sudden? She's been on her own on that farm in Tennessee for as long as you've known her. She sick or somethin'?" Frank picked his wing back up and took another messy bite.

"No, not that I know of. I just need a break from everything, you know. I'm sure Trish would be happy to have the extra shifts, what with me outta the picture for a few days." She bit her lip and slid into the chair opposite him. "And I was thinking, the allowance Daddy gives me to cover the holidays could help us out while I'm not here working," she added.

"I guess." Frank mulled it over, then beamed at her. "Well, alright then honey, you go, but you just promise me one thing," he grabbed her hand across the kitchen table and squeezed it just a fraction too firmly.

"Yeah?" she replied, twitching.

"You don't go without leavin' me the recipe for this chicken."

"Deal," Lucy replied, freeing herself as politely as she could muster from his loosening grip as she got up to leave. Reaching the doorway, she looked over her shoulder to see Frank devouring another piece of chicken.

It was a full two weeks after the day of Dorothy's fall when Harry next saw the blue truck drive into his parking lot that Monday morning.

"Hi Shona. How's the old girl doing? Turning cartwheels again yet?" he yelled over to Shona as she pulled up a few yards away from him.

Jumping out of the truck, Shona grinned as she caught the oily rag Harry had thrown at her full in the face. "Yeah, she's doing OK. Doc said she was lucky. It coulda been much worse." Shona's smile faded as she let that thought cross her mind. "Thank you for letting me take some time off to tend to her."

"That's OK, I know how hard it is to manage when you're a leg down," he grinned, tapping his own affliction.

"How's things been around here?"

"Better. Giving you guys Friday afternoons off was one of the best decisions I ever made. Done wonders for morale. And it's made me a goddamn hero around here." He threw his arms wide in the direction of a group of workers who took their caps off to salute him.

"Yeah, you got that right," Shona replied, smiling. "Anyways,

I'll get started on that one over there." She pointed to a truck that was parked up on the ramps and picked up a wrench on her way over.

"Hey Shona, you're back?" Jonny called out then ran quickly over to her.

"Yeah. So, what's new around here?"

"Nothin' much. Same ol' place. All the better for havin' you back though. Say, can I treat you to lunch later? Just us this time. I've kinda missed you bein' around." Jonny turned his cap over in his sweaty hands as his cheeks began to redden.

"Thanks, Jonny, I'd love to, but I got loads to catch up on here."

Jonny's smile faded. "Oh, OK. But one day you're gonna say yes to a date with me, I swear." He smiled, then sauntered off, leaving Shona to get started on her first job of the day.

Lucy's eyes lit up when she saw Shona walk in through the doors to the bar the following day after work.

"Well, ain't you a sight for sore eyes. How's Dorothy? I heard about her fall."

"She's fine. Thank you for the flowers, they were beautiful. Really cheered her up." Shona smiled and sat down at the bar.

"Well, I meant to come over before I went to Tennessee, but Frank wanted me to do a few last jobs for him before I left," Lucy said, snipping the cap off a bottle of Coca-Cola and setting it down in front of Shona.

"You remembered," Shona grinned, downing a long slug.

"Of course, how could I forget? You're the only one I know who comes into this bar and leaves sober," Lucy chuckled, clinking her own shot glass with Shona's bottle.

"How was it at your aunt's place?"

"Well, I came back, didn't I?" Lucy replied, winking. "She

talked some sense into me, said I should knuckle down at college and give myself the best chance of making something of my life."

"And what about Frank?" Shona broached. "Will you stay with him?"

"I guess so. For now. But I ain't gon' be working all hours behind this damn thing." She tapped the bar top. "I gotta concentrate on my studies properly now."

"That's great, Lucy. I'm real pleased for you," Shona said. "You'll make your ma and pa proud."

After half an hour of playing pool and sharing stories about their weeks apart, Lucy leaned against her cue and perched on the edge of the table.

"Why are you always looking around you? Who do you think's gon' walk through that door, Rock Hudson?" Lucy asked.

"Huh?" Shona replied. "Oh, sorry."

Before Lucy could ask her next, more probing question, Norm walked over to them both.

"Whaddaya think? Thirty dollars in prize money should have them piling in from all over," he said, holding the flyer he'd drawn up for the pool competition and pinning it up on the wall behind them.

"Say now, you've beaten me in every game we've ever played, Shona. You should enter. That's a tidy lil' sum of money you could make there."

"Yeah. It would be," Shona replied.

"You'd clean up. I ain't never been beat this many times, and I'm really trying." Lucy laughed. "You'd be talked about for miles around. Heck, it might even make the press. You'll be famous."

Shona froze. *Famous?* Leaning against the pool table, her head began to spin. Lucy's smile faded, seeing Shona's muted reaction to her enthusiasm. Just as she was about to ask what the problem was, she heard her name hollered from the other side of the room.

"What's up, Trish?" she asked, walking over to the bar.

"What's up? I'm just getting a little tired of you slacking off around here. I work my fingers to the bone cleaning up out back, then I come in here and find you, not even back a day yet from your nice lil' vacation, playing pool and having a good old time." Trish's eyes blazed as she rested her mop against the bar.

"Trish, what's got your goat? Tommy not well again? I thought that new treatment was working." Lucy reached out her hand to lay it on Trish's shoulder.

Trish brushed it away. "Yeah, it's working. But it ain't gonna cure him. I need to take him to the hospital every two weeks and that costs money. I'm pulling double shifts here to afford it and then I see you goofing around, not a care in the world. *That's* what's got my goat. And to top it off, every night you go up those stairs, I hear you in that room complaining to Frank that you don't wanna do this anymore. Well, if that's the case, then why don't you just get out of the game permanently, not just for a week when you feel like sunning yourself on vacation."

"Look, before I left, I spoke to Frank to tell him to give you all my guys. That should help with money, right?" Lucy cocked her head to the side as she processed one element of Trish's earlier speech. "Wait a minute, you been hanging around outside my room?" she asked, her eyes narrowing.

Shifting her weight from one leg to the other, Trish softened her tone. "Look, just forget I said anything. It's not easy for me. I'm juggling a lot of shit right now. Sorry. Don't tell Frank, OK?" She picked up her mop after Lucy nodded her assurance, then headed back into the restrooms.

"What was that all about?" Shona asked as she walked over to Lucy at the bar and sat down on a stool.

"Don't matter," Lucy sighed, rubbing her eyes.

"Oh, OK." Shona nodded and began fiddling with one of the paper napkins on the bar top.

"What's that you're making outta that napkin? Looks like a bird or something," Lucy asked, watching Shona fold down each corner.

"Oh, nothing. Just something my momma taught me. How come's Trish is angry with you?"

"She's just a little stressed about..." Lucy paused, remembering the sordid subject of their conversation. "Well, let's just say you ain't the only one around here who don't wanna talk about stuff."

"I guess so. Alright, I'll catch you later. It's chicken pie tonight, I can't miss that." Shona grinned and got up to leave.

"Heaven forbid you miss a chicken pie, Shona," Lucy called after her.

Frank emerged from the back room with a man in a gray flannel suit carrying a clipboard.

"Look, Frank, rules are rules. You can't run a business with the kitchen in that state. That basement wall needs total rebuilding too. It's not safe. If we have another downpour like the one a few months ago, the whole damn roof'll come down with it," the suited man warned.

Frank flashed a smile at Lucy as she walked over to them, her brow furrowed as the scale of the problem facing them was becoming more apparent.

"Don't worry, honey, I'll take care of this. You go start dinner." He raised his eyes to the staircase next to the bar. Lucy complied, feeling the sting from the next look Frank gave her.

After she was out of sight, the building inspector stepped closer. "Look, Frank, all us guys know what goes on in this bar. That's none of my concern. All I care about is that it's safe. Max

Whitfield won't stand for any more complaints about this place, y'hear? He's already got the measure of you from what he's hearing around town and it wouldn't take much for him to close you down. Understand?" Seeing Frank's eyes twitch, the building inspector softened his tone. "Put the money into smartening this place up... and fix that damn wall. Then you won't have the pleasure of seeing me again." He grinned.

"Why the hell do folks around here seem to think they got the right to tell me what to do *in my own bar*?" Frank seethed. "Get outta here."

Feeling the shadow of Frank drape over him, the building inspector did the wise thing and stepped past him. "Get that wall fixed, Frank."

Chapter 21

Shona was hammering away underneath a truck when a familiar voice chirped from above.

"You got a minute?"

"Sure." Shona slid out and stood up, brushing herself off.

"I owe you an apology. Yesterday... it felt like I was a little rude to you. When you asked me about Trish? It's just, well, she's taken me into her confidence and..." Lucy stood there twirling a strand of her loose hair around her index finger.

"Hey, don't worry. It's forgotten," Shona replied, squatting back down to sit on her creepers. "I hate too many questions being asked about me too. I guess I should practice what I preach, huh?"

After a few moments of watching Shona get back to work, Lucy had an idea.

"Say, can I buy you an early dinner tonight? I can't promise it'll be as good as Dorothy's famous pie now." She smiled, biting on her bottom lip as she waited for Shona's answer.

"You don't have to, it's fine really. It's none of my business what you and Trish were arguing about."

"I know, but... Look, at least let me treat you to a burger at the bar after work, OK? You gotta let me win a few games of pool back; my ego can't handle it."

Seeing Shona's resolve crack made Lucy's heart jump.

"OK then. I'll see you later." Shona smiled up at Lucy who skipped away in triumph.

"Baby, please, just one last time. For me? Don really wants to see you again. He's a nice guy and he pays a lot for your company."

Frank had spent the best part of half an hour trying to sweet talk Lucy.

"OK, Frank. But this is the last time, OK? I don't wanna do that stuff anymore. You promise?"

"Honey, I promise. Now go get ready, he'll be here just after five. And Lucy...?"

"Yes, Frank?"

"I love you."

"See you tomorrow, Harry," Shona called out as she headed over to her truck at five thirty that afternoon. Hearing his muffled response from inside the office, she smiled, dropped her lunch box on the passenger seat and walked across the road to the bar.

"Hey Norm, Lucy around?" Shona asked, after looking around the bar for a few seconds and not seeing her.

"She's upstairs," he replied, keeping his eyes fixed on the lipstick stain on the rim of the glass.

"Thanks. Try a bit of vinegar on that," she suggested, winking as he looked up at her in surprise. "Where did you say the stairs were?"

"Just around the end of the bar, turn right, you can't miss 'em," Norm replied. "Oh, and hey, thanks for the tip," he added.

"No problem."

Shona walked all the way around the perimeter of the bar, eventually finding the bottom of the staircase. Grabbing the handrail, she skipped up the stairs, two at a time, then followed the balcony walkway over the top of the bar area, turning left along the corridor that led to the rooms. Most of the doors were closed but, as she passed one, the noises coming from inside were too intriguing for Shona's curiosity to resist.

Bending down to peek through the keyhole, she recoiled in horror.

Inside, Frank was sitting in an armchair with one girl kneeling in front of him, her head face-down in his lap, while another girl was leaning over and kissing him. Recognizing them as two of the girls she'd seen working behind the bar, Shona felt sick to her stomach.

Just as the thought about how upset Lucy would be to know Frank was cheating on her, she heard another noise further down the corridor. Tiptoeing, and hoping she wouldn't hit a creaky floorboard, Shona stopped outside the room where the strange grunts and groans were coming from. The door this time was slightly ajar.

Looking in, Shona's mouth suddenly went dry.

Chuck's hulking figure stood in one corner, with only a thin screen obscuring his view of the bed. He was obviously there as some kind of security but couldn't resist a look through a tiny hole in the screen every few seconds.

Keeping as quiet as she could, Shona inched closer to look through the crack in the door. Inside, a brown-haired woman wearing nothing but a red lacy bra, was lying on the bed facing away from the door. Sprawled on top of her was a naked man, his smart blue business suit flung all around the bed in his haste to get on with it. Blinking several times to try to make sense of what she was seeing, Shona stood on the creaky floor-board she'd been terrified of finding.

Chuck snapped his body around from the screen and tore open the door. "What the...? What the fuck are *you* doin' up here? This is a private party!" he roared at Shona, who fell backwards as the door was ripped away from her grasp.

"I was... I was just looking for Lucy... I'm sorry, I..." Shona stuttered, in total shock and fear of Chuck's massive frame bearing down on her.

"Oh yeah? Well, as you can see, she's busy." He pointed over to the bed and glared at Shona.

The bottom of Shona's stomach suddenly felt as if it had been set on fire.

Oh my God, no. Not now. It's happening all over again, she thought, as her memories flew through her brain like missiles. With her head spinning out of control, she looked at the bed where Lucy was lying and clamped her eyes shut. Feeling the burn in her throat and her eyes stinging, Shona slumped against the doorframe and doubled over. Retching uncontrol-lably, she then vomited onto the floorboards.

"*Goddamn* it, you better clean that up." Chuck grimaced as Shona tried to stagger away. Grabbing her shoulders, he lifted her up a foot off the ground and threw her down the hallway. "Get the hell out of here, *now*!"

"What the hell's goin' on? Can't a guy get some damn peace around here?" Frank roared as he emerged into the hallway. Lucy shrieked in horror. Desperate to get to Shona, she tried to wriggle free of Don, but he grabbed her waist with both hands.

"No, goddamn it, not till I've finished," he growled, yanking her back.

After a few more moments of Don's grunting, Lucy was finally able to prize herself free from his grip after he sprawled himself backwards on the bed with a huge grin plastered over his well-groomed face. Grabbing her skirt and shirt, she threw them on, then slipped on her sandals and pushed past Chuck.

"Shona... please, wait."

Shona had already barged her way past a bemused-looking Frank and was already at the bottom of the stairs and stumbling towards the exit.

Ripping open the front door, Lucy watched helplessly as the blue truck roared off, kicking up dust as its shape became a blur on the horizon. With absolutely no way of catching up with her, Lucy set off on the mile-long trek to Dorothy's house in the hope that by the time she got there, Shona might have had time to calm down.

~

"What the hell's goin' on, Chuck?"

Frank, after watching Don leave the room half-dressed and scuttle down the hallway past him, looked over to see Chuck picking up the last few items of the clothing Lucy had left on the floor by the bed.

"Lucy," Chuck replied, standing up. "She bolted. That broad from your uncle's garage came in and saw what was goin' on up here. God knows why but Lucy ran after her. She's probably gone to the old lady's place... that's where she's gone a couple of times before."

"Did he pay?" Frank asked as he walked up to the bed, his eyes narrowing when he saw the delicate lace panties Chuck was clutching. "What you doin' with them?"

"What? Oh yeah. He paid. Not full whack though, he only got half of what he was promised but..." Chuck put his hand into his pocket and took out the money. "Here."

Frank grunted as he held the thinner than he was expecting wad of bills. A thought suddenly crossed his mind. "Say, Chuck.

How do you know she's been to the old lady's place before? You been followin' her?"

"Yeah," he said in a quiet voice, his eyes lowered to the frayed carpet.

"Well now, you really *are* keepin' a close eye on my girl, ain't ya." He walked over to Chuck and then reached up to pinch his fingers and thumb between his collarbones until the big man winced. "I appreciate that, my friend. You're lookin' out for your buddy. Thank you, Chuck."

The corners of Chuck's mouth twitched as he caught a glimmer of menace in Frank's dark eyes. Letting him go, Frank strolled back over to the bedroom door and pocketed the money.

"Oh, Chuck?" he said, without turning back to face him.

"Yeah?"

"Take the panties outta your pocket and put them back on the bed."

Lucy stood outside Dorothy's cottage, frozen to the spot, trying to summon up the courage to knock on the door. Completely distraught at what Shona had seen her doing, she'd run the whole way over to try in some way to explain. But no amount of words said in the right order was ever going to remove the image she'd imprinted on Shona's mind.

It was useless even knocking. Neither Dorothy nor Shona would answer the door. Disgusted with herself, she turned back towards the road.

Chapter 22

Lucy sat at the breakfast table in the little kitchen above the bar, staring into space. Frustrated that she hadn't been brave enough to knock on Dorothy's door last night, she hadn't slept a wink, completely embarrassed and horrified at what Shona had seen. The irony of it all was gut-wrenching. On the same night she'd promised herself she'd stop, she had been seen by the one person in town she prayed would never discover her sordid little secret.

Stirring her coffee into a whirlpool, she didn't even notice Frank enter the kitchen and stand behind her chair.

"You OK?" he asked.

"Hmm?" Lucy replied, not lifting her eyes from her cup.

"Last night. You didn't get in until late. Did you find your friend?" Frank's demeanor was eerily calm.

"What?" Lucy snapped her eyes back into focus, perplexed by his question. "No." She looked up at him, tears in her bloodshot eyes. "Oh, Frank, I didn't want her to see me like that. She's my only friend and I've gone and ruined it now." She put her head on the table and sobbed.

Frank watched her for a moment, unmoved.

"It's probably for the best. If she's too square to understand what we gotta do to make ends meet, then she ain't no real friend." He walked over to the table and kneeled beside her. Stroking her hair, he softened his tone. "Shhhh... please don't cry. You know it makes your eyes all red."

"Is that all you care about, Frank? How I look? Can't sell a wreck, can you?" Lucy snapped, lifting her head to face him.

"Of course it's not. But you're the best bartender I got, baby. You're keepin' the roof over our head. If it wasn't for you and how... hard you're workin', I don't know where we'd be. I need you, darlin'." He held her face in his hands. "Hey, how about I let you take a few nights off, huh? And a promise is a promise. I'll let Trish have your guys from now on, OK? Whaddaya say?" His eyes had a kindness in them she hadn't seen since the day they'd met.

"You mean it?" she asked, wiping her nose on her sleeve.

"God's honest, baby. I'm gonna keep you all to myself from now on."

It was just over a week from that night and Lucy still hadn't had a chance to properly explain to Shona what had gone on inside that room. It seemed a massive coincidence to her that every day since that night Harry had sent Shona out on deliveries that took up the whole working day. Aching to put it right, Lucy had gone round to Dorothy's most evenings, but the old lady wouldn't let her in the house. She knew Dorothy was protective of Shona, but recently she'd been even more so.

It was Friday morning, May 3, and, returning from Wreckers for the fifth time that week, Lucy walked up to the bar and sat on a stool. Resting her head on her palm, she wasn't in the slightest bit interested in what Norm was rattling on about.

"Hey boss, I was just telling young Lucy here about the big

news going around town!" Norm hollered over to Frank, who had just descended the stairs.

"Damn right, Norm. I just been on the phone hearin' about all the ideas for the fair from the plannin' committee. They want the bar to be front and center. Pool competitions, food and drink, poker night, you name it. We'll make so much money it'll be obscene." Frank slapped Norm hard on the back, making the middle-aged man stumble forward a step. "That Max Whitfield is the best thing to happen to this town in years." His beaming face changed as he looked over at Lucy, who had barely said a word to him all day. Taking a deep breath to steady his voice, he walked up next to her

"What's eatin' you? That blonde still not talkin' to you?"

"No. I can't catch a second with her to explain what happened last week. When's the fair?" Lucy asked.

"July, I think," Norm replied.

"That's right. Gives us just over two months to prepare and get this place spruced up proper. A gold mine is coming to town, I tell ya."

Lucy smiled in all the right places, but her mind couldn't stop turning over.

"You're late tonight again. I don't like you out on that recovery truck past eight o'clock."

Dorothy placed a large bowl of clam chowder on the table in front of Shona, who looked exhausted as she picked up her spoon.

"I don't mind. Gets me out of town for a while," she replied, her voice barely audible. "Harry sends one of the guys with me anyway so it's cool. I like the freedom. Anyway, now we're into May the nights are starting to get lighter. No need to worry 'bout me."

"You not hungry?" Dorothy asked, noticing Shona staring at her untouched bowl. Smiling, Shona dipped a piece of bread in her bowl and began to eat. "She came by again earlier. I told her you weren't here," Dorothy said, dropping two lumps of sugar into her coffee cup and stirring.

"Probably for the best."

"Shona, no matter what happened in the past, I can see you're a good person inside."

"That means a lot, Dorothy. More than you know," Shona replied, reaching over the table and clamping her hand over the old lady's.

Chapter 23

Shona and Lucy hardly spoke to each other during the following week, with both of them working at different ends of the days. In the mornings Lucy would head off to college, she would wave over to Shona, to receive only a cursory glance and the merest nod back. A day had rolled into two, and then three. Every time Lucy saw Shona return from a call, she would head across the street to Wreckers, but by the time she'd arrived Shona would have melted into the evening again.

Then late Friday afternoon, two weeks after the incident in the bar, Lucy looked out of her apartment window and saw Shona pulling the heavy wooden garage doors together. Knowing the other mechanics would have left hours earlier, Lucy saw her opportunity and raced down the metal steps of the fire escape.

"Hey."

Shona spun around to see Lucy standing on the edge of the sidewalk behind her. She lifted her hand to wave and waited for Shona's reaction.

Taking an eternity to respond, Shona squeezed out an apathetic, "Hi."

"Been so long since I talked to you, I think I've forgotten how to. I've missed you." Lucy half-smiled.

"I been busy," Shona replied, turning back to the doors to wrap a chain through the handles and clunk the padlock closed. Pulling on it once to check it was secure, Shona took a huge intake of breath and headed towards her truck, striding straight past Lucy who stared open-mouthed at her.

"Coincidence, though, isn't it? After months of us getting on so well, then that night you see me..." She paused. "And all of a sudden you're *busy* all the time?" Lucy scolded, her hand resting on her hip as she stared at Shona. "What is it with you? You think I've been lying to you all this time? Well, that's rich. Who the hell are you to judge me? Given how closed off *you* are to spilling your secrets." She paused as she saw a flicker of acknowledgement to that fact on Shona's face. "I ain't proud of what I done, you know. You think I like what I had to do for money?"

Shona bowed her head. After a moment she turned around. "You didn't have to do *that*."

"It's not fun for me, you know. Frank says he can't keep that bar going without my help." Lucy tried to make eye contact with Shona. "I'm trying my best. I told Frank, that night you saw me, it was gonna be the last night I'd do the extras. And then you go and see me, don't you." She shook her head in anguish, then wiped her nose on the back of her sleeve. "I'm even going to college every single day now. I ain't let my aunt's advice go completely to waste," she added, hoping that would make a difference.

"Is that 'cos you wanna go there or because your parents'll stop sending you money if you don't?" Shona shot back.

"Wow, that was harsh," she said. "But you're right. The dean called me into his office a week ago wanting to discuss my attendance record since Christmas." She raised an eyebrow, not needing to elaborate further.

"He tell your parents?" Shona asked, her tone a little more sympathetic than before.

"No. But he said he would unless I attended every day from now on. I gave him a sob story, turned on the waterworks, you know. I'm lucky. The dean is one of my father's oldest friends. They were at Yale together. How do you think I got into college in the first place with my high school record?" Lucy hesitated, her gaze drifting off to the horizon. "But..."

"But what? That's good, isn't it? He's given you a second chance at making something of yourself. Anyone would kill for that opportunity," Shona replied, half-smiling.

"I just... Oh Shona, I don't know," Lucy cried out, spinning around. She clamped her hand over her face and exhaled in frustration. "It just feels like... You know? There's just something missing. Can you understand that? I know I'll go to college and I'll get my teaching diploma one day, but I just think I need to get out and travel more. See new things, new places." She paused and looked at Shona. "Be more like you."

Shona's eyes met Lucy's. "Believe me, you do not want to be like me."

"Why? What's so wrong with you, Shona?"

They both stood staring at each other for the next five seconds, the tension between them almost tangible until Shona blinked first.

"Look, would it really be so bad to go home to your parents and tell them the truth? Your mom will forgive what you did. Moms always understand." Shona wrapped her fingers around her pink pebble necklace, then stepped closer to Lucy, who closed her eyes and shook her head.

"What, and tell her I blew my chance of getting a real career and making her proud? Shall I tell my school principal mother that her only child, her precious daughter, decided that a better option for her future was to hook up with the first good-looking guy she met, then let him talk her into fucking guys for money?

Then, on top of that little bombshell, I tell my well-to-do surgeon father that his sweet little angel also swallowed drugs to relax her while she did it? And now she can't function properly most days without them 'cos the flashbacks of those guys pawing at her make her feel physically sick and, on top of that, she lied to them on the phone about how great school was? Yeah, I'm sure they'd really enjoy hearing all that, don't you?" Lucy swayed, her face staring at the sky. "Just because one day she fell for a guy at a bus station who told her she was beautiful. Now, here I am." She swept her arms out wide.

Shona moved towards Lucy and held her gently by the shoulders to calm her down. "They might not understand why you lied to them before. They might not get why you almost ditched college for Frank. But they wouldn't want you to be doing what you were doing that night I saw you, Lucy. They'd just want you to come home. Maybe start college again next year."

Lucy stared at Shona, not sure whether her words were comforting or critical. Suddenly, from nowhere, she found the courage to ask Shona the question she had been so curious to ask for all the time she'd known her.

"So, if you really believe all that, why are you running? Why can't *you* go home?"

Chuck stood outside the bar watching the two women across the street. Lucy had been waving her arms around one minute and, just as he was about to march over there, it all seemed to calm down. But within seconds the hairs on the back of his neck began to bristle when he saw Shona step forward and lay her hands on Lucy's shoulders. Fighting his natural protective instinct, Chuck also noted a different sensation running through his blood.

Jealousy.

~

Shona flinched at the bluntness of Lucy's question. Incapable of fighting the panic she felt in that moment, she backed away and stood facing the garage doors, her breathing labored from the pounding in her chest.

"Every time you used to come in that bar, you'd look around as if the devil himself was after you. You almost passed out when I mentioned that D.C. guy from Louisiana until you found out what the D.C. stood for, and I don't think you could even point Tennessee out on a map, let alone convince me that you lived there all your life. You think I don't notice all these things?" Lucy stepped forward towards Shona, who leaned on the garage doors holding her stomach as it lurched and twisted inside her.

"You don't know nothing about me," she muttered.

"'Cos you won't let me know nothing. I thought we were supposed to be friends? All those months we hung out together before Christmas? Pretty much every day. Did they mean nothing to you? Friends trust each other." Lucy took a step towards Shona who had turned deathly pale. "Whatever it is, Shona, you can tell me. What are you so scared of?" Noticing Shona's body sliding down the garage doors, Lucy lurched forwards. The second her hands reached Shona's waist, Shona ripped herself away. Her eyes were brimming with tears.

"Why can't you just leave me alone, huh? I don't want you hanging around me anymore. Go do what you wanna do, I don't wanna see it. It's none of my goddamn business, alright? Just leave me out of it." Shona stumbled towards the truck and without even a glance back to Lucy, floored the gas pedal.

Chapter 24

By the time June came around, many households were still behind in their preparations for the town fair coming their way in five weeks. Numerous house fronts and porches were still in the process of being repaired and repainted and all the local businesses were being spruced up with new awnings and bunting.

Traipsing along the sidewalk through the main center of town that Thursday afternoon, Lucy looked over to Wreckers. She'd lost count now of the amount of times she had said "hi" to Shona and received only a faint nod back for her trouble. Their friendship had waned to a point where it now seemed almost irretrievable.

"Well, good afternoon, Miss Lucy. How's the studying going?" Jake greeted her from the top of his stepladder as he scrubbed the grocery store window ledges.

"Hi Jake," Lucy replied, still staring over to the garage. "It's going well, thank you for asking."

"Good, good. I'm glad to see you doing something better with your time than working in there all hours," Jake added, stroking his bushy moustache and nodding sideways to Chasers.

Lucy smiled, but deep down she knew he was right.

~

There were only four weeks to go to the fair and Max Whitfield was starting to get twitchy.

"Smith, I need a word. Now!" he bellowed as he swung the doors to the bar wide open and scanned the area inside. His cane clipped the bare wood floorboards as he limped over.

"Hey Max, what can I do for you on this fine Saturday mornin'?" Frank drawled as he leaned back in his booth.

"Don't give me that sweet talk, Smith," Whitfield replied, sitting in the booth and tossing his fedora onto the table, almost knocking Frank's glass into his lap. "I got high hopes for this fair, then I walk past this place and it's *still* showing no signs of improving its appearance. That shitty paint you insist on using is chipping away again, that front window is still cracked and what the goddamn hell is that smell?" Whitfield pinched his nose. "You got a blocked toilet or something?"

"Yep. Don't worry, Max, it's on the list." Frank smirked. "Although, I might need a bit more money to get that sorted out now too."

Whitfield threw his arms out in indignation. "What about that money I already gave you, huh?"

"I invested it," Frank replied, spreading his legs out in his seat.

"I bet you did." Whitfield shook his head and looked down at all the empty shot glasses and bottles that littered Frank's table. "Look, Frank. There's nothing to be gained from us butting heads on this one. I want this place to look good, I'm sure you do too. So, here's my proposal. I'll arrange for the council to release more funds to have this place fixed up, kitchen, bar area, everywhere. Even the john. But, in return, I want forty percent of the profits from now on."

"What? You gotta be kiddin'," Frank scoffed, going to pour himself another drink from the half-empty bottle of scotch on his table.

Whitfield smiled and, with the tip of his cane, held the bottle back. "Now, you know that's the best offer you're gon' get. I've seen the building inspector's report and it don't make good reading." He paused. "I can get him off your back too."

Frank smacked his lips and leveled his stare at Whitfield. "No."

Allowing Frank to pour his drink, Whitfield curled his lip and sat back in his seat before making his next move. "Unless... you want me to tell the inspector you have no intention of fixing up this place? I wonder how he'd feel about that? Probably shoot straight down here, that's my guess."

Frank snarled, slamming his glass down after downing his shot. "You can't do that."

"Sonny boy, have you forgotten who I am? I can do whatever the fuck I like in this town now, right?" Whitfield smirked. "Do you have the slightest comprehension of just how easy it would be for me to shut you down? Hell, I could even get you charged for the illegal activity you got going on up there," he added, flicking his eyes to the balcony walkway above their heads. "I'll be back tomorrow for your decision," he whispered, getting up and leaving Frank to seethe.

Chuck walked up to Frank's booth to find him glaring at the exit. "What'd Whitfield want?"

"We're runnin' out of time. Get those friends of yours together and collect up whatever paint, wood, nails you can find. We need to get this place perfect, fast." Frank focused his eyes on Chuck. "Whaddaya say, *partner*?"

Chuck's face illuminated. "Really? You mean it?"

Frank nodded.

～

"Can I come in?"

Lucy had been standing on Dorothy's front porch for three minutes and thirty-eight seconds that Saturday afternoon, trying to convince her that she meant no trouble before the old lady finally tutted and opened the door.

"Alright. But Shona's not here, she's gone for a walk. Like I told you on the porch. Three times," Dorothy said as she left Lucy to close the door behind them.

"That's OK. It was you I came to speak to," Lucy announced. Dorothy turned around in surprise and stared at her, her arms folded and resting on her apron.

"Me? And why's that?"

"I wanted to ask you something. About Shona."

Dorothy turned away and headed into her kitchen. "Did you close the door properly?" she called behind her.

Perplexed at the old lady's dismissal of her request, Lucy walked back to the front door. Noticing the gap around the edge where it wasn't quite fitting in the frame properly, she pushed hard on it, clunking the door into place. She then walked into the kitchen and leaned against the counter.

"So, what I wanted to ask was—"

"Was it shut? Shona keeps patching it up, but I think I'm gonna have to get a new one." Dorothy tasted the soup she was heating through, nodded, then set the pan to one side. Looking up at Lucy, her wrinkly blue eyes hardened. "Shona told me about you. What she'd seen you doing that night. It upset her to see you like that."

Feeling her cheeks redden, Lucy looked down at the floor. "I wanted to explain at the time. I came here but I just couldn't face knocking. And since then, I just ain't been able to find the words..." Lucy's eyes welled up with frustrated tears, but Dorothy was unmoved.

"Shona ain't mad at you. It's not like that." Stopping herself before she said too much, Dorothy turned back to the counter and pulled out a loaf of bread from the crock.

"What do you mean?" Lucy asked, leaning forward.

"What did you expect? She thought you worked behind the bar. Then she finds you upstairs... giving yourself away for money." Dorothy gripped the bread and sawed off two large slices. "She knows you're worth better than that. You think she doesn't care about you? Well, I think how she reacted shows she cares *more,* don't you?" She turned around to face Lucy, still brandishing the knife and punctuating every word with it. "She don't mean to ignore you when you speak to her, Lucy." The old lady sighed. "The reason she won't talk to you about it is because she doesn't know *how* to."

Lucy blinked back the tears as she took in what Dorothy was saying. "I know how that feels. Believe me, I do. Sure, I'm going to college every day now, being a good girl and all. But when I'm there... I can't really talk to anyone. They don't think like I do. About being a free spirit, you know? They are all college brains, full of textbook quotes and research talk. I ain't ever met anyone like Shona. She's..." Lucy paused, trying to find the right word, "different."

"Yeah, you're right, she is. And she's pleased that you've got yourself all sorted out now, but maybe... Oh, I don't know, maybe it's best all round if you two just get on with your lives." Dorothy looked up at the clock. "Look, she'll be home soon, and I don't want you here when she gets in. She's had enough trouble in her life without you adding to it. If you really want to be her friend, then you'll give her time and space to figure all this out alone." The old lady motioned to the door.

"OK. I'll go. But please, can you do one thing for me?"

"What?" Dorothy snapped.

"Please just tell her I'm sorry. And I miss her friendship. But if she truly wants me to leave her alone, then I will." Lucy turned and walked back towards the front door, the question she'd come to ask going completely ignored.

"Damn door. I promise I'll get it fixed this weekend. I got a piece of wood outside that'll replace the bit that's broken this time. That other bit ain't gonna take another nail hammered into it."

After a minute or so into her greeting, Shona noticed Dorothy still hadn't even turned around from the stove.

"You had a visitor. Lucy," she muttered, filling their bowls with soup.

"Again?"

"Again." Dorothy turned around. "Said she wanted to ask something."

"What did you tell her?" Shona asked, licking her lips and holding Dorothy's stare. The second or two it took for her to answer was torture.

"I never gave her the chance to ask," Dorothy replied, placing the bowls on the table and sitting down.

Feeling sick with anguish, Shona edged down into her seat. "But if she did...?"

"Shona, why did you confide in me?"

"Because I thought I could trust you."

"Then you don't need to ask whether or not I told her anything, do you?" Her mouth twitched into a faint smile. Ripping off a piece of bread, she dunked it into her soup. "Now eat."

Chapter 25

The inevitable influx of strangers to Riverside was playing on Shona's mind more and more as each day closer to the day of the town fair ticked by. Dropping her wrench on the concrete floor of the garage for the fifth time that Tuesday morning, she let out a huge deep groan along with several expletives.

"Hey there, you OK?" Harry called, popping his head out of the office.

"Yeah," Shona lied, rubbing the thumb she'd caught on a wheel arch.

"Getting crazy out there, ain't it?" he said, walking out of the office with his hands in his pockets. He nodded his head towards the street. "Old Jake has been rambling on for days now about how good business is with people getting their ingredients from him for their bake sales. Max Whitfield seems to think that there'll be people coming in from far and wide which should be good for us with the car wash. Bonuses all round, I reckon." Harry smiled, hoping the thought of an extra few dollars would cheer Shona up out of her melancholy, but it appeared to have the opposite effect. "Why so glum, Shona? I thought you'd enjoy a bit of fun around here for a change."

Shona half smiled. "Just not too keen on a lot of fuss is all."

"Look, how 'bout on the day I get my guys to wash the cars out front and you stay back here. I got a few jobs you could keep yourself busy with."

As if by magic, the tension in Shona's shoulders seemed to be released. "Really? I mean, if you need me to do that then—"

Harry held his palm up to stop her rambling. "No problem. Listen, it's almost five. Go home. You've worked real hard today."

Shona nodded her thanks and went to grab her jacket. As she was walking over to the truck, Harry called after her.

"Yeah?" Shona hollered back.

"You're a real asset to this place, girl. You remember that." He waved as he watched Shona jump into the truck and honk the horn as she roared off.

Lucy had told herself she was going to make a conscious effort to give Shona the time and space that Dorothy had advised her to do. But, unable to fight the urge any longer, she made the mile-long walk over to Dorothy's house later that Tuesday evening. Not expecting to see Shona in the front yard crouching behind the truck staring at the tailpipe, Lucy breathed deeply to steel herself and think of a good opening line.

"If you find a potato or something in there, I can swear it wasn't me." She giggled, waving over to her. Seeing the blank look on Shona's face as she looked up, Lucy wished she'd gone with a simple "hi" instead.

"What you doing here?"

"I just came over to say hi," Lucy replied, sweeping a strand of hair from her eyes.

"You not *working* tonight?" Shona felt a twinge in her gut at the memory.

"No. I told you, I ain't doing that stuff no more." She paused. "How was your day?"

"OK. Busy. Everyone going on about this damn fair." Shona paced her way around the truck from back to front to turn over the engine. Revving it loudly, she completely drowned out Lucy's next question.

"I asked if you're going to the fair?" Lucy repeated when Shona had switched the engine off.

"No. I don't go to those things."

"You don't go anywhere. What do you do for fun?"

"I told you before. Ride horses."

"Don't sound like fun to me."

"Well, the last dose of fun you offered me was to meet you in the bar. Then I went upstairs and look what I saw." Shona leveled her stare at Lucy, who looked down at the ground. "I guess we both have different interpretations of the word fun." Shona regretted her words the second they crossed her lips. "Hey, look. I'm sorry. That was mean. I shouldn't have said that." She wiped her oily hands on a rag, then ran her hand through her bangs.

"No, I deserved it." With tears welling up in her eyes, Lucy saw no point in continuing the conversation. She nodded her goodbye and left Shona to her repairs.

"You two sorted things out?" A croaky old voice sounded behind Shona as she watched Lucy depart.

"Huh? Oh, no. Ah, damnit. I said something I shouldn't have. She didn't deserve that." She turned around to face Dorothy, who looked at her through her wise old eyes.

"Well then, you need to apologize. Friends are hard to come by, Shona, and if that young girl is adamant that's what she wants to be then there's nothing wrong in it, you know what I'm saying?" Dorothy stared long and hard at Shona.

"She asked if I was going to the fair," Shona said, kicking at the ground.

"And?"

"I said no."

"Why?"

"Dorothy, are you really that surprised that I wouldn't wanna go? Knowing what you know about me?" Shona raised her eyebrows.

"I suppose not."

"How 'bout you? You wan' go?" Shona walked round to the driver's side door, slammed it shut, then placed her wrench back in her tool belt.

"Good God, no. Too much noise. All that hustle and bustle ain't no place for an ol' codger like me. Plus, I can't be bothered with all those people spending money they don't have on things they don't need, to impress people they don't even like. No thank you."

Shona grinned. "That's one thing we do have in common, then," Shona said, sniffing at the air. "Well, along with the love of freshly-baked cornbread."

Shona held out her arm for Dorothy to take. The two of them headed up the porch steps and into the house, following the mouthwatering aroma floating on the cool evening breeze.

Slipping into the almost see-through lacy material of the dress she'd been told to wear that night, Trish stared at herself in the mirror, yet again hating the sight of what stared back. She applied her mascara, then her scarlet lipstick and plumped up her red curls, sighing as she inspected the result.

"You look so beautiful, honey." Doria appeared at the bedroom door clutching a glass of water in her trembling hand. "But do you really have to wear *that*?"

"Mom, all bar staff have to look good, or their customers will go somewhere else to drink and gamble away their wages.

Plus, I get better tips," Trish replied, fixing her hair one last time before finally being satisfied. "I'll be home around two, OK?"

"Tommy's so lucky to have a mom like you. You work so hard on your feet all night. You must be tired, darling. I wish I could help more." Her mother lifted the glass to her lips, her hands shaking so much that the liquid almost dribbled down her chin.

"Mom, you do help me. I couldn't work at all if you weren't here. The best thing you can do for all of us is to just promise me that the only thing that goes in that glass is water. You promise? I can't do this without you." Trish walked over to her mother and wiped her chin with her handkerchief.

"Thank you. I'm trying real hard and it's not easy, but I get stronger every day and I have you to thank for that. You and that beautiful lil' boy up there. I just wish I'd looked after you when you were his age, like you look after him now."

"Mom, listen. I need you to look after yourself too, OK? Who knows, if this fair is a big success and the tips roll in, things might be a bit easier." She kissed her mother on the cheek and went into Tommy's room to read him his story.

Her mother stood outside the bedroom door listening to her daughter's soft reading voice and her grandson giggling in all the usual places. Gripping the glass of water, she wished she could shake the overwhelming urge to put just one drop of something stronger in it. Even after months of fighting it, the need was greater than ever. The thought of her daughter working all night in that seedy, decrepit bar filled her with shame. She was almost certain that her daughter's job included more than just cleaning up and serving the drinks.

～

Max Whitfield breathed in the cool evening air as he stood outside Chasers. Receiving a very firm "no" to his last offer to help finance Frank's renovations, he ran his eyes all over the windows and weatherboarding. *Good, but not great,* he thought, clenching his teeth before pushing open the door.

At the far end of the bar, Frank saw Whitfield enter, then swaggered over to him. "Mr. Mayor. How d'ya like the new paint job? Shines like the sun, this place now, don't it just?" he smirked, holding out his hand for Whitfield to shake.

Whitfield shook Frank's hand, softening his glare when he looked across to Joanie and then Lucy.

"I gotta admit, as much as it pains me to do so, Smith, it looks OK out there. For now. But I think we might still be able to do a bit of business together anyway." Pulling on his arm, Whitfield switched Frank's body around to face the bar. "Your girls. How many you got?"

"What? Oh, 'bout five all together. Some work different shifts so they're not all here yet. Why d'you ask?" Frank's eyes narrowed.

Whitfield gestured to Lucy, who was bending over the bar to reach a glass. "That one there. She's a real peach. And the others, if they're as stunning as her, I reckon this place could be worth something," he muttered, half to himself. "I reckon I could bring a lot of my guys in here, for a discount of course."

"Let's talk in private," Frank replied, leading Whitfield across to the back room.

When they were a few feet from the door, Chuck reached out and pulled Frank to one side. "I don't like him."

"Who? Max?" Frank replied.

Chuck grimaced. "Yeah. I don't like the way he looks at Lucy. It's not right."

"Yeah well, that's my business, not yours. Anyway, I'm more concerned with how you're lookin' at him. Dial it down a notch, will ya," Frank hissed.

"You asked me to protect her. So did Lucy. I'm just doin' my job," Chuck protested, his shoulders becoming tenser.

"Look, she'll be OK. I'll sweet talk her into comin' outta retirement," Frank said, winking. "I've got a deal to make with Whitfield and I promise I'll save her for the best ones, OK? And after all, she still comes home to *me*. So, they can look all they want, they can't touch her unless I say so. That's what'll keep us in business, right? Partner?" He slapped Chuck on the back, knocking the big guy forward. "Just keep it quiet for now, don't you go tellin' her nothin', OK?"

"Whatever you say, boss," Chuck replied.

Chapter 26

"Momma?"

A tiny voice, thick with a heavy wheeze, called out into the air the following afternoon. After a couple of minutes of silence, the little boy peeled his bedsheets back and placed his bare feet on the cold, wooden floor of his room. In the corner he saw Doria leaning at an odd angle in a rocking chair.

"Grandma? Wake up." Tommy pulled on a fistful of her cardigan, stepping back when she slumped forwards. As she did so, her half-empty mug crashed to the ground, sloshing the remnants of her drink all over the floorboards.

"Mom, you OK?" Trish called from downstairs. Receiving no answer, she put the plate she was washing down on the drying rack. Drying her hands on a towel, she headed up the stairs, climbing each with more haste than the previous one.

"Mom!"

Rushing over to where her mother was hanging out of her chair, she threw her arms around her and sat her upright. She turned her attention to Tommy.

"Baby, you're too sick to be out of bed, you'll get cold. Now scoot back under those blankets," she commanded her son, who obeyed. Keeping one curious eye on his grandma, the little boy climbed back into bed.

"Mom, wake up. Come on, please?" Trish slapped her mother's face until she groaned and came to.

"Wha-a-a-at? Whasss happening?" she slurred, opening her eyes a crack.

"You tell me." Trish realized her knees were wet. "Mom, you dropped your water... Let me get you some more, I'll..." She stopped mid-sentence at the very familiar, unmistakable whiff of something she'd hoped she'd never smell again in her mother's mug. Blinking the tears back, Trish lifted her gaze up to her mother's watery, red eyes.

"I'm sorry, honey. I don't know what happened. I've let you down," she mumbled.

"Why now, Mom? What's happened? I can't leave Tommy alone with you if you can't stay sober. You know that." Trish's heart was breaking having to chastise her own mother, especially seeing the look of sadness and embarrassment in her eyes. "Look, all I need is a bit more time to save up, once that fair brings more business into the bar. Please, Mom, I just need you to fight this." Trish paused and held her mother's face in her hands. "We can get you back in the program, if that's what you want?"

Doria wrenched her face away from Trish's grasp. "I don't need that stupid program. A load of self-indulgent nobodies all sat in a circle bleating on about how hard they have it. No thank you. I just had a slip-up today is all. I'll be fine tomorrow." She nodded her head and straightened her back in her chair.

Trish stood up and thought carefully about leaving her son in her mother's care when she went to work later. But faced with little choice, she checked on Tommy, then returned to finish the dishes.

"Don't move!" Lucy yelled, racing across the street.

It was just after four that afternoon when she'd exited the grocery store and, out of habit, looked across to Wreckers where she'd seen Shona trying to pin a flag string to the top corner of the garage doors.

"Fuck, you nearly fell over," she gasped.

Looking down in surprise, Shona's panicked face broke into a relieved grin. "Goddamn. That was mighty close, I could feel the ladder slipping but I couldn't stop it," she said, her legs shaking as she descended.

"Yeah, I saw. Well, seeing as though I just saved your life and all, you wanna come over to the bar for a cold drink?"

"Thanks, but I can't. I gotta go and do one last delivery for Harry. Say, if you're not doing anything you can come keep me company? If you want to, that is?" Shona offered.

"Sure, I'd love to," Lucy replied, almost before Shona had finished speaking. She walked over to the blue truck and hopped in.

"How's things been at college?" Shona asked after five minutes of awkward silence passed between them on the journey over to Birchfield.

"It's been good, actually. I was helping out in this one first grade class for a couple of days. I didn't think I'd like it, with them being so young and all, but I really did. I think I'd like to teach that class someday."

"It's real nice to hear you thinking of the future, Lucy. Go out there and teach. Damnit, you got one life, start living it." Shona looked over at Lucy and within seconds they were in fits of laughter.

"Well, alright there, John Dewey, I might just do that," Lucy giggled.

Chapter 27

"Frank Smith, are you in there? I need to talk to you!" Trish hollered at the closed front door of the bar on Saturday morning. After waiting a few seconds for a response that never came, she headed up the fire escape. Knocking on the heavy wooden door at the top, Trish hollered again until it snapped open.

"What the hell do you want? It's the middle of the night!" Frank roared, rubbing his head.

"It's nine o'clock in the morning, but I ain't here to be your alarm clock, Frank. I need to get paid."

"Yeah, well, that bar needs new roof tiles, so I'll be keepin' what you made last night. Otherwise you won't have a place to work, got it?"

"Frank, you can't do that. I got a kid to feed."

"Yeah, well, we all gotta make sacrifices. Now, beat it!"

He slammed the door in her face, the force of the backdraft nearly knocking her down the steps.

"Whoa there. You OK?" Lucy appeared, laden with grocery bags, at the top of the steps just in time to stop Trish from falling.

"That damn boyfriend of yours ain't paying up. I don't know what I'm gonna do."

"I wish I could help, but every time I have a bit extra, it gets taken from my room," Lucy said, shaking her head.

"Yeah well, maybe you should keep it in a drawer that locks next time," Trish replied. "Look, hon, I gotta go. You tell that Frank I'll be back later and I want what he owes me," she called back over her shoulder.

"I wish I knew for sure where she goes sometimes. College finishes at three but she didn't get home last night till after six. Now, I got my suspicions but..." Frank muttered as he stood at the bar next to Chuck.

"She goes on delivery errands with Shona, then back to her place for dinner. I followed her," Chuck replied. "For you," he added.

Frank slammed his fist down on the bar. "I *knew* it. Goddamn that broad. Why the hell does Lucy wanna spend more time with her instead of me? What's she got that I ain't, huh?" He took a long drink from the bottle of bourbon that Norm had just that minute taken off the optics to clean. "I need that Shona gone, Chuck. You hear me?"

Chuck nodded.

The first morning of the fair brought with it the most beautiful sunny day the town had seen for a long time. Even at 7 a.m. when Shona sat down on the porch swing to drink her morning coffee, the weather was already stiflingly hot.

"Make sure you take extra water. It's gon' be a record by midday," Dorothy said, handing Shona her lunch box and a larger canteen than the one she usually took.

"Thanks. But don't worry too much. Harry said I can do some jobs out back, so I'll be out of the sun," Shona replied, packing the canteen into her satchel anyway. "You remember me telling you?"

"Oh yeah. Probably for the best, in more ways than one, huh?" Dorothy gave Shona a knowing wink, then wandered off down to the chicken run to collect eggs.

Feeling the nerves twist her gut, Shona declined breakfast and threw her satchel into the truck. Dorothy watched her drive away, not surprised that Shona was feeling apprehensive about all the strangers that would no doubt be sniffing around town in a few hours' time.

"Smith, you in here?" A deep voice echoed through the empty bar. Looking from side to side, the man eventually caught sight of Frank through the half-open back room door. "Oh, you're in here. Alright, well, I need to know what's happening tonight. What time am I telling my guys to be here for?"

Frank looked up from his desk and grinned. "Hey Barney, long time no see." His smile faded. "Jeez, man, what happened to your face?" He pointed up at the huge scar on Barney's forehead and the smaller ones around his left eye socket.

"Oh, this?" Barney replied. "Last time I was here, some guy jumped me. I'd just finished with your girl, Lucy. I went outside for a smoke and *wham*. Took me months to just be able to walk straight afterwards."

Frank slouched back in his chair, shocked at his associate's injuries. "I never heard nothin' about that. You usually can't take a shit in this town without somebody hearin' about it."

"Well, I was hardly gonna report it to the police now, was I? Can't have the wife findin' out what I was doing here. The guys found me and took me to the hospital. Told Wendy I'd been robbed."

"You see who it was?" Frank asked.

"Nope. But I swear he'll kill someone next time. His eyes when he was beatin' me... they were wild, like he was possessed or somethin'. I thought it was somethin' to do with the hooker, but she's your girl, right?"

"Yeah. So anyway, get here tonight for around eight o'clock. Tell your boys to bring lots of dough. I'm feelin' lucky," Frank bragged, getting up to show Barney out.

As they reached the exit, Barney caught sight of Chuck twenty yards away, painting the last of the weatherboards on the side of the bar. The color drained from his face as, across the distance, Chuck's eyes met with his own.

With his blood running cold, Barney gasped and grabbed on to Frank's arm. "He works for you?"

"Yeah. Why?"

"'Cos he's the one who tore me up." Barney pointed to the scars on his face. "That son of a bitch gave me the beatin' of my life, cracked four of my ribs and now I can't see straight anymore."

Frank could hardly believe his ears as he looked over at Chuck. "You sure? Yeah, he's a big guy and he ain't right in the head, but he wouldn't hurt a fly. I've known him forever. You sure?"

"You're goddamn right I'm sure. I remember now. Those eyes. I'd know them anywhere." Anger had taken Barney over completely now. "I'm gonna tell my boys to take their money elsewhere. I ain't comin' back here again. Not while that crazy bastard's around."

"Hey, c'mon Barney, don't get all bent outta shape. I'll talk to him... *Barney!*"

Frank's protests fell on deaf ears as Barney limped away in the opposite direction.

~

Each evening Lucy had to work behind the bar was becoming tawdrier than the last, especially after spending her days actually starting to enjoy college. Frank had taken the nights away from her, but said she was too good at the performances not to dance anymore. It was a sort of compromise. Lucy knew that while college was going well and Frank was being kind to her, she had to be grateful she had a place to stay. But lately her heart twisted with every dance she gave and every man she let near her.

After college that Friday afternoon, she meandered through the fair stalls and hot dog carts, finally reaching the corner of town. Looking over at Wreckers, she saw that Shona was nowhere to be seen.

"Harry, is Shona around?" she asked, stepping into the cool shade of the office.

"Oh, hi Lucy." Harry looked up from his pile of paperwork. "Yeah, she's over there. I got the feeling she ain't one for crowds, so I let her do some repairs out back."

Lucy went over to where Shona was lying on her back on a set of creepers, only her brown leather boots visible from underneath the truck she was fixing.

"My guess is it's the shift linkage system," Lucy announced, running her hand over the hood of the truck.

Shona slid out and stared upwards. "How d'you know that?"

"I didn't, but what a guess," Lucy replied.

"Sure was," Shona praised, a wry smile on her face as she held out the cable she was just about to start fitting. "You watching the parade tomorrow?"

"Maybe. You?" Lucy replied as Shona slid back underneath the truck.

"Nah, got enough back here to keep me busy all weekend."

Just then, a huge hiss rang out followed by a splat. "Shit!" Shona's wrench clattered to the concrete as she slid out, her face covered in transmission fluid.

"Here. Use this." Ripping off her thin white cardigan, Lucy thrust it into Shona's face to wipe off the surplus. Momentarily unable to see a thing, Shona had no choice but to let her, her hands reaching blindly for Lucy's forearms.

"It's OK, just let me get this off you," Lucy murmured as she cleaned up Shona's face. Blinking several times, Shona eventually cleared her vision to find herself met with Lucy's concerned brown eyes.

"Better?"

Shona coughed. "Yeah. Shit. Thank you."

"No problem," replied Lucy, not realizing she was still

holding on to Shona's forearm with one hand and wiping away the remaining drops of fluid from her hair with the other.

Shona smiled after a moment. "I think you got it all."

"Oh, sorry. Yeah." Lucy blushed. "Listen, you wanna go grab a soda? Before my shift starts?"

Shona thought about it, wondering how many people were already outside milling around. "Maybe later," she said, not wanting to openly disappoint Lucy right there and then. "Um… I just gotta go clean up."

"OK, well, you go make yourself a little less flammable and I'll go get you a soda. Don't be long," Lucy ordered, not registering Shona's reluctance. She smiled over her shoulder as she departed.

"Shona?" Harry called over, breaking her out of her thoughts. "Can you put the sign out front? It's starting to get a little busier on the streets. We might draw in some business."

Grabbing the 'Car Wash Today' sign that Marcie had made, Shona walked out onto the parking lot, wincing as she felt the hot sun hit the back of her neck.

"Hey… Shona!"

She looked up to see where the yell and come from. Sitting across the street on the backrest of a bench, Frank was waving over to her, with Chuck and a few of his other friends sitting beside him. Chuck's eyes lasered their glare through her. Realizing she had no intention of walking over to him, Frank jumped down from the bench and strode over to her.

"You know, it really used to piss me off when I saw my girl comin' out of this place after wastin' her time talkin' to you. But you know what? I think I've got it all wrong. It's actually given me an idea." He circled around her like a lion stalking its prey. "Do you know how many guys have come up to me to ask what your story is? Whether you're *available*?" He emphasized the syllables in his last word. "So, maybe I've been lookin' at this situation all wrong. I've seen the way she looks at you. Hell, she seems to want to spend all her goddamn time with *you*, so why don't we all make a bit of money out of this?"

Shona scrunched her fists up, using every ounce of her concentration to remain calm.

"Oh my, the thought. You two? *Together*. They'll come from miles around to watch that. I mean, you're actually quite pretty underneath all *that*..." He rolled his wrist over as he searched unsuccessfully for an appropriate adjective. "Just need to get you in somethin' a little more... feminine. You're my goldmine, lil' lady."

"Leave me alone, Frank," Shona squeezed through her clenched teeth.

Seeing Harry approaching behind Shona, Frank mock-saluted him and swaggered back over to the bench.

"He giving you trouble?" Harry asked.

"Nah."

"Yeah, well, whatever it was he said to you, his pal don't look happy about it."

Shona looked over towards the bench to see Chuck glaring over at her and Frank whispering in his ear. If looks could kill, Shona would be stone dead on the ground.

"He don't like anyone, that guy. I wouldn't take too much notice. He's an idiot. Always has been," Harry remarked. "If you ask me, Frank should spend less time fooling about with Chuck and those loser friends of his and more time straightening himself out."

"Does he know about fixing trucks?"

"He ain't got a clue. I tried teaching him when he was a boy, but he never took to it. Marcie's always saying maybe I should try and train him up as an admin clerk? Says it'd get him away from that bar... and those losers." Harry nodded over to the bench where the crowd of guys were still pointing and laughing.

Harry remained quiet for a minute, lost in thought.

"You OK?" Shona asked, tapping him on the arm.

"What? Oh, yeah, fine. You still OK to work late?" Harry mumbled, his eyes still fixed on Frank.

"Yeah, no problem."

"OK, well, why don't you go grab a quick soda with Lucy while those guys are off causing trouble somewhere else." Harry nodded over to the bench that Frank, Chuck and their friends had now left empty. They were disappearing around the corner at the opposite end of the street.

As Shona left the parking lot, Marcie appeared behind Harry holding two glasses of ice cold sweet tea.

"Getting busy out here," she said, scanning the area in front of her. "Oh, by the way, I was counting the takings earlier. Did you take twenny dollars from the safe yesterday?" she asked, knowing in her heart he had and what he'd done with it.

"It's the last time, I promise," Harry replied. "He's got a big poker game tonight, convinced he's gon' win. I told him that's all he's getting and not to ask again."

Marcie sighed. "I hope he does win. For all our sakes."

Chapter 29

"So, tonight's the night?" Doria said, watching her daughter slip into a tight navy blue dress that accentuated her every curve. Although she thought the dress was way too revealing, especially more so now it was threadbare, it was her daughter's best one.

"Yep. Hopefully we'll be so busy tonight that I'll earn more money in tips than ever."

Doria stared at her daughter. "I'm proud of you," she whispered, licking her dry lips.

Trish stopped adjusting the straps of her dress and turned to face her mother. "For what? Working late while my sick mother looks after my even sicker son?"

Seeing her crumble in front of her, Doria moved over to her as quickly as she could manage and scooped her up in her arms.

"For doing what you need to do for your son. For all of us."

"I couldn't do it without you, Mom."

"Shush now, it's the least I could do. You've had to clean me up when I've had a relapse. You've looked after me when I've been sick and when I'm falling over. No child should have to do that for their parent. I've let *you* down, not the other way around." She stroked her daughter's hair and kissed the top of her head.

Smoothing her dress down, Trish fixed her tear-smudged make up in the mirror. "We're a family. We do what we need to. But after tonight, maybe we can look at takin' a little vacation? Something to look forward to, huh?"

Doria smiled through her tears and nodded.

~

Swaggering up to the front of the assembled group, Frank grinned and hooked his thumbs through his belt loops. It was four o'clock in the afternoon.

"Right, ladies, I know I'm preachin' to the choir here about how important this evenin' is for us all, but this place is gon' be crammed and I need you all lookin' and actin' your best. There's a lot of money comin' into this place tonight. Understand?"

He stared at each one of his girls, then lingered his gaze longer on Trish, who nodded. Switching his attention to Lucy, who was sitting at the bar staring into space, he finished his pep talk and walked over to her.

"Did you hear what I said? I need you in top form tonight. You're my best girl, you know that," he whispered in her ear. "No one dances like you do."

Lucy sipped her drink through a straw and nodded. Wanting to be anywhere but there right that second, her mood wasn't helped by the approach of a stony-faced Trish after Frank had walked away.

"Listen, girl. You need to paint a smile on that pretty lil' face of yours," she hissed. "I got a lot riding on tonight. If business is slow then it's gon' be me who suffers, and I can't have that happen."

Lucy glared at Trish. "Do you think I give a shit about what you got riding on tonight? I got my own fish to fry, OK?" She shot up off her stool and stormed out of the bar.

～

As soon as she stepped outside, Lucy immediately regretted it. All around her were revelers milling about eating cotton candy and pointing at everything around them that was running a sale or putting on a show. Looking over at Wreckers was natural to her now, but there was no sign of the reason why she did so every time. Wandering across the street up to the garage, Lucy struggled past the hordes of people blocking her path.

"Hey Jonny, Shona around?"

"Well, hello, Miss Lucy. You enjoyin' the fair so far?" Jonny replied, looking up from the car he was waxing.

"I ain't really seen much of it," Lucy said, scanning the area behind him.

Jonny nodded. He wiped his sweaty face with the back of his forearm. "Say, you mind if I ask you somethin'?" She didn't reply. "Thing is... Well, I was just wonderin'..." Jonny twisted his chamois around in his hands as he stumbled over his words.

"What is it, Jonny? I'm in kind of a hurry."

"About Shona. Has she said anythin' to you...? About if she's datin' anyone right now?"

His words hit her like a thunderbolt.

"What?" Lucy's full attention was now completely focused on Jonny's hopeful green eyes. "Why?"

"Well, you know I think she's real' pretty and I've been tryin' to find ways of gettin' her to go on a proper date with me for months now but I'm too chicken-shit to ask her outright. Whenever I try and broach the subject, she keeps changin' it. You know what she's like for doin' that. But sometimes it seems we get on so well that... Oh, Lucy, do you think I should go for it?"

Lucy blinked several times, her mind racing. There was no doubt about it, Jonny was a good-looking young man, only twenty-six years old, and no one in town had a bad word to say about him. He would make a perfect boyfriend and any girl would be lucky to have him.

But Lucy couldn't bear the heartbreak of that girl being Shona. Not now that she was starting to feel like Jonny was.

"Oh, Jonny, I really don't think you should. I think she's already seeing somebody. But she told me in strict confidence, so don't you go saying anything to her, you hear?" The lies tumbled out of Lucy's mouth before she had chance to process them.

Disappointed, Jonny nodded, then returned to the car he was polishing with much less gusto than before.

"Hey, Pearson. I hope you're not hittin' on my girl," Frank called over from outside the bar. Jonny waved back, then moved on to the next vehicle as Frank crossed the road. "Shouldn't you be gettin' ready by now? That bar is gon' be full soon." He kissed her on the cheek.

"I'll be over there soon," she protested, wiping her face.

Looking over her shoulder at the garage, Frank clenched his teeth. "Sweetie," he began, his cold tone incongruent to the smile he forced onto his face. "I need you tonight. You understand? Can you put me first for one goddamn night?" His grip pinched the soft skin of her hand.

"OK, OK. I'll go get ready." Squirming free of his grasp, she walked away past Jonny, who was now sitting down on a tire staring at his boots.

Suddenly time stood still. All around her the world seemed to pulse and Lucy felt her heartbeat quicken just that little bit, beat by beat. A flush of warmth through her cheeks, and then her mouth went dry. She looked again at Jonny and instinctively knew he was picturing in his mind the same pair of blue eyes as she herself was picturing right that second. He was wishing for the same miracle as Lucy was: that the woman he had fallen for would somehow notice him and confess she felt the same way back. The anguish of not being able to communicate this to Shona was written all over Jonny's face. Lucy recognized it immediately.

She felt it too.

~

"Get the hell off me, you stupid son of a bitch."

Lucy quickened her pace up the fire escape after hearing the anguished cry from inside her apartment. Throwing open the door, she recoiled.

"What the hell are you doing in here?" she yelled, then motioned to Chuck to release his grip.

"Sorry, Miss Lucy, I caught this one goin' through all your drawers."

"What the..." Lucy paused to take in the scene in front of her. Dismissing Chuck, she closed the door behind him and turned to face the intruder.

"So it's you who's been stealing from me? Why?"

Caught red-handed and with no way to explain, Trish sank into the armchair next to her and buried her face in her hands.

"What's goin' on up there?" Frank asked as Chuck descended the internal stairs and sat at the bar next to him.

"Trish has been stealin' from Lucy. I caught her."

"What?"

"Yeah, she had about twenny dollars in there." Chuck took a slurp of his drink. "But I got it back for her," he added proudly.

~

"All this time I thought it was Chuck going through my stuff and taking my money. But you? Look, I know we ain't seen eye to eye lately, but why would you do that?" Lucy raged.

Trish got up out of the armchair and looked at her through tear-filled eyes. "I work goddamn hard to keep everything together. Tommy's sick, and that new technique they've been trying out, to clear the crap out of his lungs, is starting to work real good for him. But it's expensive and he needs it every two weeks. His no good father ain't no damn help." Trish paused and hardened her stare at Lucy. "Then there's you with everything going for her. Frank gave you all the good guys, the ones who didn't rough you up. Then you go and announce that all you wanna do from now on is dance. And he lets you. And you're still not happy. You still mope around this place with your head up your ass, acting as if you got it tough?" The anger in her words was completely undiluted.

"That ain't no reason to go stealing. It's not my fault you got problems at home," Lucy shot back.

"Not your fault? How can you say that?" She paused and put her hand on her hip. "Did you know Frank and I were together for a few years on and off before you came along? *I* was his best girl. *I* had what you have right now, and *I* goddamn appreciated it, not like you. The way I figure, you stole my boyfriend so it's only fair I steal something off you too." Trish crossed her arms and stared at Lucy.

Lucy perched on the armrest of the sofa. "What? I didn't know about that. When I met Frank at the bus station, he said he was single. If I'd have known, Trish..."

"We were together, but we broke up more times than I can remember. Oh, it don't matter. He's obsessed with you now. We dated, fooled around, you know? But any time the idea of getting married came up he got scared and became distant. He was never interested in ever becoming a father either, but stupid me thought he'd change his mind one day if I stuck around long enough." Trish sat down on the sofa next to Lucy and picked at the seam on the armrest.

"I'm so sorry," Lucy whispered, but it made no impact.

"I was his star once. *Me*. After you came along, though, all I got was the grubby little men. You got the rich, young businessmen and I got the shit. How's that fair, huh?"

"Can't Tommy's father help out? Where is he anyway?" Lucy asked, leaning forward.

Trish wiped her eyes and set her face. "Doesn't matter," she said vaguely. "He's a loser anyway. He don't deserve to know how amazing his little boy is."

Feeling the awkward pause between them, the anger diminished from Trish, leaving her feeling just the shame of what she'd done. Seeing this, Lucy reached into her skirt pocket.

"Here." She held out the twenty dollars.

"What? I can't take that," she said, folding her arms.

"Take half then. We'll call it teamwork," Lucy insisted, counting out the bills and passing them over to Trish, who took them.

"Thank you. I'd better go do something with this mess before tonight," Trish said, pointing at her own face.

"You'll look gorgeous, like always. But please talk to me next time. Don't keep it all inside. If I can help, I will, OK?" Lucy whispered, walking her to the door leading to the stairs above the bar.

"Lucy?" Trish began, her hand on the bannister as she stood on the top step.

"Yeah?"

"Can you talk to Chuck, please? He likes you. Ask him not to tell Frank about this. I can't lose my job. Not now."

Lucy nodded her agreement and watched a grateful Trish descend into the noisy bar below.

～

"You wanna tell me what the hell is goin' on up here?" Frank appeared at the door minutes after Trish had passed him on the stairs. His voice was eerily calm.

"Trish just came up to see me about tonight, that's all," Lucy lied.

"How much did she take?" Frank said, flicking his eyes to her open top drawer.

"What?" Annoyed that Chuck had already spoken to Frank before she could get to him, she thought fast. "Oh, no, honey, you got it wrong. I said she could borrow some money from me." She held her breath, waiting for his reaction.

Walking up behind her, Frank reached into her skirt pocket, taking out the remaining ten dollars from her stash. "You expect me to believe that? I spoke to Chuck. He told me what happened in there. At least *he* tells me the truth."

"Frank, please. That's my money. I earned it fair and square."

"Wrong. It's *my* money. And I need it for the game tonight. These hands are hot, honey. I can feel a big win comin'." He walked back towards the door. "Oh, and don't worry. I saw Trish on her way downstairs, got back the rest of the money she stole. I'll triple it tonight, you just see if I don't."

Lucy looked at Frank in horror. "You had *no* right to do that. I gave it to her. She needs it for her son. How can you be so heartless?"

"Why should I give a shit about some snot-nosed runt? Now get ready."

"You OK, boss?" Chuck asked when he saw Frank return to the bar deep in thought.

"I want you on watch tonight. Keep a close eye on Lucy. I don't want any jerks goin' near her unless they're payin' for the privilege. And if that broad from across the street comes sniffin' around her then you let me know, got it?"

"Sure thing, boss."

Harry stood outside Wreckers, his long day finally at an end. The crowds had dissipated, with the men descending on Chasers for the pool tournament about to start and the women and children grabbing dinner at the diner across the street. Sending his boys home with a few dollars' bonus in their back pockets, he realized one member of his workforce hadn't gone home yet.

"Leave that where it is for tonight. We'll need it again tomorrow," Harry said, smiling at Shona who hadn't stopped working out back all day. "Here." He handed her a thin wad of bills. "Little bonus. Why don't you go over to the pool competition? The guys are in there. I'm sure they wouldn't mind a run for their money. Especially Jonny." His eyes twinkled.

"I'll pass. But thanks for the bonus." She picked up the last of her tools and placed them in their correct slots in the tool chest. "See you tomorrow, Harry. And thanks again." Shona waved with the hand she was holding the money in, slung her jacket over her shoulder and headed over to her truck.

"You'll break his heart, girl," Harry called after her, then nodded towards the bar, smiling.

"He'll get over it," Shona called back, honking her horn as she sped away.

~

"Look, just go over there for an hour or so. It'll be fine. It's been over a year since you left Louisiana..." Dorothy paused. "You got friends now—and Lucy—just stay close to them." She looked over to Shona who was sitting on the couch staring into space. Dropping her glasses and the TV guide into her lap, she sighed and toughened her tone. "You don't wanna sit with me watching oaters all night, do you? Go have some fun."

"Nah, the place'll be crammed by now and I've already had my fill of the crowds today. Anyway, *Jim Bowie* is on later. You know you can never work out what's going on without me," Shona replied, cocking an eye sideways to see Dorothy purse her lips.

"I managed perfectly well before you came along," she chastised. "Now *go*. You're too young to be old."

Shona thought about it for a moment, but, after seeing the old lady's keen eyes encouraging her, she rose up out of her seat. "Alright then," she said, pretending to sound reluctant, "I'll go 'have some fun'."

"Good. Now *scoot*. And don't forget to pull that damn door shut properly!" Dorothy yelled after her, smiling as she heard it clunk securely into its frame.

Pushing open Chasers' door, Shona found herself met by a wall of noise. The bar was full to bursting, with most people crowded around the pool table at the opposite side to the bar area. The cheering got louder with each ball that was slotted home, then hushed again as the next one was carefully lined up.

"You came?" A happy, surprised voice separated itself from the dull roar of the crowd. Lucy shot across the floor towards Shona, leaving her customer with only half of the dance he'd paid her for.

"Yeah. Dorothy talked me into it. Again."

Lucy tossed her hair out of her glowing eyes. "Well, I'm really glad she did. Come and get a drink—my treat." She led the way through the crowds over to the bar and instructed Norm to clip the top off a bottle of Coca-Cola.

Bending over at the pool table to take his final shot, Frank's eye was drawn away from the 8-ball. His confident grin melted when he saw who Lucy was standing with. Anger flooded through his body, his cue now shaking as the fire burned from his eyes. Moments later, he pulled back and thundered the cue tip through the ball, nearly ripping a hole in the baize as he skewed his shot.

"Goddamn it." The 8-ball finally came to a halt an inch from the corner pocket.

"Well, that's just too bad, Smith." Max Whitfield's son Michael eyed up the thirty dollars of prize money on the edge of the pool table and nailed the easiest shot he'd ever had.

Throwing his cue on the table, Frank fought to control his frustration as he shook Michael's hand. His attention was then drawn by another man seated at the bar.

"Is my mother joinin' you this evenin'?" Frank asked after walking over.

"She's worried about you," George replied, his eyes staring straight ahead as he sipped his rum and Coca-Cola.

"Like hell she is. She's shacked up with you when she should be waitin' for her husband to come home."

George slammed his glass down on the bar and grabbed Frank's shoulder. "For God's sake, Frank, when are you gonna grow the hell up? He ain't coming home, y'hear? Your mother is trying in every way she can to soften that blow to you, but it's high time you got the message."

Wrenching the hand away, Frank heard his name shouted over from the back room door. "Save your advice for someone who gives a shit. I'm busy. I'm about to make more money than ever."

~

"The guys'll be playing for hours before I'm needed for anything else. You wanna keep me company for a while?" Lucy offered.

Shona nodded. "Sure, why not."

"You *may* even have a little fun, who knows."

After waiting for their drinks, they clinked glasses and took a sip. Looking towards the pool table where another game had just begun, Shona turned to face Lucy. "So... does it not bother you that Frank uses you to dance for those guys?"

Surprised by Shona's blunt question, Lucy took a moment to answer. "I have to do my bit, especially when we're busy. He sees it as business. Simple as that, really," she replied, taking a slow sip of her drink.

"And what do you see it as?" Shona asked.

"My way out," Lucy said softly. She tapped her glass with her long red fingernail and looked at Shona, who had raised her eyebrow at Lucy's response. "What I mean is, I have to keep Frank happy so I have a place to stay while I finish college. I only have a week left of this semester and I don't have anywhere else. I'm thinking of transferring up to Tennessee for my second year, stay with my aunt maybe?" She winked and sipped her drink. "But I'd prefer it if I didn't have to do that, of course."

"What, leave?"

"No, I mean what I do here. On that dance floor." She paused, seeing Shona swallow a lump that had clogged up her throat. "But if I had the choice, no, I wouldn't wanna leave either. I like this town. And since I met you, I've started to like it even more." Lucy paused again, her heart thudding. "You know, I wish you hadn't seen me do what I was doing. I'd give anything to take that moment back."

"Me too," Shona whispered.

The crowd around the pool table suddenly erupted into cheers as the 8-ball dropped into the corner pocket, almost drowning out Norm as he announced the start of the poker game. Fresh from his victory, Chuck grinned as he picked up his winnings from Michael, who really shouldn't have accepted that 'one-for-the-road' bonus game. As he caught sight of Lucy leaning into Shona as he walked past the bar, the dollar bills felt the crushing force of his now-clenched fist.

~

Leaving the game to fetch a fresh tray of drinks, and relieve the cash register of any dollar bills, Frank saw Trish laughing and joking with Joanie. Striding over to them, he grabbed Trish by the elbow then led her away.

"I don't want you anywhere near the register today, you hear me? I can't trust you not to line your pockets again with my money," he growled.

"Well, ain't *that* the pot calling the kettle black. Maybe if you paid me the money I work damn hard for, I wouldn't have to," Trish replied, freeing her arm and rubbing the red mark he'd left.

"You better watch your damn mouth. Don't *ever* forget how easy it is to replace you," he hissed back, jabbing his finger in her face.

"How could I? You done it to me already, remember." Trish swiped Frank's finger away and nodded over to the bar where Lucy was still talking intently with Shona. Leaving him to fume, she stormed off into the bathroom. Setting off to follow her, Frank's arm was pulled back.

"Frank? I'm Jimmy. Max Whitfield mention me?" The man now standing in front of Frank, smiling expectantly, was dressed immaculately in a dark blue three-piece suit. A long gold pin held his blue striped tie in place against his perfectly pressed white straight collar shirt.

"Yeah. He said you'd be poppin' by tonight," Frank lied, not wanting to lose this smartly-dressed stranger's business.

"Well now, I came over to introduce myself but then I saw

those two mighty fine young ladies at the bar." He pointed over. "They both yours?"

As he turned his head to follow Jimmy's pointing finger, an idea began to blossom in Frank's brain.

~

"Doesn't that ever piss you off?" Shona asked.

Lucy rolled her eyes in response to the guys raising their drinks at her. Just then, her attention was caught by Frank beckoning her over.

"I'll be back in a minute," she said to Shona, who nodded.

Walking over to Frank, through the usual whoops and cheers from the crowds of guys she passed, Lucy was surprised when she saw his smiling face. "You win?"

"I'm doin' alright," Frank replied. "Listen, I got a guy over there askin' about Shona. Like, what's the deal with her?"

Lucy shuffled her weight from one foot to the other, raking a hand through her hair. "Whaddaya mean 'the deal'?"

"She could make me a lot of money."

Lucy stared at Frank, open-mouthed at his lewd suggestion.

"And the two of you together? Wow," Frank added.

~

"Sorry about that, Frank had some... um... business to talk through. You OK?" Lucy asked, returning to the bar. Her eyes studied Shona a little closer this time, taking in all of her features.

"Yeah. Everything OK with him?" Shona pointed over to Frank who was in deep conversation with Jimmy.

"Frank says he's got some guy asking about you."

"Huh? Who is it? Why they asking about me?" Shona replied, fidgeting in her seat and turning to look.

"Like are you... available?" Lucy had wanted to ask Shona this question for a long time now, but it still sounded awkward, no matter how delicately she tried to put it.

"Oh... I thought you meant they thought they knew me." Shona ran her hand through her hair and over the back of her sweaty neck, completely oblivious to Lucy's keen eyes.

"No," Lucy laughed nervously. "Why? Are you worried?"

"'Course not," Shona said. Draining her drink, she swept her hair out of her eyes again and got up off her stool. "Look, I gotta go, it's way later that I thought I'd be out 'til. That guy over there keeps staring too. Must think I work for Frank."

Lucy ran her finger around the rim of her glass. "Would that be so bad? I mean, I'm sure you could use the extra money."

The smile on Shona's face vanished. "What do you mean?"

"Frank was saying... That you could make some serious money." Plucking up the courage to finally say the words, Lucy swallowed hard. "With me."

~

Little Tommy scampered out of the house wearing only his red and blue pajamas and slippers. Stopping at the edge of the road to look both ways, he shivered and wiped his dripping nose with the back of his hand. He hugged his little white teddy bear close, bowing his head to whisper in its fluffy ear.

"We gotta find my momma, Brumas."

~

Shona stared at Lucy for what felt like an age. All the noise from the bar seemed to bleed away, muffled now inside her woolly head. She leaned in close, keeping her voice low. "I am *not* a whore," she said, forcing the words through her clenched teeth.

Lucy felt the color rush to her cheeks. Her stomach twisted and the look on Shona's face was one she prayed she'd never see again.

Heading towards the exit, Shona covered the distance so fast that Lucy struggled to keep pace with her.

"Wait... I shouldn't have said that... Shona, wait!" she yelled, grabbing her arm as Shona swung the exit door open wide.

"It was a mistake coming tonight. I should've stayed in. Goddamn it, why don't I listen to my gut?" Shona snapped.

Chuck appeared behind Lucy.

"Frank needs you in there. Now," he growled. "Please," he added, his tone politer this time.

Chapter 30

Only fifty yards from the bar and exhausted, Tommy sank to the ground in the middle of the road, his lungs burning. Seeing him stumble, Shona skidded to a halt, jumped out of the truck and raced over to him.

"Hey, lil' buddy, this ain't no place to be at this time. What you doing out here all alone?" she murmured, scooping up his fragile little body in her arms, his hand still clamped around the paw of his bear.

"I need to find my momma. She works in a bar. Can you help me?" Tommy asked between wheezes.

Carrying him over to the entrance to Chasers, Shona placed his feet on the ground. "What's your momma's name?"

"Mom."

"'Course it is," Shona smiled as she pushed open the door and led him inside.

~

"Momma?" a tiny voice rang out.

"Tommy? What in God's name are you doing here?" Trish shrieked, rushing over to embrace him, hardly noticing Shona back away and leave. "You OK, sweetie?" She smoothed his dark hair down over his sweaty brow and checked him over as he coughed up the mucus that had settled on his chest. The merriment around them ground to a halt, with silence descending over every person in the bar. Confused looks were followed by small pockets of laughter as the drunker of the men in the bar pointed over at Trish and her pajama-wearing son.

"Grandma fell down. I heard a bang."

"What?"

"She wouldn't wake up," Tommy continued between coughs.

Trish scooped her four-year-old son up in her arms and ran out of the bar.

~

"Mom? Mom!" Trish yelled after racing through the open front door. Lowering Tommy to the ground, she rushed into the kitchen to see her mother face down on the floor.

"Oh my *God*, mom, what have you done?" she cried, noticing the empty bottle of vodka lying smashed in the sink with some of the contents still pooled underneath it. Reaching her mother's side, Trish's shoe crunched on a shard of glass. With her thumb and forefinger, she picked up the bottom half of the broken glass and put it to her nose.

Her brow wrinkled in confusion.

Carefully wrapping her lips around the smoother of the cracked edges, she tasted the last dregs of liquid remaining.

Water.

Looking along the length of the body below her, she saw her mother's foot partly wedged underneath a loose piece of linoleum by the door. Slowly lifting her eyes, Trish felt her heart slice in two.

The telephone receiver was dangling down by its cord. On the wall next to it was the note she'd scribbled before leaving for work.

I'll be home by 1 a.m. If I'm late, call me.

"Oh, Mom, I'm so sorry. I'm so sorry I was late," Trish wailed, draping herself over her mother's lifeless body.

Chapter 31

"Whoo. You're *goddamn* right it is. *Full house!*" Frank yelled, slamming his poker hand down on the table. Sweeping his hands across the table, he raked in the money and grinned at the groaning men he'd just beaten. "It's been a pleasure, boys. Wanna try and win your money back?"

As they were nodding, Lucy burst through the door. "Frank, I need to talk to you. *Now*."

"Later," he replied, shuffling the cards.

"Please," Lucy insisted.

Exhaling, Frank slammed the deck of cards down on the table and slid his chair out. Following her back out of the room, he grabbed her by the arm. "This better be important," he snarled.

"Trish had to go home. Her kid showed up, something to do with her mother."

"What? She just left?"

"Frank, did you win?" Lucy asked, ignoring his question when she noticed the lump of cash in his top pocket.

"Yeah. I told you I felt lucky tonight."

Her eyes imploring him, Lucy pulled Frank towards her. "Please call it a night. Don't gamble it away. That could see us

OK. It'll pay for everything, give everyone a bonus. Get this place fixed up good. Like you wanted it to be... for your daddy."

Frank, his attention devoted to staring at the poker table through the crack in the door, heard only the last sentence. "Listen, you concentrate on what you do and leave me to do what I do," he growled, casting her arm away from him.

"Hey, Smith! You in?" Max Whitfield called out from inside.

"Frank, please don't do this," Lucy begged.

"Call Trish. I want her back here workin'. *Now*." He looked at her for a moment, then called back over his shoulder to the guys in the room.

"Deal me in."

It was eight a.m. that Saturday morning when Frank, after only about three hours of sleep, wandered into the kitchen, his hand ruffling through his tousled black hair as he poured himself a coffee from the pot.

"How much did you make last night?" a voice asked.

Looking over at the table, he saw Lucy seated, sipping her coffee. "About two hundred," he replied.

"How much did you lose?" Lucy murmured.

Frank paused. "I'll make it back," he affirmed, turning his back to her.

"How much, Frank?"

Slamming his mug down on the counter, Frank swung round to face her.

"Why you always stickin' your nose into my business, huh? How much did *you* make last night? Or were you too busy cozyin' up to blondie? You think I didn't see you?"

"I got a right to enjoy the fair as much as the next person, Frank. You don't own me."

"*Yes I do!*" he roared in her face. "You live in *my* house so you do what I tell you to do. Unless you want me to make a call to your parents?" Pulling his head back, the menace on his face was all too clear.

So was the look of dread in Lucy's eyes.

"Didn't think so. So, in the future, you keep *that*," he jabbed his dirty fingernail at her nose, "out of my affairs, OK?" Ripping his leather jacket off the back of a dining chair with so much force it crashed to the ground, he stormed out of the back door to the apartment.

~

Chuck had been gazing up at the window when he looked across to the top of the metal staircase where Frank had just emerged.

"Hey boss, you got a minute?" he shouted, standing up sharply.

"No!" Frank yelled back, stomping down every one of the steps.

"Oh. Well, you see, I just wanted to ask... well, what's gonna happen now. You know, after last night." Chuck's words, tentative though they were, were still irritating enough for Frank to stop in his tracks.

He spread his arms wide. "Why is everyone so *goddamn* interested in everythin' I do around here?"

"Word is, you lost a lot of money at the table. I was wonderin' what that meant for our plans," Chuck continued.

"Our plans? Oh, you mean us being partners?" Frank smiled and slapped a grinning Chuck on the arm. "I can't be partners with you now, buddy. You're a liability. You think I wouldn't find out about what you did to Barney? He came to see me yesterday, said you nearly snapped him in two."

The grin melted from Chuck's face like a stick of butter on a freshly roasted corn cob. "But you said we were gon' run this town. You promised." His voice quivered with a mixture of disappointment and thinly veiled rage.

"Oh, come on, Chuck. Don't kid yourself. The only reason you hang around with me is because of the money, the status and the free beer. You really expect me to believe you wanna put the work in to make this place succeed?" He got up into Chuck's reddening face, the point of his finger punctuating every word. "You're a bum. You always have been. I've carried you all my life and I'm sick of it."

"That's not true!" Chuck yelled back.

"It *is* true. You've always wanted everythin' I got, includin' Lucy. You think I ain't noticed how you stare at her all the time? You musta *loved* it when I got you to stand guard while she was fuckin'."

A thin bead of sweat dripped down the bridge of Chuck's nose as he fought to contain his fury.

"Like she'd ever look twice at an ugly bastard like you. You know what? That girl over there's got more chance with Lucy than a basket case like you will *ever* have." Frank pointed across the street to where three mechanics were waiting for Harry to open up.

Just then a blue truck pulled up and Chuck's eyes landed on the one person he hated more than Frank right that second.

～

"*Norm*? Where the hell are the takings from last night?"

Ripping open the cash register, Frank lifted the levers and pulled out the tray, but there wasn't a single bill left. All he found were piles of nickels and dimes.

Norm wandered out of the back room and leaned on his broom. "Sorry, boss, but you had it all last night."

"Damn it..." Standing with his hands on his hips for a moment, the same idea he always had in this situation dawned on him.

"I'm gon' ask the old man."

"Frank, what you doing? Where you going?" Lucy shouted from the balcony above the bar.

"None of your damn business. *God*, why is *everyone* interferin'?" Frank raged, kicking over the nearest bar stool and storming over to the exit, almost dropping the bottle of beer he'd swiped from the bar on his way past.

"Wait!" Lucy shouted, racing down the stairs to catch up with him.

Outside, Frank stared over at Wreckers, his mouth clenched as he watched Shona and Harry chatting as they filled buckets with soapy water. Like a hunter stalking his prey, he walked over.

"I need more money," Frank bellowed, gesturing to Harry with his beer bottle. Lucy caught up with him and gripped onto his other arm to drag him back. "Get off me, will ya," he growled, shaking her off.

"I got nothing left, boy. You've had everything," Harry said, thrusting both hands deep into the pockets of his overalls.

"Not good enough. Where's the safe?" Frank swigged his beer, his eyes black as coal.

"Look, whatever mess you got yourself into this time, you need to sort it out yourself. I'm done."

Looking up from her crouching position by the standpipe, Shona tried not to listen, but Harry and Frank's raised voices made it impossible not to hear. Out of the corner of her eye, she saw Lucy trying to calm Frank down. A bit further to the right of them she spotted Trish walking over from the other side of the street, holding the tiny hand of the little boy she'd helped last night.

"Look, old man, you need to open that safe," Frank warned, stepping closer to Harry.

"Frank, I need to talk to you," Trish interrupted, walking straight up to him, her eyes bloodshot.

"Not now."

"I need my money. I got nothing now," she said, squeezing Tommy's hand.

"You'll get paid when I pay you, understand?" Frank replied, staring down with contempt at the little boy by her side.

"No, Frank. I need it now. I got responsibilities." She paused to take her handkerchief out of her pocket. "My mother passed last night. I got nobody to help me now."

Harry and Lucy looked in sympathy at Trish, who had now let go of Tommy's hand to blow her nose on a tissue. The little boy stood by her side until something caught the corner of his eye.

"Look, Momma, a kitty cat," Tommy grinned, watching as it walked out into the road.

Frank took another long swig from his beer and leered at her. "Well, maybe you shoulda asked your guy to use somethin' before you opened your legs for him. You wouldn't have been left with that lil' runt then, would ya?" He threw out his arm towards Tommy.

Trish looked at him in horror.

"How can you accuse me of not being careful, Frank, with all the guys you throw at me night after night? I'd have been pregnant a hundred times over if that were the case. No. There has only ever been *one* person I've slept with who never used nothing."

She looked into his eyes and stepped one pace closer.

"*You.*" She paused. "Five years ago."

"What?" Frank breathed, looking down at Tommy as if he was registering the little boy's thick black hair and his familiar-looking steel gray eyes for the very first time.

"He's yours, Frank. Tommy's your son," Trish confirmed.

Marcie emerged from the office.

"What's going on over there?" she shouted, her hand on her hip. "You better not be after any more money, Frank Smith. You've damn near cleaned us out."

"Marcie..." Harry warned, shaking his head at her.

"What? No, Harry, I'm sick of you pussyfooting around that man. It's high time he understood the sleepless nights we've been having with him rinsing our savings whenever he goddamn feels like it," Marcie continued.

"Marcie, I really don't think now is the time..." Shona chipped in after emerging from behind the standpipe. She motioned towards Frank and Trish, who were still staring wordlessly at each other.

"It's exactly the time. Now, you listen to me. Harry's been sick with worry—"

"Yeah? Well, maybe he should be more worried about his brother, my *father*, who's still fightin' to get home. *Maybe* he should think himself lucky he never had to go through what my father had to go through *every goddamn day*—"

"For God's sake, Frank, Harry *is* your father!" Marcie yelled.

Cocking his head to the side and staring at Marcie, then at Harry, Frank could barely take a breath, let alone voice his thoughts. Finally, after what felt like an eternity, Harry nodded.

"It's true. I'm sorry we never told you, but you were so hung up on your fa—" Harry paused. "My brother coming home one day that we—"

"*We?*" Frank at last croaked back.

"Your mother and I." Harry lowered his head in shame once again. "We just didn't have the heart to tell you the truth about him."

"What truth? Come on, you may as well spit it all out now!" Frank roared.

"He wrote your mother three years ago. Said he ain't never coming home." Harry ran his shaking hands through his graying hair. "He made a new life for himself over in Korea after the war ended. He's got a new family now."

Frank's legs crumbled beneath his trembling body. Staggering from side to side, trying to process what Harry was telling him, his emotions were visibly in tatters.

"But that can't be... Why would she still send over the letters I've been writin' him? Huh? Why would she make me go through that if she knew all of this?" Angry tears fought their way out of his blazing eyes. "Wait a minute. Is *that* why he ain't comin' home? Did he know I wasn't his boy, huh? Did he know about you two screwin' behind his back?"

"No, he did not, and you mind your mouth, boy." Harry cast an embarrassed look over to Marcie, who flashed him a reassuring smile. "It was one time almost thirty years ago. That no good brother of mine made her so damn unhappy that she couldn't help but look for some comfort elsewhere."

"But it doesn't make any sense. Why didn't he tell me in his letters back to me?"

"For God's sake, boy, you ain't that dumb, surely. Ain't you figured that one out yet?" Harry yelled at him. "It's your *mother* who's been forging those letters to you."

Norm looked through the front window of the bar at the argument escalating across the street.

"What's goin' on out there, Norm?" Joanie asked, appearing behind him.

"Not sure. But my guess is we're gon' need the law down here soon. Frank looks fit to be tied."

"I'll wait by the phone," Joanie offered, leaving Norm to keep watch.

~

"What the fuck? You lyin' son of a bitch." Frank smashed his empty beer bottle into smithereens on the concrete and launched himself towards Harry.

Yelping, Tommy jumped in shock, then backed away into the road.

Only Shona looked up just in time.

"No... Kid, stop!"

She launched across the road right in the path of a Buick that had rounded the corner so fast there would have been no time for it to brake. Scooping Tommy up in her arms, Shona dove out of the way with only milliseconds to spare.

"Tommy!" Trish screamed, frozen to the spot with fear.

"Shona!" Lucy clamped her hands over her mouth, unable to breathe until she saw Shona safe on the other side of the street, lying on her back with Tommy wrapped up safely in her arms.

"It's OK, It's OK," Shona whispered in Tommy's ear as he clung onto her, terrified from his near miss. Burying his face into her shoulder as Shona walked past Frank, Tommy reached out his tiny arms as she lifted him into Trish's grateful embrace.

"Oh my God, thank you so much. If you hadn't reacted so quickly..." Trish said.

Frank's face had drained of all its color as he tried to process the events of the last five minutes. He stared at Harry and then at Tommy, his world and everything he thought he knew turned completely upside down.

~

A minute had passed before anyone could really speak. Reeling from shock, Frank had run off, leaving everyone else to pick through the debris of the bombs that had just exploded.

"Here. It's not much, but it might help. After all, this little guy... he's my grandson, I guess?" Harry mumbled, handing over a ten-dollar bill to Trish.

"Thank you, Harry. You're a good man," she replied, pocketing the bill. "I'd better get him home. He's had a nasty shock."

Nodding, Harry said his goodbyes, then slung a weary arm around his wife.

"I'm sorry it came out like that, honey. I know you wanted to tell him your own way," Marcie began.

"He had to know," he replied, leading her back into the quiet of the office.

Only Lucy and Shona were left standing in the parking lot.

"You OK? That can't have been easy to hear," Shona said, not quite sure how to comfort Lucy.

"Yeah, I'm fine. Maybe it's for the best all around. We were never gonna last, me and Frank. Who knows, this might make him finally grow up. Well, a bit maybe?" Lucy replied, mirroring Shona's tired smile. "Listen, I'm glad I got to see you this morning. I wanted to say I was sorry... about last night?" Waiting for the recollection to appear on Shona's face, Lucy continued. "It was inappropriate for me to suggest that you and I should... Well, anyway. It was a dumbass thing to say. Will you let me make it up to you?" She walked a pace closer to Shona, who focused her attention on a pebble on the ground. Lucy looked at her, wishing she could explain better, but the words just didn't want to come.

"OK, well, how about you come over and have dinner with me one night this week? Me and Dorothy, that is," Shona replied, looking up from the pebble.

Lucy beamed. "How about tomorrow night? I'll pop over to the diner on my way and pick something up." She grinned after receiving a nod of acceptance, then headed back over to the bar.

Shona watched Lucy depart. After all her years of running, she was starting to feel settled.

She'd finally found not one, but now two friends to brighten her lonely world.

Chapter 32

"Chicken's your favorite, right?" Lucy announced, holding out the still-warm, tin foil package as Shona opened the front door the following evening.

"How d'ya know that?"

"Janine in the diner. Says you order it regular as clockwork."

"You been checking up on me, huh? Well, better not tell Dorothy I said that. I told her nothing beats *her* pie." Shona winked, breathing in its delicious aroma.

"I'll set it down in the kitchen," Lucy offered, heading down the hallway. "Where's Dorothy?"

"Upstairs, just resting. She thought you'd be here a bit later." Shona cast her eyes up to the clock on the hallway wall. It was just after six, only twenty minutes after Shona had returned from cleaning up after the last day of the fair. "You look nice. You got work later?"

Lucy stopped at the kitchen door, her smile fading at Shona's assumption that her new yellow summer dress and white saddle shoes were for the benefit of a customer.

"No, no work tonight. I told Frank I was busy. He didn't seem to care." Lucy's voice lost its bounce. "Don't seem to care about nothing at the moment, not after what he found out yesterday." She turned around. "So, I'm as free as a bird tonight." Placing the pie on the counter, Lucy walked back down the hallway to find Shona in the front room.

"Do you think he's taken it all in yet? You know, having a son and all?" Shona asked, squatting cross-legged on the armrest of the couch.

"I only saw him for a minute. He's pretty much ignored me all day." She sat down on the sagging cushions of the couch at the opposite end to where Shona was perched. "But, anyway. I wanted to ask you something, Shona." Lucy straightened her dress over her knees and swept a strand of light brown hair out of her eyes.

"OK?" Shona replied, folding her arms.

"You seemed pretty jumpy last night. After what I said. About us," Lucy began.

Shona coughed and cleared her throat.

Lucy sighed. "I've never met somebody who is so full of mystery, you know that?" She grinned, shaking her head in disbelief.

"I just keep myself to myself. Better for me that way." Wrapping her arms around herself, Shona breathed in deeply.

"Shona—"

"Shame to let that pie go cold. You hungry?" Shona interrupted. Jumping up from the armrest, she bounded towards the kitchen, with Lucy scurrying behind. "Oh, did you manage to shut the door OK? I still need to fix it properly," Shona called back over her shoulder.

"Um... yeah, I think so," Lucy replied, casting a distracted glance at the door on her way past. "Shall we get Dorothy?"

"No, she's probably fallen asleep by now. She seemed pretty tired this morning. We'll save her some." Shona peeled back the foil of the pie. "Damn, that smells so good," she said, taking the two plates off the drying rack.

"You fit some more in?" Lucy asked, slicing off another piece of pie and lifting it towards Shona's empty plate.

"I wish. That was delicious, but I'm as full as a tick," she replied, leaning back in her dining chair.

"I'll save this for Dorothy then." Lucy folded the foil back over the remaining half of pie and placed it on top of the warm stove. "I don't know about you, but I need a comfier chair to stretch out in while this goes down," she blew her cheeks out as she patted her full stomach.

After each of them plopped down on the couch, they both took a few moments to settle.

"I meant what I said yesterday, Shona. I'm really sorry for what I suggested," Lucy began, playing with the threads on the armrest. She looked up at Shona, then lowered her eyes almost instantly.

"We're better than that. You concentrate on finishing your last week at college and then go do something that makes a difference. Frank don't get to decide anymore what you do. Only *you* do." Shona's eyes glowed as she tried to ignite the spark back into Lucy's downcast face. "Go do what makes you happy, Lucy. You deserve it. Frank's got a new start now. You can have one too."

Lucy placed her hand on Shona's knee, losing herself in her stunningly deep blue gaze. "I don't know if I can. Frank says I'm damaged goods. I've tried so hard to make friends at college, but they're all so different from me. There were times when I'd get home and he would make me feel so bad about myself... He only wanted me to go there so the money would keep coming in from my parents. He never really wanted the best for me. Oh, Shona, I don't know where to start trying to be myself again." She wiped away a tear. "Frank used to say sometimes that I was useless... That I was ugly—"

Shona reached her hand out and clasped it over Lucy's. "Are you serious? You're beautiful. The others in that bar ain't got nothing on you." She squeezed her hand.

"Really?" Lucy wrapped her fingers around Shona's. "It means everything to me that you think that."

"Why?" Shona whispered.

Taking the deepest breath imaginable, Lucy locked eyes once again with Shona. "Because I've wanted to do this for so long..."

Lucy leaned into Shona until their faces were almost touching. At the very last second, she looked up towards the doorway.

Her blood ran ice cold.

~

Holding the piece of splintered wood that had come away in his hand, Chuck looked at Lucy, then at the back of Shona's head, his expression murderous.

Lucy pulled back. "What are you doing, Shona?" she shouted. "I knew it. I knew you were one of those screw-ups." She pushed Shona away from her. "Get off me." She jumped up from the couch with her face twisted in disgust, then backed up towards the wall.

"What?" Shona replied. Turning to look around, she saw the giant hulking figure of Chuck and the three friends he'd brought with him.

"That's all the permission I need. Boys, let's get her," Chuck ordered, launching himself at Shona.

One man jumped over the couch and pinned Shona's arms behind her back. "No, please... Lucy, help me!" Shona screamed.

But Lucy was nowhere to be seen. The door she'd escaped

through was slowly closed behind her by the third of Chuck's friends.

"You come onto *my* turf, bringin' your dirty ways into *my* town, hit on *my* friend's girl..." Chuck spat out, punctuating every accusation with a sickening blow to Shona's stomach, smiling as he heard the first of her ribs crack. He wrapped his pudgy, sweating hand around the back of Shona's head and yanked it up to face him. "I'm gon' tell *everyone* what you are. You're a monster! You won't get away with this. You've been groomin' Lucy for months now, then you go forcin' yourself on her? Now, well *now* you're gon' pay. Boys!" He let go of Shona's hair, wiped his sweaty brow and kicked her to the ground. "She's *all* yours. But make it look like we're robbin' the place. And be quick. Mess some stuff up."

Descending on Shona like wild animals, his friends took turns kicking and punching her until a commotion at the top of the stairs made them freeze.

"Stop that! Stop that *right now*! Get out of my house!" Dorothy shouted down, rattling her stick between the bannisters. "I'm calling the police." Staggering down the stairs, the old woman brandished her stick, hitting it against anything that made enough noise for the attackers to think twice about continuing their assault.

"Come on, Chuck, let's scram." One of his friends grabbed him by the forearm. Chuck snarled, turning to give Shona one last sickening kick to the ribs, then pushing his way past Dorothy who recoiled against the front room doorway.

Sweeping everything they could find off shelves, sideboards and tables, the men ran out of the house. Shona, semi-conscious and bleeding on the carpet, gurgled and coughed as she fought to stay conscious.

Dorothy shuffled over to Shona and knelt painfully at her side. "Come on, girlie, don't you dare think of going to sleep. I'll get the doctor. Stay with me," she pleaded, tapping Shona's face.

As she picked up the receiver to dial the operator, a familiar face appeared at the open door.

"I was just passing," the man said. "I was told there was an injured woman in here?" He spotted Shona on the floor and knelt next to her.

"Oh, thank God you're here, Doctor Henry. Yes, please... Help her," Dorothy begged, her own head starting to feel woolly as the adrenaline started to ebb away. She leaned against the wall and looked at the bloody mess below her.

"Ma'am, we're gon' need an ambulance. Can I use your telephone?"

Chapter 33

Sitting on the bench outside Chasers, Lucy had no idea how she'd gotten there or at what time. Looking up at the clock above the garage doors, she saw it was almost seven a.m. and, after another sleepless night at Trish's house, she felt drained. Unable to take her bloodshot eyes off Wreckers, her heart ached.

"You'll be glad to hear I've put the bar up for sale. You and everyone else in this town, that is. No doubt Whitfield'll make me the lowest offer he can," Frank said as he sloped up next to her.

Shivering from the cool breeze, Lucy vaguely acknowledged his presence. "I don't care anymore, Frank," she murmured.

"You never did really, did you?" He paused. "I heard what happened with Shona. I reckon Chuck did us all a favor riddin' the town of that pervert. All that time you thought she was your friend and all she wanted was to have her dirty way with you? Not nice to find out you've been betrayed, is it? Bet you feel real' stupid now, don'tcha?" Frank taunted.

Lucy shook her head. "Frank, really. You have no idea what you're talking about."

"Hell, she must have been as happy as a pig in mud when

you told her my plan for you two." He shook his head. "Good job Chuck was there that night. I heard he almost killed that bitch to save you. Got himself in a whole heap of trouble now, but I'm sure the police'll see sense."

Lucy let a tear roll down her pale cheek. The lie was killing her. "I guess. What about you, what are you gon' do now?"

"The old man over there said he wants to train me up as one of his clerks. He says I have to be a role model now for my boy. Make an honest buck for once. Fatherly advice, huh?" Frank spat on the ground.

"OK," Lucy said. "What's that?" she asked, looking down at the object in his hand.

"Found this in my stuff. Thought I'd take it round to Trish's, give it to the kid, you know?" He held out a small wooden tractor and spun the wheels with the tip of his index finger. "Had it for years. Don't make much sense to keep it now. You think he'll like it?" There was the tiniest glint of light in Frank's dark eyes as he spoke of Tommy.

"I'm sure he will. I gotta go." Lucy stood up, smoothed her skirt down and walked aimlessly away.

❧

Poking at the bacon on his plate, George exhaled and lay his fork down on the table.

"Honey? What is it? You haven't seemed yourself all mornin'." Gloria lowered the coffee cup from her lips.

"You told me about the letters. You told me why you wrote them. But why didn't you tell me Harry was Frank's real father?" George asked.

"Oh, honey, I didn't mean to keep it from you. I just hoped that one day Harry would tell Frank himself. And I just couldn't bear to see Junior go through any more rejection. I hoped he'd never find out that I was the one writin' the letters and one day

238

he'd understand the gentle hints I was droppin' in them. But he didn't give up on Senior and I just couldn't keep it goin' anymore. He had to know once and for all. Marcie did us all a favor. Least now we all got a chance to put everythin' right." Licking her lips, she put her cup down on the kitchen table and looked at him. "Are we OK?"

"At least now he has a father. Harry's a good man," he replied.

❧

As he walked up to Trish's house, Frank licked his palm and ran it through his already slicked back hair. After straightening his shirt collar, he climbed the few steps up and knocked on the door.

"Frank. Hi," Trish greeted, her eyes red and raw.

"Hi. Look, I know the kid probably won't wanna see me, and hell, I don't blame him, but... Well, can you give him this?" Frank held out the wooden tractor.

Trish looked down at the toy.

"Why don't you come in and give it to him yourself?" Trish leaned back to allow him enough space to pass, but he looked behind her and took one step down.

"Umm..." He paused, then ran a hand through his hair again and over his eyes.

"Momma? Is he here?" Tommy appeared at Trish's side, his little face wide with amazement as he stared up at Frank, who looked down at his son.

"Yeah, baby, your daddy's come to see you. And look, he brought you a toy." She reached down and passed it to her son.

"My pa gave that to me when I was about your age," Frank whispered, kneeling down to face Tommy. The little boy looked down at the toy, then back up, his expression blank. With embarrassed tears pooling in his eyes, Frank got back to his feet and started to stride away.

"Daddy," a tiny voice squeaked.

Frank turned around just in time to catch the running figure of Tommy who jumped into his arms.

Frank gasped, tears streaming down his face. "My son... My son."

Chapter 34

"Please, Dorothy, don't hang up again. I just need to know how Shona is. Please."

Lucy gripped the receiver with both hands, fresh tears tracing their way down through the dry tracks on her cheeks.

"I told you yesterday, she'll be out of hospital in a week or so. But she don't wanna see you, so don't you go down there. The nurses know not to let you anywhere near her." The old lady paused for a moment to wipe her nose. "Shona told me what you did. How could you? After what she's done for you."

"Please... I just need to expl—"

Dorothy clicked the receiver back onto the hook, leaving her hand on it for a few seconds.

"She bought it." She turned around to face Shona standing behind her.

"Thank you, Dorothy," Shona whispered through her cracked lips.

"We got a week or so to get your strength back up, then we'll head to the next town's bus station and get you as far away from here as possible," the old lady continued. "See how you feel in a few days' time, then when you're well enough we'll go at the crack of dawn, before even Buddy wakes up. Just you keep away from the windows and stay indoors, you hear?"

Shona tried to smile but flinched as the effort rippled through her bruised and broken body. "I can't believe I have to hide out, just because of what people think I am. It's not fair, Dorothy. I ain't done nothing wrong." She bit back the tears and stared at the old lady, whose eyes were also brimming.

"I know you ain't, my darlin'. I know."

A week later, the old blue truck rumbled along the road, sounding better than it ever had. Shona was crouched down in her seat, out of sight until they reached the open freeway.

"What are you gonna do now?" Dorothy asked after several minutes of silence between them.

"Keep running. Like I always do," Shona replied, leaning against the windowsill. "I just won't trust anyone again."

The truck hit a pothole, rattling the two of them in their seats. Shona groaned at the burning sensation shooting through her healing ribs. She had escaped with her life that night, but it had been close. After spending two days and nights in the hospital, the swelling around her eyes had finally eased just enough for her to be allowed to go home to Dorothy's, where she'd spent the last week regaining her strength.

"It's so unfair that *you* have to do the running. You ain't done nothing wrong," Dorothy said.

"I'm starting to get used to it now. Don't worry."

"I do worry, Shona. Some things you can't run away from." She looked over but saw only the side of Shona's head as she fixed her gaze on the horizon ahead. "Please, will you just promise me one thing?"

"What?"

"Don't tell *anyone* what you've told me, you hear? Never again."

"I just wished I didn't have to leave. I can't believe Lucy did that to me. I thought she was my friend. But she's been setting me up all this time for some weird kick. She never cared about me." She swallowed hard, the tears of betrayal almost choking her. "I loved it at Wreckers too. What are you gonna say to Harry? I've let him down." She sniffed and wiped her nose on the back of her hand.

"You leave that to me. I'll call him when I get home. I'll tell him you're sorry," Dorothy reassured her.

"I don't know how to thank you for everything, Dorothy. I'm really gonna miss you."

"I'm gon' miss you too, young lady."

Dorothy stared straight ahead, the two of them sitting in silence as they drove the last few miles.

~

"Lucy?"

Wearing a powder pink pencil skirt, silk blouse, matching fitted jacket and pink pillbox hat, Lillian Adamson looked down at the solitary figure sitting on the bench outside the diner. She barely recognized her pale-faced daughter.

Lucy didn't need to look up. Her eyes filled with tears as her mother's soft voice poured into her ear like nectar.

"Mom..." Lucy lifted her eyes. The late morning sun had created a halo of light around her mother's head. "Oh, Mom, I've really messed up this time. I'm so sorry."

"Shhhhh... it's OK, sweetie. We got a long journey back to Monterey so there's plenty of time to talk it all over. Every-thing's going to be alright now, honey, I promise." She crouched down in front of the bench and wrapped her arms around her daughter's painfully thin shoulders. After a minute or so of stroking the back of Lucy's hair, Mrs. Adamson stood up and picked up the heavier one of her daughter's canvas bags. "Come on now, let's get you home."

Slinging her other smaller bag and her purse over her shoulder, Lucy slipped on her cat-eye sunglasses and followed her mother to the car. The moment she saw her sack-suited father standing by their maroon Chrysler Imperial, waiting by the rear door to open it for her, her eyes welled up once more.

His brown eyes, so similar to her own, were now glazed over. The warmth she was used to seeing in them now cold. The hardness in his handsome face was almost too much for Lucy to bear.

"I think you've got some explaining to do, young lady," he said, pressing his lips together as he opened the car door.

"Honey, what is it? You ain't been the same since Mrs. Clark called you this morning," Marcie whispered into her husband's ear, wrapping her arms around his neck. "I know what you're thinking. It don't add up, does it? The whole damn town's calling Shona a 'pervert', but we knew her for over a year and... well, I just can't bring myself to believe it." She shook her head in disbelief.

"Me neither," Harry agreed, taking a long sip from his black coffee. All week he had tried to process the sheer amount of abuse they'd received from the townsfolk who were raging at them for hiring Shona in the first place.

"I blame that Lucy. She was always hanging around here, bugging Shona every day. I wouldn't be surprised if she set this whole damn thing up. Probably jealous of how much Jonny liked Shona and not her, so she got that thug Chuck to take her outta the picture. He always was a loose cannon. From what I heard, he was obsessed with Lucy and would have done anything for her. Police have got at least three other guys who'll testify that he beat them up too—right after he'd seen them in the bar with that girl. He's a damn animal." Marcie screwed up her face as she finished her sentence.

"Then why the goddam hell are we believing *his* version of events, huh? Lucy's gone; so has Shona. There's no one left who can explain what actually happened that night." The more Harry thought about it, the clearer his decision became. "You know what, Marcie, I'm gonna keep my own counsel on this one. Shona was one of the best workers I ever had come through those doors and until I hear a piece of hard evidence of her wrongdoing, she'll always have a special place in my memory."

Harry blinked several times as Marcie slipped her arm through his.

"Me too," she whispered.

~

"So, where to next?" Dorothy asked, passing Shona a string bag containing a couple of soda bottles and two candy bars.

"Just the next state, I think. I'll find my way from there. Do what I always do, I guess."

"At least they've caged that animal Chuck. He always was bad news, but you didn't deserve this." Dorothy's voice quivered.

"Don't help me much now, though. Word would have already spread. People will believe what they wanna believe. Don't matter it's not the truth." Shona paused and wiped her eyes with her palm. "I won't ever be able to set foot in this town again. It'll probably be worse next time."

Hearing the "last call" announcement, Dorothy held onto Shona's arm. They walked slowly over to the bus stand.

"Oh, I almost forgot to give you this." Dorothy fumbled in

her cardigan pocket and pulled out a now-creased postcard. "As you weren't able to make it up those stairs to sleep in your bedroom these last few days, with your ribs the way they are, I thought I'd try to be helpful by packing up your stuff this morning." Dorothy smiled as she held the card close to her chest, trying to break the news to Shona gently. "But I clean forgot to pack those beautiful postcards you had pinned up next to your bed. I know you were really fond of them, especially this one next to your pillow. I know it's your favorite. I remembered the second we were leaving the house, so I grabbed my copy that I had pinned up by the front door. I've still got yours to look at when I get home so it's just fine." Dorothy held out the postcard to Shona.

Holding the postcard in her hands, Shona gazed down at the image of a beautiful white beach house with blue painted window frames and a long veranda that stretched the whole way around. At one corner of the house was a ramp leading down to the white sandy beach below.

"The beach house, Dorothy—"

"The one we stayed at in Gulfport, yeah." Dorothy sniffed, the tears beginning to roll down her cheeks now too.

"You're right, this postcard was always my favorite. Thank you. I'll treasure this. Always. And one day, I'll have my own beach house just like this one and you'll come stay, you hear." She grabbed the old lady and hugged her tightly.

After breaking apart, Dorothy clasped her hands around Shona's face. "You know, your mother would have been so proud of you, Shona," she said. She straightened Shona's jacket collar for her then smoothed down the front of her denim overshirt.

"I miss her so much. I just wish I could talk to her, tell her... You know." Shona ran her fingers over her pink pebble necklace as a lone tear trickled down her face.

"Listen, I will *always* be here for you, OK? Just you make sure you stay safe, write when you can and don't trust *anybody*."

"I won't. Not again."

They hugged, tighter this time, with Shona kissing Dorothy on the cheek, before hauling her weary body up the three steps onto the bus. As it pulled away, Shona waved and took her last glimpse of the old lady, who brandished her stick in the air until the bus finally disappeared out of sight.

Shona leaned back in her seat, not entirely sure what her next move was going to be. How was she going to stay safe this time? She couldn't understand how she had gotten into this situation, just when she had settled, and now she was on the run. Again.

Looking down at her ticket, she ran her finger over the destination printed in black, bold ink. The destination that was chosen simply because it was the first ticket out of town, the place that was to be her next chance of survival, to be invisible: *ALABAMA.*

EPILOGUE

The bus to Alabama had dropped Shona off just over the state border. With the little bit of money she had, she'd found a room for a few nights in a motel, before continuing her journey. The following few weeks were spent doing any odd jobs she could find, moving from farm to farm. They didn't pay much but Shona was content to trade a living wage for a safe, warm place to sleep each night. One week became two and slowly, as time began to pass, the pain she felt from what had happened in Riverside began to ebb away.

Just over six months after leaving Mississippi, Shona found herself, once again, back on the road. She'd found a new place to work, cleaning out barns and tending the livestock in Alabama, staying there until just after Christmas 1957, but sure enough, as time went on, the townsfolk began to ask the questions she was used to people asking her. Sensing they were getting to close to uncovering her secret and keeping true to her word to Dorothy that she'd never trust anyone again, she packed up her satchel in early February 1958 and found herself on the road again.

In front of her, the long featureless highway stretched out

for miles ahead and, with no other option than to keep going, she pulled her cap down low, wrapped her dusty jacket around her and set off on her long walk, through near-darkness, to find another town to call home.

FEEDBACK

Thank you for reading 'Shona'. We hope you enjoyed the book? Please now scan the QR code below to leave your feedback.

• Open the camera or the QR reader application on your smartphone.

    • Point your camera at the QR code to scan the QR code.

    • A notification will pop-up on screen.

    • Click on the notification to open the website link

MEET ME AT 10

Liked *Shona*?

Want to know what happened to her during her time in Alabama?

Read your FREE sneak-peak chapters from book 2: *Meet Me At 10* now to find out...

SOME SECRETS CAN'T STAY HIDDEN

MEET ME AT 10

THE
SEQUEL TO
SHONA

VICKY JONES
AND
CLAIRE HACKNEY

CHAPTER 1

Trudging along the seemingly endless straight road, Shona Jackson shivered as she felt the temperature in the air around her starting to fall. Jagged hills on both sides of the road loomed over her, their interweaving faces sliding down into plush greenery. The emerging crescent moon brought with it fears of being stranded in its wake, surrounded by darkness with her path ahead illuminated only by the occasional glare of speeding truck headlights. Hunger pangs groaning within her reminded Shona that she had little choice but to push onwards in search of civilization.

Running a dry tongue over her parched lips in a vain attempt to lubricate them, she wrapped her coat around her body to keep out the icy chill as the roar of a truck engine sounded in the short distance behind her. She stepped to the side of the road, safely out of the truck's path. She held a hand to her eyes, preparing herself for the expected whoosh from its heavy tires and for the cloud of dust that would no doubt be kicked up by them to choke and blind her temporarily. But there was neither a whoosh nor a dust cloud.

The truck was slowing down.

Its headlights remained on as the truck creaked to a halt,

the driver's hulking silhouette darkly framed by the windshield.

Edging forward, Shona pulled her crumpled cap down to just above her eyebrows and tucked her short blonde hair safely behind her small ears. Nervously, she hooked her thumbs underneath her coat collar, folding it up around the soft skin of her neck and pinching it against her chin.

"Need a lift?" shouted a gravelly voice from the driver's side.

"Um–" she replied in her deepest voice, looking from side to side as she assessed her predicament.

"Look, I ain't got all night, son."

"Sure, thanks."

Stifling a relieved grin at his assumption, Shona reached up for the door handle, climbed up the three steps into the cab and slammed the door. She sat on the passenger seat furthest away from the driver, his malodorous stink making this a necessity if nothing else.

"Where you headin', boy?"

The driver was easier to see now under the cab's overhead strip light. Shona discreetly grimaced as she noticed his pudgy white belly overhanging a pair of ripped jeans, the waistband of which had long since given up the fight. His straggly brown beard appeared to have yesterday's food still clinging to it and dark, grubby sweat patches adorned the armpits of his grimy red t-shirt, completing his stomach-churningly feculent look.

"Just the next town, sir." She lowered her chin as she spoke, hugging her battered old brown satchel close to her chest.

"Well, that ain't no five-minute journey, boy. What the hell y'doin' out here at this time?"

Shona cast a surreptitious glance at the driver's watch. It was 10:55 p.m.

"My ride bailed."

He peered over the bridge of his blotchy red nose at his passenger, an air of suspicion crossing his eyes. He grunted, then returned his attention to the pitch-dark road up ahead. Hoping he wouldn't pry too much, Shona tucked her satchel underneath her weary head and leaned against the door, then pulled her cap down over her eyes. The fingers on her right hand traced along the doorframe until she found the handle as the motion of the truck began to rock her into a deep, well-needed sleep.

~

After what only felt like five minutes to Shona, the truck hit a massive pothole in the road. The driver's subsequent swerve jolted her awake. She rubbed her tired, red eyes and squinted into the bright lights of the oncoming cars, shaking her head a few times to clear it after being snatched from her dream. It was then she looked up at the driver's staring eyes and recoiled in horror when she realized her cap had fallen backward, revealing her heart-shaped face and high cheekbones. Her satchel pillow now lay in the footwell, having dropped from underneath her head after the sharp swerve. Her coat had slipped open, revealing her delicate neck through the open top buttons of her checked shirt, and the thin straps of her bra peeking beyond. Shona, realizing her cover had been blown, buttoned up her shirt as quick as she could and pointlessly straightened her cap.

"You're a *broad*?"

The driver's face contorted with confusion, his nicotine-stained fingers gripping the truck steering wheel as he fought to control the swerve.

"Please, sir, I'm sorry. I didn't intend to trick you. I just wanted to get to the next town, and when you thought I was a guy, I guess I just went along with it." She shrugged.

"What game you playin'? You tryin' to make me look like an idiot?" he growled.

"I didn't mean to. I understand if you don't wanna take me any further." Shona looked through the windshield into the darkness with no way of guessing where in the hell they were. She hunched her knees into her chest and curled up into a ball, shrinking into the darkest corner of the cab.

The driver sat with his eyes fixed on the road ahead, his gray teeth grinding as he shook his head with embarrassment at his earlier assumption. After a few minutes his indignation appeared to fade as he chewed on his bottom lip, seemingly deep in thought.

It wasn't noise this time but silence that woke Shona again that night. Still dark out, the truck was now parked in the middle of nowhere, with no sign of civilization or any kind of landmark. She turned her head left in the hope of gleaning an explanation from the driver, but as she did so her eyes widened with revulsion, the dim light of the cab revealing a sight that turned her stomach.

"What the hell y'doin'?" Shona stared in horror.

The driver had fixed his black beady eyes on her, his body reclined into a more *comfortable* position. His pants were wide open, exposing his fat, hairy thighs. The cab window had misted up from his hot breath as he steadily rocked his hand backward and forward inside his stained underwear.

"There's one way you could earn your ride," he drawled.

Shona kept her eyes on the driver as she tried to plan her next move.

"I'm sorry. I don't want *that*." Holding her left hand up, she reached down to the footwell with the other, feeling around for the strap of her satchel.

"Come over here, help me out, darlin'. You're a real pretty

girl and I've had a long journey." His eyes rolled back in his head.

Scrabbling along the surface of the door, Shona's shaking fingers finally located the metal handle. At that same moment, the driver lunged towards her and dug his dirty nails into her neck, forcing her downwards onto him. Gagging from the stench of his body odor, she struggled with all her might to keep her face out of his lap as he squeezed her throat tightly. She spread her arms out wide, her right hand gripping the dashboard, her left clinging desperately onto the seat next to him as she fought to stop him entering her mouth.

"No!" she squealed.

As the driver's arousal reached fever pitch, his grip began to increase in pressure around the back of her thin neck. With a frustrated grunt and a fistful of Shona's messy blonde hair, he jolted her head fiercely, causing her sweaty hand to slip from the dashboard. Shona's head fell forward, but instead of falling onto his lap, she found herself met with the top of his chubby thigh. Instinctively, she bit down on it so hard that within seconds the rancid taste of blood oozed into her mouth. Yelping in white-hot agony, the driver lashed out, punching her square on the right side of her jaw. Flying back into her seat, she slammed her head against the door window, cracking the thick glass. Through blurred vision, she watched the driver grimace as he tucked himself away, inspected his injured thigh, then wiped his bloody hands on his grubby jeans.

With the driver distracted, Shona grabbed her satchel and wrapped her fingers around the door handle. Her heart pounded as she took a final look across at the driver, who was now staring murderously at her as he tried to stem the blood flowing freely from his bitten thigh. His face twisted in pain as he buttoned up his jeans, then bent forward and reached into the glove box. Panicking, she pressed heavily against the door, relieved to hear its hinges groan as it opened behind her, sending bitingly cold air rushing into the stuffy cab. She stumbled down the steps, landing in a crumpled heap on the ground. With a tight hold on her satchel, Shona sprinted away as fast as her trembling legs could carry her.

Running in a zigzag formation, she ducked as the crack of a gunshot pierced the silent night air and whizzed inches past her ear. Then another. Then a third. She dropped to her knees behind a mound of fallen rocks to catch her breath, listening for any further shots. In the distance, she heard the truck's engine restarting and then the whoosh of wheel-spinning tires as it skidded away, its headlight beams disappearing into the bitterly cold night.

A few hours and several miles later, Shona sighed with relief as the dawn finally began to break. Tentatively, she touched the back of her throbbing head with her fingers, groaning when she saw the dark red blood that had coated them.

Just as her exhaustion threatened to overwhelm her, she spotted a river in the distance. Knowing it had to lead into a town somewhere, she headed towards it. With the sun beginning to pour its light into the sky, landmarks that the darkness had hidden were now illuminated. She could see a shed-like building on the horizon and began to make her way over to it, treading cautiously over uneven rocks littering her path. Approaching the shack with caution, she reached out for the latch on the wooden door, hearing a welcome click as it bore no resistance. Over in the far corner, a small pile of hay looked as good a place as any to snuggle down and get some longed-for rest. She lay down, placed her satchel underneath her pounding head and instantly fell sound asleep.

CHAPTER 2

"Who the hell are you?"

Shona jolted awake as the metal barrel of a shotgun cast its long shadow over her.

"What? Oh, I'm sorry, sir. I was dog-tired last night. I've been traveling and I found this place. I'll move on, I'm sorry–" she sat upright and reached for her satchel.

"Don't you move, not one inch. You plannin' on stealing my animals?" He edged closer, the shadow of his gun now crossing the beam of sunlight that had been burning her dry eyes. An old man, with tousled white hair and weathered skin, stood glaring at her.

"No way, sir, I just needed to rest."

She held her hands up in surrender for the second time in less than six hours.

"Get up." He gestured with his gun, keeping his suspicious eyes fixed on the young blonde girl he'd found on his property. Shona rose, wobbling slightly from the ache still thundering around the back of her head. He lowered his gun a little and backed up until he was almost outside the shack. In the dawn light, his sharp gray eyes softened when he saw the girl he was pointing his shotgun at was injured.

"You been in a fight or something?" He furrowed his brow, noticing the angry bruise on her right cheek.

"Some jerk tried to attack me. I ran, and I been hiding out here to rest until I move on, sir." Her bright blue eyes pleaded with him for mercy.

He lowered his rifle, his aggression towards her waning. "Well, you won't get much rest out here. The cows are gon' want that bale of hay you're lyin' on for their breakfast soon. Come back to the house. M'wife can make you some food for your journey. I'm Tom, Tom Bird, and you are?" He unloaded the cartridges from his shotgun, placed them in his top shirt pocket and slung the open gun over his forearm.

"Shona Jackson, sir."

"Would you like some more sweet tea?"

Ruby Bird's smile had straight away put Shona at ease after Tom returned to the house for his breakfast with a stray in tow. She put down the jug in front of her guest, readjusted the handmade shawl that was draped around her neck and smoothed back a lock of graying hair into the bun on top of her head as she busied herself in the kitchen, ensuring there was plenty of food on the table.

"Thank you, Mrs. Bird."

"Please, call me Ruby," she said, tapping Shona's forearm.

"So, Shona...heck, that's a strange name for these parts. How'd you end up with that one?" Tom chuckled as he buttered his toast.

"Well, sir, my momma had some real good friends when she was a girl, called Shane and Fiona. They came over from Ireland, y'see, to start a new life. So, I guess when I came along she just decided to honor them by namin' me *Shona*. Heck, I guess y'could say I'm all mixed up!" She grinned back at Tom, who nodded his head and took a huge bite of his toast.

"So, what's next for you, lil' lady? What are your plans?"

"Not sure really, sir. Just keep on movin' on until I figure somethin' out." Her voice tailed off. She had no idea where the hell she was.

"Tom, call me Tom. I'm not one for formalities," he said.

Shona smiled. "OK, Tom. I don't have any exact plans. It was just to find a job, somewhere to sleep. Live the simple life, y'know?" She leaned forward to take another bite of her toast, her elbows planted firmly on the table.

"Can you sew?" Ruby asked as she sipped her coffee.

"Pardon me, ma'am?" Shona spluttered.

"Can you mend clothes?" she elaborated.

"I'm sorry, no ... but I can mend vehicles, any kind you put in front of me! I may be a girl, only twenny-four, but I know more about trucks than any man. I can ride too, tame any damn horse you give me, I swear I can." Her keen eyes shone.

Looking at each other, Ruby and Tom chuckled at her enthusiasm, overlooking the fact that she was chewing her toast heartily with no regard for table manners.

"Where you from, Shona?" Ruby asked, clearing the breakfast plates off the red and white gingham tablecloth.

"Claybank, Louisiana, ma'am."

"Never heard of it." Tom took another bite of his toast.

"Nobody has." Shona chuckled. "It's a small town. I worked on a farm with my father until I was sixteen."

"Why'd you leave?" Ruby asked, sitting back down to face her.

"Yeah, and how the hell did y'end up all the way out here in Alabama?" Tom added.

Shona's smile faded. "See now, that's a long story."

CHAPTER 3

"Linda!"

Larry Bruce bellowed at the top of his voice in the direction of his secretary, who was working away at her desk.

"Yes, Mr. Bruce." She raced over to his office and cowered in the doorway, peering at him over the top of her narrow-framed glasses.

"Linda, get the sheriff on the phone right now! Tell him to come straight over here," he growled, eyeballing the three terrified men standing in front of him.

"Right away, Mr. Bruce," she squeaked, adjusting her glasses to write down a quick note on her miniature notepad, then hopping back to her office.

Bruce's mustache bristled with anger as he glared at the men in front of him. One had beads of sweat on his forehead which slithered down his nose, his eyes wild with panic.

"Sir ... please, may I speak?" he begged.

"Shut your damn filthy mouth, you son'bitch," Bruce spat. "Y'go crawling to Ellis for a job, knowing he's the easy touch when it comes to you coloreds, then have the audacity to thieve wallets from the good, honest white folk here?"

Bruce erupted out of his chair and glared at the petrified

man. "I hope they rip your ass apart in prison where you belong, all chained up!"

"Mr. Bruce, I swear to Almighty God, I don't know about no wallets. Ain't seen 'em, none of us have!" The sweating black man fell to his knees.

"Get your sorry ass up." Bruce flicked his booted foot at him.

In desperation, the man dragged himself upright and stood next to the two others. The elder of the three looked towards Larry Bruce but dared not make eye contact. Instead, he focused on a large, elegantly framed photograph of a smiling young man on the wall above Bruce's head.

"Mr. Bruce, sir, I promise on my own dead son's grave. We ain't taken those wallets. Search us, search our bags, search our lockers."

Larry Bruce smirked.

Ten minutes later, Linda's voice rang out again from just outside the door.

"Mr. Bruce, sir, the sheriff's here."

Sheriff Landon's intimidating figure almost filled the doorway as he entered Bruce's office, flanked by his scrawny-looking deputy.

"Y'know what to do, sheriff. I'll leave this matter in your ... capable hands." Bruce winked at Landon who responded with a tip of his hat. He unclasped the small leather strap holding his revolver in its holster and motioned to his deputy to slap the iron handcuffs onto the black men, so weak with dread that they didn't struggle as they were led off.

"Anything else, Mr. Bruce?" Linda asked, about to return to her desk.

"No, thank you. Close the door behind you," Bruce replied, opening his desk drawer to retrieve his ever-present bottle of whiskey. Underneath the bottle, three black leather wallets he'd arranged that morning to be taken from the lockers of his workers nestled snugly underneath. Pouring himself a large measure, he slouched back in his chair and swigged it down in one deep gulp, smiling to himself in satisfaction at an excellent afternoon's work. It was his mission to rid his business of colored workers.

His plan had been a success so far.

CHAPTER 4

"This is Storm."

Tom patted the neck of the feisty chestnut-colored mare stomping her hooves on the ground next to her stable as if she were about to be let loose in a race. He and Shona were standing in the back field behind the farmhouse, a stunning expanse stretching as far as the eye could see. Their shadows lengthened as the afternoon sun lowered in the clear sky.

"Storm?" her eyebrows raised.

"Yep, every time we let her out, she moves like a damn whirlwind. This beast really is untamable." Tom held on tightly to the reins as Storm bucked at him, proving his point.

Shona laughed and patted the animal who threw her head to the side in response, almost taking Shona's arm out its socket. She back-kicked the wall of her stable door several times, sending loud thuds echoing across the flat ground.

"Yeah, I can see that," Shona grinned.

She scanned her eyes over the landscape that surrounded her. It headed down towards the Weaver, a fast-flowing river with gorgeous Cahaba lilies and wildflowers blooming on its banks. The Birds' land was used for growing crops and grazing their farm animals, generating most of their stable but meager income. Tom smiled as he left her lost in her faraway thoughts.

When she returned to the farmhouse a while later, she sensed she'd interrupted Tom and Ruby talking in the kitchen. She turned on her heel to head back outside.

"Shona, wait!" Ruby gestured towards her. "Tom and I have just spoken, and we wanted to ask if you would like to stay here a night or two, just until you find yourself somewhere more permanent, I mean. We'll have to clear some space in the barn across the way, but it's warm."

"Really?" Shona couldn't contain her excitement long enough to even allow Ruby to complete her offer. "My God, yes, please! I'll help with the animals for my keep. I don't have no money yet, but–"

"That's OK. Ruby and I would just appreciate any help you can give on the farm. We're not getting any younger!" Tom glanced over at his wife, a cheeky smile sweeping over his kindly face.

"Speak for yourself, Bird!" Ruby jabbed a finger into his belly.

"I'd like that. I surely would. Thank y'all so much!" Shona beamed, leaping at Tom and Ruby and wrapping them both in a tight hug.

CHAPTER 5

"Mr. Bruce, sir! What an honor to be chosen to work alongside a fine gentleman such as yourself, who I respect and, quite frankly, am in awe of."

The dashingly handsome Kyle Chambers ran a hand over his perfectly coiffed jet black hair and flashed a well-rehearsed smile exposing his bright white teeth as he extended his muscular arm to shake Larry Bruce's hand. He wore his best gray flannel suit, white button-down collar shirt and tapered, pleatless pants. Aiming to impress his new boss, Kyle's outfit was completed by a striped tie and shiny black leather wing-tipped shoes. At thirty-four years old, he knew he was finally onto a good thing as he glanced eagerly around Bruce's lavishly decorated office.

"I'm sure you'll do well here, Kyle. I like the way y'think. Hell, you remind me of myself at your age," Bruce replied, walking around the back of his desk.

"Thank you, sir." Kyle felt the swell of confidence grow larger in his belly.

"Great. I'll ask Linda to give you details of when you'll start work. By then, my daughter Chloe will be home from college. She's gon' be my number two, but y'know, we'll see how you do and who knows," Bruce said, pouring a celebratory drink for the two of them. "I'll be training her to help run this place once I retire, but I need a man to, y'know, take this company forward. I mean, who in the hell heard of a woman being in charge? Investors would run a mile. But she's my only child to pass my half of this place on to after my son died five years ago. Just twenty-three years old he was."

Bruce paused for a moment, remembering the tragic day he'd found his son lying dead in a pool of blood, his arm ripped clean off by the threshing machine a colored worker was trapped in. He'd never come to terms with the fact that the colored man had lived and his son hadn't.

"I won't let you down, sir!" Kyle assured him.

~

Ruby joined Tom and Shona in the sparsely furnished barn, her arms laden with cotton towels and thick flowery blankets to make the place feel more like home. A weary-looking single mattress lay on top of some wooden pallets, keeping it off the hay-strewn floor. It wasn't much, but it was more than Shona had had in a long time.

Perfect, she thought.

"Shona, do you wear dresses at all?" Ruby asked, trying to be as tactful as she could.

"Dresses? No, ma'am, I don't. I guess I dress like I do 'cos I travel around so much. That way, guys don't give me no trouble, y'know?" Her cheeks flushed bright red.

"I was only asking as I could fix you a few new things to wear if you like? I saw you only had a little bag, so–"

Ruby gestured towards the battered-looking satchel lying on the floor next to Shona's new bed.

"Well, Shona, until Ruby here can make you some other kinda clothes, I'll lend you some pants, shirts, overalls and stuff.

Will that make you feel more comfortable?" Tom smiled, sensing her embarrassment.

"I'd really like that, thank you," she replied.

Clearing space and tidying the area, they smiled at each other as they created a little haven for Shona and basked in the warm glow of the longed-for family feeling that was enveloping the three of them.

CHAPTER 6

"Larry? What can I do for you?"

Jeffrey Ellis poured himself a glass of his finest red wine from a crystal decanter, relaxing in his chair in the palatial home he shared with his wife Marjory, who was resting upstairs after another bout of illness. Holding the phone to his ear, he sipped his wine, savoring its flavor.

"I've had to get rid of those damn coloreds you sent my way. They've been thievin'." Bruce tried hard to sound disappointed.

"What?" Ellis lowered his glass. "I heard good things from the guy they came from. You sure?"

"Oh, yeah, I turned them over to the sheriff like the last ones. You can't change 'em. They don't appreciate what you're tryin' to do for them, Jeffrey," Bruce continued in feigned dismay.

Ellis reclined back in his chair, deciding, as usual, to give Bruce the benefit of the heavy doubt.

"Fine. Got anything else for me?"

"You know about us taking on Kyle Chambers. I think he'll do well. Other than that, the numbers are looking good. There is one thing; I'm looking to buy some replacement machinery. Damn tractors keep breaking down, so I'll need to buy new parts. We can't keep up with the orders if things ain't working right!"

"Sure, go ahead. I dropped some cash off on my last visit. There should be plenty in the safe."

"That's great, Jeffrey. Oh, and say hi to Marj for me. I hope she's feeling better soon."

"OK, Larry, see you when I'm next in the office."

Ellis put the phone down and drained the last of his wine. Bruce sat back in his chair, a satisfied smile creeping over his face.

CHAPTER 7

"D'you know anywhere I could find work 'round these parts?" Shona asked, glancing up from the hearty breakfast Ruby had prepared the following morning.

"Tom?" Ruby aimed her spatula in his direction as she heated up the pan to fry more eggs.

"Daynes is a tough town, Shona. I mean, opinions have changed a little since the war ended, but it's still pretty much unheard of having a woman working with trucks, even one as hardworking as you. I know your old place back in Mississippi let you, but that's rare. There are some bone-idle people in this town, but they'd rather die than let a slip of a girl show 'em how to do their job properly! But we're only a coupla years away from the '60s so who knows, maybe things'll change."

"Want some more?" Ruby put the freshly fried eggs in the serving dish next to Shona's plate as if to offer some crumb of comfort.

Tom put down his knife and fork and wiped his mouth with his napkin. "Well now, see, there's this one place over the other side of town, coupla miles from here. I mean, I ain't worked there or nothin', but I've heard from people. They got trucks, tractors, you name it coming and going. It's a cotton plantation with a workshop on the side doing repairs and stuff. All depends if you get the chance to speak to the *nice* guy."

"Nice guy?" Shona said.

"Yeah, his name's Jeffrey Ellis. He co-owns the business but lets that no-good Larry Bruce run it day-to-day. It's Ellis you need to find. Don't bother speaking to Bruce. The things I've heard about that man would make your hair curl! He runs the whole of Daynes through fear alone. Me and Ruby try to stay away from town as much as we can nowadays, away from that son'bitch's influence. Ruby used to be the town's nurse until about five years ago, but then Bruce made the place feel so damn dangerous for her to be out at night on call. Nah, it's Ellis you want. I hear that even coloreds get a job after speaking to him–"

"Ellis tries to give 'em a chance first, y'know?" Ruby chipped in, trying to sound optimistic.

Shona leaned forward, drinking in every word. Her keen blue eyes widened at the prospect of getting a job that would help her to stay longer with Tom and Ruby and allow her to save some money to figure out her next move. After a few moments of contemplation, she raised her eyes to Tom and Ruby.

"Where can I find this Jeffrey Ellis?"

CHAPTER 8

"Hayward, what the hell's in your glass? You're talkin' like you're drunk already."

Henry Conway stubbed out his ever-present cigar in the ash tray next to him later that evening as he laughed at another ridiculous idea coming from James Hayward, a man notorious for his harebrained schemes to make even more money for himself. The two men frequented the Copperpot Inn weekly to meet with Jeffrey Ellis and discuss their numerous investment deals. It was a high-end establishment, known for its select clientele and innate respect for privacy. Hayward and Conway were Ellis's business acquaintances, but he'd over the years tried to distance himself from their vacuous *double-your-money* scams and instead build a business he could be proud of.

"Can I help you ... *Miss*?" The immaculately presented woman at the front of the house pursed her lips as she eyed the visitor up and down. Shona flicked her floppy blonde bangs out of her eyes and stood up straight, pulling at her clothes to try and make herself look more presentable. She was grateful that Ruby had expertly altered one of Tom's shirts for her.

"Hello ma'am, I'd like to talk to Mr. Ellis, please." She flashed a bright smile.

"Does he know you?" The woman raised a perfectly-shaped eyebrow in disgust.

Shona took in a calming breath. "I just need a minute of his time, ma'am."

"This is an *exclusive* members' bar that is men-only. Mr. Ellis is our most valued customer and we won't see him being disturbed by the likes of ... you."

"Ma'am, I just need to talk to him."

"I will have you removed if you do not leave!"

This last interaction stopped the group of men mid-conversation. One of them, Brian Carson, went over to see what the problem was.

"Hey Gracie, you OK? She causin' you trouble?" He nodded his head towards Shona.

"Sir, I just need to speak to Mr. Ellis."

"What could the likes of you possibly want with Mr. Ellis?" Carson replied, curling his lip.

Ellis's name being spoken made his ears prick up. "What's going on over there?"

"Nothing, sir, it's all under control." He turned his head away from Shona, who, at that moment, saw her opportunity.

In one fluid motion, she ducked and headed straight for Ellis. Carson awkwardly rotated his body, reaching out to grab a fistful of Shona's shirt as she passed, but she wriggled free before he could wrap his arm around her. In two seconds, she was at Ellis's table, a swirling mixture of eagerness, nerves and adrenaline pulsating through her body. Carson raced after her, red-faced with frustration for not containing the menace that Shona had become.

"Sir, Mr. Ellis–" Shona gasped. As she opened her mouth to continue, Carson wrestled her into a headlock.

"Get off me!" she shrieked.

"Let her go. She's a woman, for Christ's sake." Ellis stood up sharply.

He snarled as he shoved Shona loose, almost knocking her into the empty glasses on the table.

"Thank you," she panted, rubbing her reddened neck. "I didn't mean to disturb you, sir. I just heard that you're a real nice guy and you've given people chances to work–" she looked intently at him.

"All this and you're looking for a *job*?" Ellis sat back down, his inquisitive eyes fixed on her.

"Yessir. I am." Shona set her jaw.

"The thing is–" Ellis rolled his hand, prompting her for her name.

"Shona."

"The thing is, Shona, I already have a wonderful secretary. I just don't have a job for you," he shrugged.

"No, sir, you don't understand, I can work on your trucks! I can repair any vehicle you put in front of me! I can work in the fields picking the cotton like I used to do with my father. I'll be the hardest worker you've ever had." She punched her fist into her other hand, ignoring the derisory sniggers around her.

"*Trucks*? I must be drunk hearing this trash." Hayward took another swig of his spirit.

"I'm serious, sir. I wouldn't let you down," she continued.

The tables' gaze switched from Shona to Ellis. After a lengthy pause, he finally spoke.

"I give chances to people who won't waste 'em, young lady. I can show 'em through the door, but then it's up to them. If they steal, they're out. They don't show up for work one day, they're out. If they're late, they're out. They refuse *any* kind of work given to 'em, Mr. Bruce has my blessing to toss them out. It's tough in there."

"I can handle it, sir," Shona assured him. "I've worked with men before. They'll see how hard I work. I just need the chance...please?"

Ellis's fingers were interlocked, his elbows planted on the

table, the tips of his two index fingers resting against his pursed lip. He admired the courage of this young girl, who had fought her way to stand in front of him. "Shona, I'm gon' give you a chance. It's up to you from here. I'll arrange for somebody to let Mr. Bruce know. You can start Monday morning. Report at the front desk at 6:30, OK? Don't you be late!"

Her face erupted into a huge grin. "Mr. Ellis, I swear I won't let you down, sir ... I promise! Thank you!" She tried to contain her excitement but it was impossible. Turning to leave, she grinned even wider as she passed the astonished front of house assistant at the door.

"You do realize, Jeffrey, you've just fed that lil' girl to a pack of damn wolves. God help her!" Hayward whispered to Ellis who silently watched Shona exit the Copperpot.

CHAPTER 9

"Get that son of a bitch!"

That same evening, the elder of the three huntsmen led through the open fields of Daynes, three miles from the Ellis and Bruce site. They were closing in on their target, but he was too fast. He needed to be. He was dead if they caught him.

Stopping for a moment, he looked frantically from side to side. Panting and sweating profusely, he placed his hands on his knees as panic raged through his exhausted body. The three men had split up and strategically blocked off his exit, closing in around him and pushing him closer to the edge of the rushing Weaver. In the distance, the escaping man could hear the unmistakable sound of ferocious barking.

"Let him go, boy!"

Turning around, he watched in horror as a bloodthirsty canine headed straight for him, baring its razor-sharp teeth. On the last dregs of adrenaline, the man raced towards the end of the field straight ahead, his lungs perilously close to giving up on him.

"Stop him before he gets to the river, boys!"

With fatigue finally overpowering him, he fell to the ground, causing a cloud of dust to billow up from his crashing boots and give away his position. The men shined their flashlight in his direction, dustcloud particles catching in the beams. Dragging himself up, the target hopped forward a few more steps. Mercifully, he saw he'd reached the riverbank.

He was almost safe.

Suddenly, a searing pain flooded through the back of his right thigh. In agony, he looked behind him, his wide eyes meeting those of a massive Alsatian hound hell-bent on stripping the flesh clean from his leg. Its ferocious teeth glinted in the half-light, its mouth frothing as it locked its jaws on the man's bleeding thigh.

With no choice, he tore his leg out of the jaws of the beast, screaming as he did so. He jumped off the bank three feet down into the river heading to God knows where, but it had to be better than here. Keeping his head underwater for as long as he could, he fought against the strong current, trying to avoid getting knocked out by the rocks as it swept him downstream.

Giving up their pursuit, the three men and barking hound melted away into the evening. The target of their sport waited until it was completely silent before emerging from the cool waters of the Weaver, immediately feeling the intense sting rushing through his mangled leg as he continued on through the brush to find a safe place to sleep.

He was one of the lucky ones.

CHAPTER 10

"S'cuse me, I start work here today?"

Shona spoke loudly in the direction of the office behind the front desk that Monday morning. Through the half-open door she heard muffled voices, the occasional laugh and bad language, but she didn't care.

"Well, look what we got here," one of the voices eventually emerged. The man it belonged to leered at Shona, a sly grin breaking out over his unshaven face as he chewed a mouthful of tobacco.

"Mr. Ellis told me to report here and that somebody would show me around so I can get straight to work on the trucks," Shona said brightly.

"Did he now? Good ol' Mr. Ellis, he's really lost his mind this time! Boys, get out here, you gotta see this."

Two other guys appeared and stared open-mouthed at the slim, blonde-haired, pretty young woman. She wore baggy blue mechanic's overalls, which on anyone else would look grungy, but Shona's perfect figure wore them well. One of the men had no shame in ogling her, his greasy black hair flopping over his seedy eyes as he mentally undressed her.

"What can we do for you, sweetheart?"

"I'm here to work on the trucks? If you show me where I need to go, I'll start straight away," Shona replied, trying hard to mask her disgust.

"Well, I'll be damned. I thought you were our new cleaning lady! Hey Paul, you gotta see this!" All three laughed loudly.

"Mr. Ellis said I could," Shona said, straightening her back.

"Oh, did he now? You and Mr. Ellis *good* friends, then?" The first man leaned over the counter.

"I just came to work. I don't want no trouble." She raised her voice, bored with being a figure of fun now.

"What's goin' on out there? Who are you?" Paul, the workforce deputy, pushed open the door of the office behind the counter.

"I'm Shona Jackson, sir. Mr. Ellis told me to report here at 6:30 and I'd be working on the vehicles or in the fields?"

Deputy Paul's cold eyes narrowed as he rested his hand on his hip.

"Yeah, I heard about you. I don't know what game you're playing, lil' lady. This ain't no place for a broad. But Ellis is the boss and orders are orders. Come with me," he sighed.

"This is where you'll get changed."

Deputy Paul opened a small room containing brooms, buckets and old equipment. It was dark and damp with broken cupboards and shelves that were chipped and falling down. Later, he ended the tour just outside a messy tool room. "Wait in here." He pointed to a cluttered bench and, as Shona stepped inside, he disappeared.

Alone, she looked up at the clock on the wall. It was already 7:25 a.m. *Where was everybody?*

Almost gagging from the musty odors in the room, she opened the metal back door leading to the fields behind the site to let the fresh air in. Bored, Shona began to tidy, almost jumping out of her skin when a loud buzzer sounded at 10 o'clock. She stopped cleaning down the benches when she heard the sound of upbeat voices passing by outside the tool room door, which could only mean one thing in a place like this – break time!

Thinking that this would be the best time to find someone who knew what was going on, Shona yanked the handle of the rickety metal door back towards her to secure the room. As she did so, a strange noise outside caught her attention. It came from behind a large mound of used tires beside the doorway.

"Hello?" She paused as she glimpsed the worn-out boots of someone who seemed desperate to remain out of sight.

"You OK?" Shona asked. The feet quickly disappeared from view. She raised her eyebrows, then edged closer. It was then that she saw the pitiful shape of a man cowering.

He didn't get up, but just sat with his head bowed. He was reluctant to make eye contact, his dark brown face wet with fresh tears.

"Who are you?" Shona asked, wearing her sternest face. She was mindful not to get too close.

"Cuban–" He sniffed. "My name is Cuban, ma'am. I just wanted to get some water from this faucet. I don't want no trouble."

He shifted positions on the gravel, wincing as he exposed the dark red blood pool underneath his right thigh.

"You're bleedin'," she noticed, her eyes softening.

"I got chased. I managed to outrun 'em but then I got bit by the goddamn dirty dog they set on me. I'm lucky, I got away. Lord only knows how but I did." He coughed and winced again.

"Who's out there?" a scratchy old voice called out from inside the tool room. Both Shona and Cuban froze.

"It's just me–" Shona shouted back, her eyes still fixed on the colored man below her.

The half-open metal back door to the tool room groaned on its rusty hinges as an elderly man stepped outside. His wispy white hair peeked out from underneath his tatty gray cap, and his eyebrows raised in surprise at Shona.

"Who are you?"

"I'm Shona. I start work here today."

Open mouthed, he looked down at her clothes.

"Workin' here? Doin' what?"

"I can repair trucks," Shona replied brightly.

He paused, staring at her. "Who's this?" His eyes diverted as he motioned his leathery hand downwards.

"I'm Cuban, sir."

He struggled to his feet, limping on his injured leg. As he stood up, Shona realized how tall this man was, well over six feet even with his back arched in discomfort. His hands had obviously not shirked hard work in the past. Thick, calloused fingers rested on his blood-drenched pant leg, his open-necked work shirt revealing a necklace with a small crucifix on it. She could sense the sadness within him but she was not ready yet to trust this stranger.

"I'm Elbie. You, young lady, must have really sweet-talked Mr. Ellis to get in here." He smiled at Shona, then turned to Cuban with a much graver look on his weathered face.

"See you bleedin' quite badly there. I can help fix you up but that'll be the least of your problems. Thugs 'round these parts huntin' black folks like you for sport. You should keep movin' on," Elbie warned.

Cuban shifted his weight, looking uncomfortable from the throbbing pain in his thigh.

"I know what it's like 'round here, sir, don't need no lecture. I seen this town for what it is. No one need tell me what I got to lose!"

Elbie and Shona listened in silence, Cuban's words piercing the heart of their uncertainty.

"Let's have a look at that leg, get you patched up. Shona, take his arm."

Together, they half-dragged Cuban inside the tool room and sat him on a stool.

"Hand me that box over there, will you," Elbie pointed to the shelf in the corner of the room. Shona returned with the first aid box, still not wanting to engage too much with the colored man. She'd always been told by her father they were never to be trusted, but Shona never knew which of his drunken tales to believe. She was on her guard, though, just in case he was right on this one.

Elbie finished cleaning and dressing Cuban's wounded leg, using up half of the first aid box's supplies to stem the bleeding. He knew the man needed stitches but judging by how quickly Cuban pulled his pants up and thanked Elbie for his trouble, he knew he wasn't willing to go to the hospital.

"Alright, now that we got that dealt with, I'd like to know who the hell's been moving things around in this tool room, huh?" Elbie frowned.

Shona held her breath.

"Well, I guess that was me, sir." She ran her hand through her hair, sweeping it out of her eyes. "You see, they left me here to wait for my orders and I don't like to be idle. I was just tryin' to clean the place up a bit–" Shona was rambling now.

"Whoa there–" Elbie held his hands up. "I was just gon' say thanks, it looks good! Folks normally treat this room like a dump. Just one thing, though, I don't want you goin' in the workshop back there, 'cos that's *my* space, got it?" the old man warned as he hooked his thumb over his shoulder.

Minutes later, the conversation paused as the three of them turned their heads to the doorway where Deputy Paul appeared.

"You got visitors, Jackson!" He flashed his dirty gray teeth in mock pleasure, tipping his head towards the voices behind him.

It was Larry Bruce and Jeffrey Ellis.

"Ah, there she is! Just wanted to see how my new girl was doing on her first day." Ellis approached Shona, followed closely by Bruce. Shona turned her head to smile her response but, as she did so, a colored face was revealed behind her.

"What the *fuck* is *that*?" Bruce snapped.

Before she realized what she was doing, Shona intervened.

"He just wanted to speak to Mr. Ellis about a job, sir."

Cuban held his breath but Shona continued, mesmerizing him with her bravery.

"Instead of sitting 'round doin' nothing, sir, I watched him clean the whole tool room! Look, see–" Shona held her arms out wide. She had no idea why she was speaking up for him, but she couldn't unsee the look of dread that was etched on Cuban's face when Bruce had spotted him.

"Shona, you not been put to work yet?" Ellis frowned.

"No, sir, I was told to wait here."

Ellis switched his attention to Deputy Paul.

"We can get her cleanin', scrubbin'–" Deputy Paul shrugged.

"Trucks," Ellis interrupted. "I want her on trucks. Let's see what she can do."

Bruce glared at Ellis.

"That one just come in?" Ellis pointed out of the tool room window at a white truck being winched off a low-loader, then dropped to the ground outside. Outwardly, it looked reasonably sound but the fact that it hadn't driven itself there didn't bode well for it. Three mechanics surrounded the stricken vehicle, scratching their heads. One stubbed out his cigarette, took out his wrench and motioned to the other two to pop the hood.

Deputy Paul nodded. "Yessir."

"See if you can get it goin'," Ellis smiled at Shona.

"Jeffrey, you lost your mind?" Bruce said in a low voice.

The group walked outside towards the truck. The mechanics attending it looked perplexed as to why the truck was resisting all their best efforts to spark it into life. The engine's problem seemed a bit of an enigma, but this didn't faze Shona. She approached Deputy Paul and gestured for the keys, his stare burning a hole in her head as he dropped them into her hand. Bruce smirked as they waited for her embarrassment to commence. Ellis exhaled, hoping she wouldn't disappoint him.

"This vehicle's expensive, y'understand?" Deputy Paul snarled.

Ellis folded his arms as Shona got to work. She stuck her head under the hood and tinkered about. Clanks and clonks sounded from the engine bay as she investigated the manifolds, sprockets and gaskets. Little grunts and groans emitted from her as she tightened her wrench around the bolts and metal tubes.

Five long minutes passed.

Shona was done. She climbed up into the driver's seat and slid the key into the ignition as everyone in the group held their breath. The engine coughed for a few seconds and then soluttered into life, black smoke billowing from the exhaust. Before long, the truck was purring like a kitten.

"Well, I'll be *damned*," Ellis blew out his cheeks.

Closing his eyes, Bruce shook his head.

"So what? Pull a few wires, flick a few switches? That's the easiest damn job you coulda given her!" He was furious.

His attention, however, soon moved away from her and, like a searchlight in the darkness, landed on Cuban who was smiling at Shona's success. He'd enjoyed the few brief moments of blending in with the crowd, but it couldn't last. Cuban met Bruce's fiery eyes, panic fizzing in the pit of his stomach.

"Let's get this bastard off our land!" Bruce snarled. "Paul, grab his arms–"

"Wait!" Shona jumped out of the truck and in front of

Cuban. He didn't stand a chance out there judging by the state he'd arrived in.

"Get out the way!" Deputy Paul growled.

"Mr. Ellis, please give Cuban a chance. Look at the difference he's made to the tool room already, and that's without being paid!" she begged.

"Paul, wait," Ellis waved his hands for Deputy Paul to cease manhandling Cuban. "Elbie, the tool room is normally your domain, right?"

Elbie nodded.

"This man here, y'think he's done a good job?" Ellis continued.

"Sir, that room–" Elbie paused. "I ain't seen it no better in a long time, do say so m'self. You could eat your dinner off that floor!" He caught Shona and Cuban's relieved faces in the corner of his eye.

Deputy Paul and Bruce put their hands on their hips. Ellis approached Cuban and spoke in a low voice.

"You got one chance. You mess it up, I ain't gon' help you. I'll leave Shona to explain my rules. If you break 'em, I'm behind Larry all the way. Understand?"

Tears glistening in the corner of his eyes, Cuban managed to croak out his thanks.

"Come on, gentlemen." Ellis turned to walk around the side of the building and back to his office. Shona noticed him limping slightly.

Waiting until Ellis was out of earshot, Deputy Paul strode over to Shona, Cuban and Elbie.

"Mr. Bruce told me to let you know that if you pull another stunt like that you won't be *able* to work, y'hear?" he growled. He stepped closer to Shona and traced down the side of her smooth face with his dirty fingernail. She stood motionless, regarding him with an icy stare. Not receiving the satisfaction of a rise out of her, he cackled as he left them and ran to catch up with Ellis and Bruce.

"So, what now?" Cuban asked.

"Don't know about you two," said Shona, "but I need to wash that dirty bastard's stink outta my face!"

Shona walked over to the faucet outside the mechanics' shed. Feelings rushed around her body like a kaleidoscope as she splashed the cool water on her face. *Humiliating one of your bosses isn't the most ideal way to start a new job,* she thought. Turning to look over at her two new friends, she saw them toeing the dust and attempting to make small talk. She smiled as she walked back over to them, her hands in her pockets.

"You're quite the brave lil' lady," Elbie said.

"Yeah, thank you. You didn't have to do that," Cuban added.

"You're welcome. It looks like we need each other 'round here?" Shona said as they made their way back to the tool room.

"You're damn right. This place, it's awful. Didn't used to be." Elbie's eyes saddened.

"What changed?" Shona asked.

"Larry Bruce, that's what! This place was run by Mr. Ellis for twenty years and he did a damn fine job of it too. But he needed to spend more time with his sick wife, so he got *Bruce the Brute* on board to take care of the day-to-day running around five years ago and then–" Elbie fiddled with his cap. "It got real dark 'round here."

"What d'you mean?" Cuban asked.

"People just came and went. If you disagreed with the bosses, well, your days were numbered. Good people with consciences left or were made to leave." Elbie's face dropped.

"Well, we got each other, right?" Shona affirmed.

"I could tell you some stories, alright. I write everything down in my diary. I started writing it when my wife passed. I made a promise I would talk to her every day." Elbie licked his lips as his emotions began to engulf him. "I write about everything that goes on here but my damn hands tremble with age now, so I have to keep it short."

The same loud buzzer from earlier sounded again.

"What's that?" Cuban asked.

"We've been summoned." Elbie's face blanched.

CHAPTER 11

The three of them were the last to reach the canteen, where all
staff briefings were routinely held. In the far right corner was a
wrought iron spiral staircase leading up to the management
offices on the balcony above. As soon as the trio walked in,
there was an ominous silence when the crowd of workers
caught sight of Cuban. As looks of disgust were thrown in his
direction, whispers, jeers and growls from the hostile crowd
began to ring out.

"Another fuckin' colored."

"Lock up your stuff, boys."

Men spat at Cuban's feet but it wasn't the first time that had
happened to him. Shona was stunned by the savagery of the
crowd, which seconds later turned on her.

"What the *fuck* have we got here, boys?"

"I'll bet you five bucks she's screwin' somebody within the
week."

From above, a man's voice bellowed, followed by a whistle
and then a hammering on the iron bars of the balcony.

"Alright, everybody, hush now!" Deputy Paul hit the balcony
bars with his wooden stick, his face maroon with the exertion

of trying to silence the mob. "We have a couple of new additions we'd like to present to you and I'm sure they'll get your usual warm welcome. I'll hand it over to Mr. Bruce."

Bruce's intimidating stare held the attention of the crowd. He appeared at the edge of the balcony in his expensive three-piece suit, showing the glint of a gold watch that would take these workers a year to save up for. His bass tones growled as he addressed the workforce.

"It's no secret I'm always looking to advance the company, but Mr. Ellis and I won't be around forever." Bruce glanced towards Ellis.

"*I* plan to be," Ellis lightened the mood.

"It's a good time to invest," Bruce continued. "The market's expanding, which is exciting for all of us. We're doing more business further afield so we need some fresh young blood to keep up with it. I've sat down with a few guys and I've picked one. Somebody who's from great stock, has good energy and thinks the way I do."

"That ain't no good thing, let me tell you," Elbie whispered.

"I'd like to welcome...Kyle Chambers."

Bruce gestured towards Kyle, who swaggered forward in a made to measure gray flannel suit. His highly polished Oxford shoes echoed on the metal platform of the balcony as he made his entrance to the crowd's applause. He muttered something to Bruce and then beamed his winning smile down at the canteen floor, giving a wave to indicate that he was ready to speak.

"It's an honor to be given a chance to lead such a fine-looking workforce. I'm sure we can do great things together."

After five long minutes of grins and smug mutual backslapping from Bruce and Kyle, the sound of shuffling feet and bored grunts began floating around the assembled workforce. Sensing they'd dragged on for too long, Bruce quickly concluded.

"I got one more thing to announce–" Bruce pointed at the crowd below him. "My daughter Chloe is finally home where she belongs. She's been studying business at college these last five years, so she can help run things when I'm gone." He went back into the management office, then returned holding his daughter's hand.

"Everybody, meet Chloe."

The applause was initially polite, but when all eyes focused on her properly, a few low whistles and murmurs of admiration followed.

Chloe Bruce shone a beaming smile at the crowd, her chocolate-brown eyes radiating warmth as she acknowledged some of the more well-mannered comments with a dainty wave. She wore a bright red fitted jacket, a red and white polka-dot blouse and a smart black pencil skirt, showing off her perfectly toned legs and significantly distracting the men standing below. She cleared her throat as her father raised his hands to hush the crowd for her.

"Well, I didn't expect *that*. Thank you, I'll keep it brief. I just want to learn the business, help the company grow, and I especially can't wait to come around and meet every single one of you."

The workforce below cheered more rapturously this time as Chloe stared down at them. She flicked her light brown mid-length hair out of her eyes as she continued to melt the crowd with her effortless charm.

But not everybody in the crowd was cheering.

~

NOW SCAN THE QR CODE ON THE NEXT PAGE TO CONTINUE YOUR JOURNEY...

Instructions:

1. Open the camera or the QR reader application on your smartphone.

2. Point your camera at the QR code to scan the QR code.

3. A notification will pop-up on screen.

4. Click on the notification to open the website link

JOIN IN!

If you would like to receive regular behind-the-scenes updates, get beta reading opportunities, enter giveaways and much, much more, simply visit the site below:

http://hackneyandjones.com

ACKNOWLEDGMENTS

This book has been a passion project, but we couldn't have done it without all our friends and family supporting and believing in us every step of the way.

Special mention to Sharon Atkinson for being so supportive in the writing group where it all started.

Many thanks to all of our beta readers, and for all the amazing support we've received from our **Hackney and Jones** Facebook group.

OUR TEAM

Virtual Assistant:
Erin Hodgson
writehandwomannz@gmail.com

Book Covers by:
WooTKdesign
wootkdesign@gmail.com

Edited by:
Gary Smailes
Bubblecow.com

Proofread by:
Melanie Bell
inspire.envisioning@gmail.com